From the corner of his eye...

Bear saw a sudden flash of light near the outer wall. He turned to look at it. A girl was floating in the air, her feet dangling, her body emanating golden yellow light. Bear smiled, thinking this was one of his friends playing some kind of trick, but the smile faded when he realized that he had never seen the girl before. She was a stranger.

He stared in confusion. The girl was looking at him. Her eyes were huge and round, and there was something sad and desperate about them. Her clothes were funny, consisting of a pale dress, girdled at the waist with a slim belt, the sleeves short and puffy, and little buckled shoes worn over plain socks. The shoes dangled in the air with her feet. She seemed about Bear's age.

Unsure what else to do, Bear raised his hand and waved.

The girl waved back. Then she vanished.

Bear continued to stare at the corner for a few seconds, then ran up to where Roma waited and grabbed her arm.

"What?" she demanded, pulling away with a jerk.

"Did you see that?" he asked.

"See what?"

"The glowing girl in the corner," Bear said.

Roma laughed, tossing her braids.

"No! What are you talking about?"

The Guardians had arrived, tall figures in black, their strange round faces half shrouded in their hoods. They were herding the children, making them form files, one kid behind the other. No one was looking toward the southeast corner.

"So, only I saw her?" Bear said, wondering if he had seen her at all.

Also by
Harold R. Thompson

Empire and Honor

Dudley's Fusiliers
Guns of Sevastopol
Sword of the Mogul

The End of the Tether

Orphans

of

Sturnus

Harold R. Thompson

ZUMAYA OTHERWORLDS AUSTIN TX

2024

ORPHANS OF STURNUS

© 2024 by Harold R. Thompson

ISBN 978-1-61271-446-2

Cover art by Getcovers

"Zumaya Otherworlds" and the griffon logo are trademarks of Zumaya Publications LLC, Austin TX, https://www.zumayapublications.com

To Ben and Maddy

Chapter 1

"Where were you yesterday?" Roma asked Bear during break.

First period had ended, and they were in the yard. Roma came up on Bear's right, seeming to appear out of nowhere. Bear recoiled a step, an automatic reaction, his mind still a little foggy.

"Bear?" Roma said, leaning toward him.

"I don't know," he said. "I think I was sick."

"Sick?" she said, wrinkling her brow. The braids on either side of her head stuck out like antennae. "All day? How could you be sick all day?"

Bear just shrugged. He really didn't know what had happened. The last thing he remembered was accompanying Miss Sweet into the corridor outside the classroom. Then… nothing. It was strange, and bothered him a little, but Miss Sweet had told him he was okay now.

"Well, allright," said Roma, apparently satisfied. She twirled away, spinning on her heels and making for the playset where Emmot and Aril were disputing the summit, playing at "King of the Wind."

Bear leaned against the wall of the school. Other children raced past him. He saw their faces, their smiles, their laughter, but didn't want to join them. He still felt a little weak. Even at the best of times, he only associated with three or four of the other kids. Somehow, that was all he had the energy for. Quite often, he even liked to be alone.

A shadow fell across the opposite wall, a sudden line of darkness. Bear watched as it crept across the yard, its edge curved like a knife. The midday eclipse.

He loved this moment, this daily hush, and welcomed it more than usual today. He needed time to think, to recover from…whatever had happened.

1

Now the world would fall silent for about an hour and a half, the birds no longer singing, the sky dimming to a deep indigo, dominated by the vast black disc that was Corvus, hanging in darkness as it passed between the world and the sun.

Someone had once explained to Bear, although he could not remember who, that the world was really a moon orbiting an enormous ball of brown gas, a massive planet almost big enough to be another sun. That was Corvus. One side of the moon always faced the gas giant, and this meant that, for a certain time every day, the giant hid the sun.

It also meant that every day brought two dawns.

Many of the other children had stopped playing and were staring up at Corvus as the sun seemed to sink into its bulk. In a moment, when the sun was completely gone, the Guardians would gather the children and send them inside for more lessons. Darkness had filled the yard.

From the corner of his eye, Bear saw a sudden flash of light near the outer wall. He turned to look at it. A girl was floating in the air, her feet dangling, her body emanating golden-yellow light. Bear smiled, thinking this was one of his friends playing some kind of trick, but the smile faded when he realized he had never seen the girl before. She was a stranger.

He stared in confusion. The girl was looking at him. Her eyes were huge and round, and there was something sad and desperate about them. Her clothes were funny, consisting of a pale dress girdled at the waist with a slim belt, the sleeves short and puffy, and little buckled shoes worn over plain socks. The shoes dangled in the air with her feet. She seemed about Bear's age.

Unsure what else to do, Bear raised his hand and waved.

The girl waved back. Then she vanished.

Bear continued to stare at the corner for a few seconds, then ran up to where Roma waited and grabbed her arm.

"What?" she demanded, pulling away with a jerk.

"Did you see that?" he asked.

"See what?"

"The glowing girl in the corner," Bear said.

Roma laughed, tossing her braids.

"No! What are you talking about?"

The Guardians had arrived, tall figures in black, their strange round faces half shrouded in their hoods. They were herding the children, making them form files, one kid behind the other. No one was looking toward the southeast corner.

"So, only I saw her?" Bear said, wondering if he had seen her at all. Was this something to do with yesterday, with being sick? Was he seeing things?

2

The girl had seemed real, though. And she had been beautiful, like something from his dreams come to life.

⁂

The school was an uneven and rambling structure made of a silvery gray material with no visible seams or joints. It housed two classrooms, a large dining hall, a small breakfast room, "play" rooms, gymnasium, washrooms, and sleeping rooms. The building had no windows to look out into the yard, which surrounded it on all sides.

The yard was, in turn, surrounded by a high gray wall without visible doors or windows, a hidden gate appearing in a different location every time it opened. The children were allowed outside the gate (or gates, maybe) now and then to romp in the grassy meadows, but that was as far as they could go. They could not venture as far as the patch of yellowpine forest to the north, nor were they ever permitted to go to the city to the east, with its jumble of distant buildings, each a stack of bland gray blocks like the school.

The classrooms were large and trapezoidal, theatres with floors that sloped upward from front to back. Ambient light came from somewhere, although Bear did not know its source. Four curved tiers of ten chairs held all forty children, the entire student population of the school. The chairs were set at intervals, with plenty of room between them. The kids sat there, looking identical in their school clothing—plain gray flannel suits consisting of pullover tunics and trousers.

Bear's chair was in the third tier. His friend Emmot sat in the second tier, just in front of him.

Guardian Number Four walked between the seated children, ensuring that everyone was settled in their proper place. His tanned face, too smooth and perfect to seem quite real inside his dark hood, showed just a hint of a smile. He wore a large white number 4 on the chest of his black coveralls.

"Miss Sweet is coming," he announced in a loud voice.

Bear sat as straight as he could in his chair. He wanted to please Miss Sweet by demonstrating perfect posture. He also wanted to talk to her after class, to ask her about the glowing girl, whether it had been something to do with his sickness, or something else. Whatever it had been, Miss Sweet would know.

She swept into the room, an explosion of textures against the drab backdrop. She was tall—taller than even the Guardians—and slim, although with a woman's shape. Today's dress was black with silver flecks, and it clung to her body and spilled around her feet. Her perfectly heart-shaped face was deep pink, with a narrow green line running down the center—along the bridge of her nose, across her lips, bisecting her chin, and trailing down the front of her neck and into her collar. Her hair was like white smoke billowing and swirling around her head.

Bear's stomach flipped, just as it always did when Miss Sweet arrived, no matter what she looked like. She was always beautiful, but beautiful in a fantastic and sometimes terrible way.

"Time to begin," she said, both hands raised above her head, looking as if she were about to sing, which was half-true, for she spoke in a sort of rhythm. "Questions and Answers!"

She paused, and Bear tensed, waiting for the first question. The class was required to answer as one, but some kids were always a bit slow. He didn't want to be one of those kids.

"Where did the human race come from?" Miss Sweet intoned.

"The planet Earth," Bear almost shouted, along with thirty-nine other children.

"Very good," Miss Sweet said, slowly climbing the slope from the narrow front of the room to the wider back, moving between the chairs. "Why did humans leave Earth?"

"Earth was corrupt and overcrowded," came the collective reply.

Miss Sweet stopped and turned. Bear had swiveled in his seat to keep her in sight.

"What is the most advanced planet in the known galaxy?" Miss Sweet demanded.

"Janus!" Bear shouted with the others. These questions were basic, and easy. He was getting them all correct, and quickly.

Miss Sweet began to walk with slow careful steps back down the next aisle. Her path would take her past Bear's seat. His heart began to thump in his small chest.

"What planet is this?" she asked.

"The moon Sturnus," everyone cried.

"And who are you?" Miss Sweet asked, her voice softer now, although no less clear and audible.

"We are the Orphans of Sturnus," Bear said, not shouting now, but proud of who he was, who they were, that they had escaped a terrible fate. Of course, he had no memory of that dark time, of the horrors Miss Sweet told them they had escaped, and that was good. That he and the others had survived made them heroes, of a sort.

"And why did the society of Sturnus fail?" Miss Sweet next asked, descending, coming closer to Bear's chair.

"Stagnation and corruption," Bear said.

He had never been sure what that meant; but it was the proper reply, and he knew it by heart, like all of the other Answers.

4

"Who rescued you from this terrible state?" Miss Sweet said.

"Janus rescued us," Bear said, and one of his earliest memories came to him, of one of Miss Sweet's faces, a more ordinary human face, saying *It will be all right now.*

She glided past his seat. He wanted to reach out and touch her, stroke the soft cloth of her dress, but of course he didn't dare.

Miss Sweet returned to her place at the head of the room. Guardian Number Four took position on her right near the entrance, hands behind his back, smooth face still smiling.

"Very good, children," Miss Sweet said. "I did not hear even a hint of hesitation in any one of your voices. Yes, you may applaud yourselves and your fellow students."

Bear clapped his hands, his grin so huge it hurt his cheeks. It was a good day when they pleased their teacher.

"You are all nearly ready for the next step," Miss Sweet said when the applause had died. "Just a little more time, but if you strive, if you make an effort, you will be ready to receive the benefits of Janus. Remember that we are an older people. We were the first to flee the Earth, the first to travel into the stars and start again. We learned much, and now it is our duty to share all that we know. It is our duty to share…to share what?"

"The truth," the class shouted, although the answer was a bit ragged. Bear was one of the slow responders, having spoken a fraction of a second after Emmot, and for that he felt his face begin to redden. He had thought Questions and Answers was over!

"It is our duty to share…?" Miss Sweet repeated, her voice rising.

"The truth!" the children bellowed in perfect unison, Bear included.

"That is correct," Miss Sweet stated, letting her arms settle at her sides.

Now Questions and Answers *was* done, truly over for the day. Bear had to admit to himself that, despite his one hesitation, it had gone well.

Next on the schedule was mathematics, just a series of equations and problems to solve. Bear removed his work card from its slot in the side of his chair. The work card was a rectangle of some thin floppy stuff, maybe a kind of plastic, but Bear liked it and thought it worked well, projecting interactive two and three-dimensional images in the air in front of him. The images filled his vision, made it easy to focus, to relax and just practice simple arithmetic at his own pace, without any fear of failure.

An hour of reading followed math. Bear liked this class even better, because he could pick whatever story he liked from the library contained in his work card. The stories were all about the planet Janus—how it was once called a "super earth" because it was larger than old Earth, with heavier gravity that, according to some tales, made its people stronger. The planet only had one city, because there was no need for any others. Its people were the most prosperous and happy in history, and they seemed to come in all sorts of colours, shapes, and sizes. If they wanted to change how they looked, they could do that, too.

Bear wondered when he would ever get a chance to visit Janus.

Reading ended too soon, as always. Classes were over for the day, and Bear followed Guardian Number Four's directions, filing out of the theatre. As he moved through the doorway, he realized with alarm that he'd forgotten to ask Miss Sweet about the golden girl.

It was impossible to go back. He would have to wait to ask her tomorrow.

He followed the children down the featureless gray corridor to a Washroom. The Washroom was a tiny featureless space, like a closet. Bear followed the child in front of him into the closet, stopping for a few seconds while strange lights swirled around him. He always imagined he felt the dirt leaving his skin and hair, but he was never sure if this sensation was real or not. He supposed it didn't matter. The room did get him clean. He could even pee in here if he wanted (although he was supposed to do that in the privy). When the lights went out and he stepped through the other side, he was "free of all foreign particle accumulations," as the Guardians liked to say.

His stomach grumbled. From the Washroom, he followed the stream of kids along another corridor to the large dining hall. This was a rectangular room, silver-gray like every other, with three long parallel tables. The tables were white and made of some hard, slick substance. Bear sat in his usual spot, in his own chair with his little circle of friends—Emmot and Aril, Roma and Kanga.

"Food!" Emmot cried, pounding the table and grinning at his closest companions. "We want food!"

"What are we having today?" Roma wondered, having to shout over the noise of many other voices.

The food came, rising from inside the table on rectangular plates in front of every child. Bear saw it was his favourite combination of meat (a brown square), vegetables (a green square), grain (a paler brown square), and a drink of opaque brown liquid the kids just called "yum."

The meal was a little bland, but that was okay, because he didn't like strong flavours.

❧

When the meal was done, the children had "free time." "Free time" could take various forms. Sometimes, it was structured, as when the Guardians

6

organized team sports, competitions between sections of the class. Bear enjoyed some of those, but some he hated. If given the choice between structured time and unstructured, he would always choose the latter.

This evening there were no sports. Bear's time was free for real. He could think about anything, or do whatever he wanted. He could go to one of the playrooms and join in an immersive game, or read, but decided instead to go out into the yard, find a place to sit, and do nothing but think and wonder.

He climbed to the top of one of the playsets, sat on a crossbar, and stared at the sky, watching the approach of second evening, counting the stars as they came out. He was feeling better than he had that morning, the weakness gone.

Now and then he glanced at the southeast corner, but the golden girl didn't appear again.

Time seemed to pass too quickly, and Bear was surprised when the chime sounded, a great ringing like that of a steel bell. He had no idea if there was a real bell hidden somewhere, or if it was just a recording, but that didn't matter. What mattered was that the chime meant free time was over.

It was time for bed.

The Guardians appeared, and Bear complied, joining the rest of the kids in the yard, forming a file, returning to the school building, winding down the corridor to his dormitory.

Ten children slept in each room. Their beds were not beds at all, but bags suspended from the walls. The bags had hard sides and were very tight, holding their occupants in a rigid form, with a hood to keep the head in place and prevent it from lolling. Bear thought it was a strange way to sleep, but Miss Sweet had told them all this was the only proper way, the Janusian way. So, he tried to do his best. Even so, he was never quite comfortable.

"Open," he said, and his sleeping bag opened. He stepped up into it, turning as it closed around him, wriggling his arms so he could hold his hands clasped together against his chest. Now he could crook his head forward as far as it could go in his hood, turning it slightly to the right. This was his favourite position, the one that worked best.

The lights in the room dimmed. A voice emanated from somewhere, the voice of Miss Sweet, saying, "Goodnight, my little birds."

Bear was tired. His day had been good, a little more interesting than most. His mind began to drift. His eyes closed, and in a half-dream state he saw the golden girl again, only this time she spoke.

Can you see me?

❦

The next thing Bear experienced was not a dream.

It was summer, the air a warm cushion filled with the soft music of crickets. Bear was at the big yellowpine table in the great room, and the windows to his left were open. He turned to look. There was still some light, despite the late hour—Mum and Dad had let him stay up—and he could see the green expanse of the lawn as it sloped down to the cliff, and the jumbled sandstone boulders beyond, and the sea.

The sea. He could smell it, the brine and the weeds and the sand. He took a deep breath, let that smell engulf him.

"Are you going to play?" his father said.

Bear looked at him, at the thin man with the sandy beard, the smile, the merry blue eyes. Mum was next to him, her dark features inscrutable, as always when they played a card game together. Mum was always the player to beat.

Bear looked at his hand. He had five cards. Three were Stars, one was Rockets, and the last was...

With sudden excitement, he realized he was about to win. He had the last Comet!

"S-s-s," he tried, unable to get the word out, but for once not caring, not humiliated at his inability to speak when he wanted. Nothing could stop him!

"Supernova!" he at last managed to blurt, slapping down the Comet.

"Oh, well, look at that!" said Mum, putting down her cards.

Dad threw his down on the table, but Bear knew his disgust was not real. Bear was laughing. From below the cliffs he could hear the waves.

Dad had risen from his chair and walked to the entertainment centre.

"Let's have some more music," he said. "Play the *Lemyn Concerto Number Three.*"

The music, soft and flowing, came from the hidden speakers in the wall.

"The *Lemyn Concerto,*" Bear repeated to himself. His father always played soft music in the background, and Bear wanted to know the names of the pieces and of the composers. Still, he was afraid he would forget, even though he remembered the tune well enough to hum it to himself.

Another non-dream came to push aside the first.

The seasons on Sturnus were not much different from each other, but late summer brought the whooping of belted owls. Bear and his father were taking an evening walk, in true night after the second sunset. The owls had always scared Bear, but he wasn't frightened with Dad around.

They made their way along the twisting lanes of their neighborhood, an area of dispersed houses on the edge of town.

"Look," said Dad, "you can look in people's windows and see what they're doing. It's like a play."

All of the houses along the cliffs had large windows, and at night warm golden light shone from inside. No one seemed to bother drawing a blind or turning the glass to opaque. Bear supposed people trusted each other here.

"Look, Dad, they're having a party," Bear said, pointing to one display. About a dozen people had gathered in their great room, glasses and bottles in hand, and Bear saw their smiles, their laughing faces, although he couldn't hear their voices. "Too bad there's no sound."

In the next house, people were having dinner, sitting in a circle and eating. And in the next, the inhabitants seemed to be just relaxing, reading or looking at their tablets.

"It's like a museum," Bear said, "a museum of people."

"Or a zoo," his father suggested.

Bear giggled.

They came to the end of the lane, and here they started down the long flight of wooden steps that took them from the edge of the cliff to the beach. Bear held his father's hand for safety, felt the roughness and warmth of his skin.

The water lapped at the strip of sand. Bear's father explained that on Earth there were tides, and the sea came in and went out; and that was true here, too, thanks to other moons nearby in orbit around Corvus, but it wasn't as extreme.

Bear tried to imagine the water coming in for more than a metre, crawling up the beach, and that thought was a little scary.

"Skip stones?" Dad suggested, and Bear agreed, so they looked for some flat bits of sandstone. When they had each found half a dozen samples, they tossed them at the water's surface, counting the number of jumps they could produce. Overhead, the great striped ball of Corvus hung like a light, fat and cheerful, hiding behind a few wisps of pink-and-white cloud but still providing plenty of light to skip stones.

Bear managed to skip his sixth stone fifteen times!

His eyes opened. He was hanging in his sleep bag. He hadn't been asleep when the memories came.

His heart was pounding, his breathing rushing in his ears. He'd forgotten his family, his mum and dad, his house, his town, forgotten it all. How had he forgotten?

His eyes darted around the dim room, taking in the shapes of the other sleeping children.

What was he doing here? Why wasn't he at home?

How had he forgotten everything?

Chapter 2

With the morning, some silent command caused the sleep bags to open, allowing the children to tumble out, landing on their feet to meet another day. Bear wobbled, throwing out his arms to keep his balance, his head spinning.

"No," he groaned, rubbing his eyes.

The room smelled strange. It was a smell he'd known all his remembered life, but now it seemed foreign. For a few minutes, he stayed put, unable, or maybe unwilling, to move. Someone bumped him, and someone else said, "Come on, Bear!"

He had no choice. This was how his days began.

He let his legs and feet carry him, following the crowd, moving without thinking, streaming out of the room toward the privy. Guardians Number Two and Number Three urged them on, calling out in turn, "Don't be late. Move quickly. You must not be late."

Bear went into one of the open toilet alcoves and peed. He stared at the silvery wall as if seeing it for the first time. Nothing seemed real. How had he come to be here, in this strange school with these children? He didn't belong here.

No, that was wrong. He'd lived here all his life, since the Janusians had rescued him.

"Move along, now, children," said Guardian Number Three.

A quick trip through the Washroom, the play of lights; and Bear was following Roma into the breakfast room. This was similar to the dining hall, except the walls were yellow, the only coloured walls in the school, and from somewhere came the sound of chirping birds. Bear sat on his bench with

10

his friends, and in a few minutes his food rose— a tray containing a square of "sausage protein" and another of "fruit." With it was a purple drink, one of his favourites, but today it tasted like nothing.

"I used to eat better food than this," he said.

Emmot gave him a dull look, then laughed.

"What?" he said. "When?"

Bear looked past him at the yellow wall. This place wasn't real. It couldn't be real. He'd remembered that he'd lived in a nice house with Mum and Dad and a dog named…

He'd just remembered the dog! And he'd gone to school, a different school…somewhere. He didn't know. He couldn't remember it all.

He finished his meal. The empty tray sank back into the table; and to his right, one entire wall opened, sliding up to some hiding place in the ceiling. The Guardians began urging the children to get up and head outside into the yard.

"Time for Warm-ups," said Guardian Number Three, not losing its tight smile.

Bear usually enjoyed Warm-ups, but now the idea made his stomach churn. None of this mattered. He had to think, to remember more. But he couldn't. He had to do what he was told, just as he did every day—form in one of three lines facing the two Guardians.

"First stretch!" said Guardian Number Three with exaggerated good cheer.

Bear reached for the sky with both hands, reached for mighty Corvus. That, at least, seemed real. He had always known the big planet.

Stretches number two, three, and four followed, and then Bear and the others had to stand on one leg, then the other. The Guardians seemed to think this was fun and made up many of these moves on the spot. The other children laughed, but Bear was silent. He just had to endure this.

Warm-ups ended. There was now some spare time before the first lesson of the day. Bear watched as Emmot raced Roma and Aril to their favourite playset and started to climb. Emmot made it to the top first, as usual, and shouted, "I'm King of the Air! You all have to call me 'Your Majesty!'"

Bear listened to Emmot's mock superiority and felt some sense of comfort. The world around him was slowly coming back into focus. Here were his fellow pupils, his friends, and the old familiar yard, those enclosing gray walls he had always known. This place was safe and held no surprises.

He took a deep breath and folded his hands behind his back, knotting his fingers. It was a warm day with a clear blue sky, and Corvus shone like a massive polished marble. He closed his eyes. The memories seemed less real now; maybe they'd been dreams after all. He'd never had a mum and dad. That was ridiculous. Miss Sweet had told them he and the other children were bred on Sturnus to be slaves, to work in factories that produced riches for a select few. They'd been rescued from a horrible existence.

Miss Sweet would never lie to him.

He opened his eyes. Miss Sweet was in the yard, strolling amongst the children. This was a rare event, and Bear watched her approach with growing anxiety. Should he ask her about the dreams? About the glowing girl?

Were the dreams and the girl connected?

Miss Sweet met his gaze and came toward him. He waited, head bowed just a little bit, but he could not take his eyes from her. Today her face was lime-green, her hair piled gold, and her wide-skirted red dress swung from side to side with each step, billowing out as if from a breeze, although the air was still. Bear thought her head seemed larger than yesterday. How could she have a larger head? He'd noticed this sort of thing before, that she changed more than just her colour and her textures and her clothing.

He gave her a crimped smile. "Good morning, Miss Sweet."

She stopped and looked at him. Her mouth was very tiny and red.

"Bear," she said. "How are you feeling today?"

"Fine, Miss Sweet," he said, instantly regretting the lie. He wasn't fine, but the word had just come out, an automatic response.

"You were sick," she said. "Do you remember?"

"I remember you telling me I was sick," he said, "but I don't remember being sick."

That was the truth, and he felt better for having told it.

"It will be all right," Miss Sweet said. "Have you had any other strange thoughts?"

He stared, and his heart began to pound again, but more from excitement than worry. Of course! He'd been sick. That may have been what made him see things. Did that mean he'd seen things before like the golden girl, the memories of a nonexistent family? Was it just because he'd been sick?

He wanted to tell Miss Sweet, knew he should tell her.

Something stopped him. He was not sure what.

"No, Miss Sweet," he said again, and heard his voice tremble with telling a second lie. "I'm fine."

She regarded him for a moment. Then she touched his shoulder with one hand, just a brief touch, and said, "That's good. We want you to be well."

She moved away, skirts flowing. Bear watched her go, relief mingled with dismay at his behavior.

He shuffled toward the playset. It was an arrangement of white tubes or pipes, piled in steps toward a high point. Emmot still sat there, still proclaiming his dominion. Bear wanted to join him, to forget his confusion, to just do what he always did. He leaned against one of the smooth tubes.

12

Someone slapped him on the arm, and he started. It was Aril, dashing past.

"Race you to the top," Aril cried, jumping for the lowest of the white tubes. Emmot was no longer the king, but was hanging from one of the top rungs, swinging back and forth, a huge grin on his broad flat face.

"You're going to fall, Emmot," said Roma as she made her way toward them. Aril was close behind her.

Other children swarmed over the playset like dull gray monkeys climbing a tree of bleached bones. Bear watched them but remained on the ground. An image flickered through his mind of another playset, of other children dressed in colourful clothing, orange and red and turquoise.

He squeezed his eyes shut. He was still sick. He should have told Miss Sweet. He shouldn't have lied.

But a little voice in his head told him why he had lied. A part of him still believed the memories were real. And if that was so, it was Miss Sweet who had lied to *him*.

More memories of the dog surfaced.

Mum had brought him home, a tiny puppy covered in tight black curls. The puppy was so small Bear could hold him in his arms, feel his soft warm body and his tiny heartbeat.

"You can choose a name," Mum had said.

"Tayor," Bear had decided, because that was one of the sounds the pup made when he pretended to be fierce.

Bear and Tayor wrestled on the floor in the den. At one point, the little dog sprang away, dashing to the far wall. Bear rolled over and sat up. Tayor dashed back, and with a pounce, dug his tiny teeth into the top of Bear's right foot.

Bear howled.

Tayor seemed to realize he'd done something wrong and ran away to hide under a table. Bear's foot was not really hurt, so he went to his new little friend and spoke to him and fondled one of his silky ears.

"It's okay, little guy," he said. "But no biting!"

Bear couldn't concentrate on his math. The memory had come out of nowhere, the scene playing out in his mind all at once, fully formed. There was no question of its being a dream. It wasn't night, and Bear wasn't sleeping. He was sitting in his seat in the big classroom.

Then another memory hit him, like a slap across the back of his head. The dog was there again, but others as well…

"We have an appointment this morning," Bear's dad said. "At the hospital. It will be fine, you'll see."

"Can I bring Tayor?" Bear asked, his voice sounding very small and whiny to his own ears, but he couldn't help that. He was afraid.

His father looked doubtful for a moment, but then Mum said, "Of course. He can help you be brave."

They took a ground car to the hospital, which was a large building of silvery metal and glass. The car carried them along a rubberized street on silent wheels. Bear remembered how it smelled, the scent of the upholstery, and Tayor's puppy smell.

The hospital had a smell, too, and that was of clean things. Bear went there a lot for checkups. He was never sure what they were checking for. Today, he went to a room with walls of gleaming white and no windows, but there were several rectangular video screens hanging in the air. He sat in a comfortable chair, and the doctor and a nurse sat on stools in front of him. Soft music played in the background, strange and sonorous, the same odd melding of tones that had been playing during his last checkup.

"Your mum and dad tell me you like music," the doctor said.

Bear nodded. "Dad plays music all the time. I know a lot of tunes now."

"That's good. It's good to be able to recognize music."

The doctor gave Bear some medicine using a cold, white ceramic thing like a little gun that he pressed to Bear's arm. It didn't hurt.

"That's just so we can see better," the doctor said.

"I know," Bear said, because pretending he knew gave him some power, some control.

The session didn't take long. The doctor looked at the monitors and said things to the nurse, and to Mum and Dad. Bear didn't pay attention to them but just listened to the music, which was soothing. He held Tayor in his lap and stroked the pup's curly coat.

When the checkup was over, the doctor gave Bear a snaptreat, something he always did. Today's snaptreat was a dragonfly. Bear cracked open the spherical package, and the simulated insect popped into existence, zipping around the room for a few seconds before dissipating.

The doctor's name was Doctor Kamra. To Bear he seemed old, his brown face a nest of wrinkles, his hair and beard white, but he was nice. He was a friend of Mum's and Dad's, and sometimes came to the house. Bear didn't go to see him because he was sick. Bear was never sick. Bear went to see Doctor Kamra because Bear was special, and Mum and Dad wanted to make sure he stayed special.

"Why am I special?" Bear asked his dad one day. Of course, he often asked both Mum and Dad this question. He liked to hear their various answers.

"Because you're our little boy," Dad said.

"That's not what I mean! Why do I go see Doctor Kamra?"

"We're all special," Dad said. "Everyone."

Bear frowned. "But if we're all special, then we're all the same, and that means no one is special."

Dad laughed.

"That's true. Well, look, I'll show you what I mean by special. I mean, I can do special things. Remember I promised you I'd make chappies for breakfast?"

Bear grinned.

"Yeah!"

"Well, here they come."

Dad moved his hands in a flutter around his head, like a magician. The chappie maker came floating into the room, a silver box that beeped and whirred. Dad continued to wave his hands. This was one of his many so-called "magic tricks," where he made various devices do whatever he wanted.

The chappie maker beeped, and its chrome top popped open. Two chappies, lightly browned, popped out and fell onto Bear's plate. Two more fell onto Dad's plate.

Tayor barked.

"You can't have chappies, Tayor!" Bear said.

"Soon you'll be able to do your own tricks," Dad said. "And bigger tricks, too. Much bigger tricks than what I can do, or your mum."

The chappies were good, smooth and sweet and buttery.

The memories came to Bear all day, like a flood, as if some kind of mental dam had broken. They were vivid, and they were real. Bear was sure of that now. He wasn't sick. He never got sick.

That night he woke in his sleeping bag and felt water on his face. He pulled one hand out of the bag and wiped away tears. This time he'd been dreaming. *Actually* dreaming. It had been a nice dream about his parents, and it had made him sad.

He knew now that he really had led a life before the school. It had all come back, or most of it. He had never been a slave. That wasn't true. He'd never needed to be rescued.

So, why was he here at Miss Sweet's school? Where were his parents? Where was his little dog? Where was his town and his friends and his house?

Something was very wrong.

Fear washed over him, and an acute homesickness that made the tears pour from his eyes. Small sobs shook his chest and shoulders and made him feel stupid. He never cried.

"Bear," a voice whispered from his right. It was Aril. "Bear, are you all right?"

"No," Bear said. "Where is everyone? Where did they go?"

"Where did who go?" Aril asked.

"My mum and dad!" Bear wailed.

Fat tears rolled onto his nose. Aril said nothing, and Bear wasn't able to stop the silent sobs from shaking his tiny chest.

"You never had a mum and dad," Aril said. "What are you talking about? We were bred in big tanks like food animals. There weren't really any mums and dads."

Bear's fists clenched.

"Yes, there were," he insisted, and the anger gave him some strength, some control, as did the realization of the probable truth. "They lied to me. Miss Sweet and the Guardians and everyone else who comes to the school."

"What are you talking about?" Aril said. "You're going to wake everyone up and get us in trouble."

Bear shook his head, even though knowing Aril couldn't see the gesture in the darkness.

"That means something happened to them, maybe to all of our mums and dads. And it also means that we're prisoners."

Yes, they were being held here. That was why they couldn't leave the yard unless accompanied by half-a-dozen Guardians.

"You had another bad dream," Aril said, his tone more comforting. "It was just a dream."

"No," said Bear.

"Bear, the Janusians rescued us."

Yes, he knew the Answers, all of the Answers for the Questions. They were there in his head, but they were not as powerful as his memories. These memories that had obliterated everything else.

"They took us prisoner," he repeated.

"That's stupid," said Aril. "Bear, nothing you're saying makes any sense. You sound crazy."

Bear turned his head so he could just see the edge of Aril's face sticking out of his hood.

"I'm not crazy. I remember my life before, Aril. Something brought my memories back, and if I have memories, then you probably do, too."

"Stop talking," another voice said. Roma.

Bear turned to look in her direction, but could see nothing.

16

"You need to try and remember," he told her.

"Oh, shhh!" Roma said.

Bear glared into the darkness. He felt hot rage rising, making his face burn. What was he going to do now? What *could* he do?

He didn't fall asleep again for a long, long time.

Chapter 3

When Bear woke, achy and bleary-eyed, the next morning, for a moment everything seemed like before. Here was a morning like every other in his sleeping room with his friends. Soon, they would get up and go to breakfast, like they always did. Maybe there would be a sporting event today.

Then realization dawned.

Everything had changed, and nothing had changed. He was in this strange place that, up until a day ago, he had liked well enough; but now he knew it was a prison, a horrible prison when compared to the memory of his true home.

And he had no way out.

The Guardians formed the children into their files. Bear obeyed, as always. He was just a ten-year-old boy, and he needed to do what he was told. He was under the control of these people who had claimed to be his friends, but who had deceived him.

Breakfast was a chore, and the yard afterwards held no interest. Bear stood apart, pressed into the southeast corner of the wall where he had seen the golden girl. Roma was spinning and dancing in front of him, trying to get him to chase her, but he kept shaking his head.

"You're no fun!" she chided.

The chime sounded, the great invisible bell. Bear went back into the school, to the big classroom. The first lesson of the day began.

Guardians Two and Three took up positions near the door, and Miss Sweet glided in. Her face was pale yellow, her mouth larger than yesterday.

It looked as if she had changed her head again. Her hair, too, was yellow, and arranged in tufts that stuck out in all directions; her dress was pale green. He wondered if she meant to look like a flower.

Bear couldn't help his admiration, even adoration, but with those feelings came a burst of acute anxiety, like an electric shock through his whole body.

"Good morning, my little birds!" Miss Sweet sang.

"Good morning, Miss Sweet," the pupils all said. Bear said it with them, because he repeated these words every day and he did not even think about not saying them.

"Today, I would like to do something a little different," Miss Sweet continued. "No Questions and Answers. You did so well yesterday that you have all earned a reward. So, retrieve your work cards and styluses."

Their work cards ejected from slots in their chairs. Bear took his and held it in front of him. The stylus was a white stick attached to one side.

"We will work on your skills in creating analog representations," said Miss Sweet. She held her hands out at her sides, as if about to cast a spell in one of her favourite Janusian tales. "Some consider this the art of drawing, but on Janus we know that the ability to draw is the ability to clarify your thoughts. That is its purpose. How precise is the image in your mind, and can you create an accurate representation of that image?"

Bear glanced to his left and right. The others were smiling, no doubt anticipating what was certain to prove an almost whimsical diversion from the usual lessons. It seemed clear to everyone they were going to get to draw pictures. They were going to have some fun.

It had been a while since their last drawing session, and that had been fun, too. Bear had enjoyed it, despite the rigid rules Miss Sweet imposed on what they could and could not depict on their cards. Those rules, those restrictions, she had explained, "Will free your imaginations."

She imposed rules again.

"This is what you are to do. I will speak the name of an object. You will envision that object. Then, you will create a representation of that image with your stylus."

Bear's work card began to glow, and the work card field, a luminous white rectangle, extended from its side. He pulled the stylus from where it was clipped to the card and touched its tip to the field. He felt resistance, and a black mark appeared in the white space.

"An eating fork," Miss Sweet said.

Bear's anxiety began to subside. This was something he liked, something he understood, and he found himself falling into it. He imagined one of the smooth white forks they were given in the dining room. They had four tines, the outer longer than the two inner ones. Using his stylus, he started to draw the fork on the white rectangle. It was important to make it look as real as possible, with the handle flaring toward its end. If his drawing was too crude, he knew Miss Sweet would make him do it again until it was right.

"Tanner, Maya, and Bayan," Miss Sweet said, "you can do better, I think! See the fork in your mind, reproduce it on your card!"

Miss Sweet had not moved from the head of the room, and Bear wondered how she could see Tanner's, Maya's, and Bayan's drawings. But of course, she saw everything.

As the lesson progressed, she told a few other children to try again, and Tanner had to try a third time. Bear and the others who had not been called out, who had succeeded on their first attempt, waited. Bear could not help feeling some pride in his work.

"Very good," Miss Sweet declared at last, clapping her hands. Bear's drawing of a fork disappeared from his work card field. He was sad to see it go.

"Now, for the next exercise, you will place in your mind an image of yourself. You will then create a likeness of yourself with your stylus."

This was considerably more difficult than drawing a fork, quite a large leap forward, and there were a few low groans.

"Now, children, negative emotions are unproductive," Miss Sweet said. "So, begin!"

Bear poised his stylus above his work field. Its tip looked like the head of an arrow.

The stylus trembled as memory drowned him.

The garden was on a hill in the town. Mum and Dad and Bear went there often, and Bear liked the fat bantan trees with their wide, shading leaves.

In the center of the garden was a statue. The statue was made of white stone, and was of a young woman in a flowing gown standing with a small four-legged animal, holding a bow and arrow.

"Who's that?" Bear asked.

"Her name is Artemis," Mum explained. "She's a goddess from an ancient story on Earth. She looked after the trees and the grass and the wilderness. The environment here on Sturnus is something many people worked very hard to create, and Artemis reminds us that we have to look after it. It's very fragile."

"Why does that animal have trees growing out of its head?" Bear asked.

Mum and Dad laughed.

"Those are antlers," said Mum. "That animal is a deer, an Earth animal. They used the antlers to protect themselves."

"Like swords growing on their heads!" Bear said.

He understood now. There were a few deer on Sturnus, although not many. They roamed around eating trees and shrubs. Bear had only ever seen pictures of them.

"Here, look," said Dad. "There's a trick you can do. See if you can make her draw back her bow."

Bear frowned. How could you make a statue move?

"I'll show you," said Dad. "It's not simply a statue. It's a posable figure."

With her right arm, Artemis drew back on her nocked arrow. Bear gasped.

"Another one of my magic tricks!" said Dad. "See if you can do it."

Artemis relaxed the arrow. Bear stared at the statue. He had no idea what he was supposed to do.

"It's okay," said Mum. "Never mind your dad. You have to be taught how to do these things."

"Bear," Miss Sweet said, "you haven't drawn anything."

He looked up from his work field. The memory of the park and the statue had been so sharp, so vivid, it was like being there again. He could almost feel the sunshine, smell the bantan trees.

"See yourself in your mind," Miss Sweet prompted.

Bear tried to stifle his alarm. His heart was pounding. He clutched his stylus and saw himself, but as he must have looked on that day in the park, amazed that his father had made a statue move. How old had he been? Just a little boy with a round head, his hair cut short, just as it was now, even all around. His skin was pale like Dad's, and freckled, his nose just like a knob or button. His eyes had been wide with surprise.

He started to draw. He had to focus, to do what Miss Sweet said. He envisioned his entire body, saw himself standing outside in the grass with no shoes. He made his head a ball, his neck just a skinny bridge connecting it to the collar of his baggy shirt. He made his shirt hang down to his baggy pants and added other details—grass under his toes, his right hand waving, a sun in the sky on his left, and the massive striped ball of Corvus on his right. And he made himself smile. He was smiling because he was not alone.

He drew Mum and Dad there with him.

He realized too late he shouldn't have done that, that it would give everything away, but he'd wanted to so much that he'd let the idea carry him. It was as if drawing them would bring them back into his life.

He wanted them back.

"Stop," Miss Sweet commanded.

Bear paused, his stylus about an inch from his work field. He didn't look up. His heart began to thud all the harder, like someone was punching him in the chest over and over, as he sensed Miss Sweet coming toward him, climbing the sloping floor from the front of the theatre.

She halted next to his seat. He could not look at her.

"Who are these other people, Bear?" she asked, her voice soft, soothing.

"Just people," he said.

"No one you know? They look a little tall to be your friends."

Bear just shrugged. He felt himself shaking, sweat pooling at the back of his neck.

The drawing of himself, standing outside in the sun, his parents at his side, winked out of existence.

He pressed his eyes closed, squeezing out a single tear. The tear sparkled as it fell through his work field to land on his lap.

"Look at me," Miss Sweet said.

Bear didn't want to look at Miss Sweet, didn't want to face her disapproval, even now. But there were punishments for resisting, and he didn't want to face those, either. Slowly, he raised his eyes to gaze into his teacher's sun-yellow face.

"Come and see me after class, okay?"

Relieved that she didn't seem mad, he just nodded.

"Okay."

The rest of the lesson passed in a blur. When it was over, Bear filed out as usual, but once in the corridor, Guardian Number Three took him out of the group to where Miss Sweet waited.

"Bear," she said, "please stand still."

He stopped in front of her, nervously trying to decide whether she still sounded friendly or not. He didn't know what was about to happen. If she asked him more questions about his picture, he decided he wouldn't admit to having remembered his old life.

Miss Sweet extended her right arm toward him, and his stomach clenched in fear. Coiled around Miss Sweet's wrist where he hadn't seen it a moment ago was the Snake, an oily black cable with three silver metal teeth at one end. This was one of the most dreaded things in the school, reserved for kids who had done something particularly bad. Why would she use the Snake on him?

He'd seen it used on others, on kids who were defiant or threw tantrums, but he'd always been good! Now, Miss Sweet, the beautiful Miss Sweet, was going to use the Snake on him because he'd drawn a weird picture.

He made an involuntary whimper, and that was all he had time for before the Snake uncoiled from Miss Sweet's arm, the gleaming end leaping for his forehead. When it touched his skin, the pain was like a blow from a hammer, radiating down his face and neck and along his shoulders. His vision went white, and the walls around him faded from existence.

When he opened his eyes, he couldn't see. He didn't know if this was because his eyes weren't working, or because the room was pitch dark. He was standing, but something bound his arms and his legs, and he couldn't move.

Terror welled up from the pit of his stomach, and he clenched his jaw and heard himself whimpering. More memories flooded in—not good ones, not ones of a lost home, but of this dark place. He'd been here before, when he'd been sick.

He'd forgotten. Or they'd made him forget?

"His brain scans are atypical," he heard someone say, a woman's voice he didn't recognize.

"How so?" said another. Miss Sweet.

"It's nothing I'm familiar with. I would have to study it further. In fact, I would like to."

"Is the nexus functioning properly?"

"Yes, it seems fine. And my repression measures are still in place. Are you sure he's had more memories? Even after the last procedure?"

There was a moment of silence, and then Miss Sweet said, "Yes. It may be subconscious, but he seems to have retained at least an impression of his family and former home."

The first woman made a strange noise, a kind of snort, and then said, "Just mind what you say. He's awake and able to hear us."

"Can't you ensure he remembers nothing of this session?"

"Obviously, I can't," said the first voice, now sounding a little irritated. "We've carried out the repression procedure on this subject twice now, and I can't recommend it again without risking damage. Or is that not a concern for you?"

"Yes, it is. This child has potential. I don't want to lose that. Not just yet."

More silence. Bear's breathing and heart rate had calmed somewhat, so intent had he been on listening to the conversation, which was baffling in some ways but also confirmed his suspicions.

"What are our options?" said Miss Sweet.

"Since the nexus is functioning properly, that is not an issue for you. This leaves us with the odd brain scan and the emerging memories. I know nothing of the first, and it may not even be relevant. As for the second, you can try a more direct approach. One question, though. Have any of the other subjects exhibited these symptoms?"

23

"None."

"That's at least something."

"We'll have to try a different approach with this subject," Miss Sweet said. "Bear, are you awake? Have you been paying attention?"

Bear didn't want to respond. He held his breath, hoping he could hide in this darkness, even though he suspected they could see him.

"You have been having difficulty, Bear," Miss Sweet continued. "You've been sick, and it's making you think you remember things that were never true. Have you been remembering things?"

Miss Sweet's tone was calm, reassuring, the Miss Sweet Bear had trusted for so long; and he felt himself relaxing. He had always answered her, and it was wrong not to do so. He still wanted her approval.

Doubts crept in again. What if he really *was* sick, and the memories *were* false?

But the other woman, the one talking to Miss Sweet, had referred to "emerging memories."

"I…" he started. "I think maybe I've remembered a little."

"Just a little. Well, you have to try to ignore those things, Bear, because they're just symptoms of the sickness. We don't know what's causing the sickness, but it's something in your brain. I don't want you to be scared, but I also want you to understand that it could become more serious over time unless we take steps to correct it. Do you understand?"

"Yes," Bear said. He wanted to at least appear to cooperate. If he cooperated, maybe he would get out of here soon. His arms were starting to ache, and there was a pain in his lower back. The more he thought about this pain, the worse it seemed to get. He tried to bend, to flex his muscles, but whatever was holding him kept him fixed in place.

The pain flared, a burning shockwave that lanced up his back and across his shoulders, just for a second. He cried out.

"Miss Sweet, there's a pain in my back," he shouted, and the pain lanced again. "Ow!"

"What is it?" said Miss Sweet. "A pain?"

"Stop it," Bear gasped. "It keeps coming. It's getting worse."

The pain flared again, in his arms this time, an intense heat from within. When it was gone, he sagged within his unseen bonds.

"It's another symptom, Bear," Miss Sweet said. "It's the sickness. Those memories you think you've been having, memories of another life—they're false, Bear. Those things never happened. And the more you think of them, the more the pain will come. You have to never think of them! Please try, Bear. It's the only way to stop the pain."

Bear shook his head. His memories had brought the pain? But he hadn't been thinking of them when he'd first felt the pain.

An image of his mother came to him. He was little, and she was sitting with him in his bedroom. She was singing a song, a song he'd loved about a little rocket who went to the moon (although which moon was never stated), a little rocket that continued on to a planet called Mars, but then turned back because it got lonely for home.

The pain lanced through him again, and he screamed, the song dissolving in a flash of red that seemed to come from inside his eyes, the first light he'd seen in this room.

"Please, Bear, stop thinking about the false memories!"

"I'm not!" he gasped, though that wasn't true this time.

"Let's do some Questions and Answers. Maybe that will help. Who looks after you?"

"You do, Miss Sweet," Bear said.

A sudden sense of calm flooded through him—calm and happiness. It was the opposite sensation to the pain. The relief was almost too much for him, and for a moment he was lost in it.

"Who will guide you to knowledge?"

"You will, Miss Sweet."

More calm, and even pleasure, a sense of hope.

"I think it's working, Bear!" said Miss Sweet, sounding excited. "Let's try another one! Who saved you from slavery?"

"Janus," Bear answered, and he started to giggle.

"Good! Remember this lesson. When you have one of those memories, I want you to run through your Questions and Answers. That way you can keep the pain away. Can you do that, Bear?"

"Yes," Bear said. The feeling of intense happiness was gone, but it had left an impression. "I can do that."

"Good."

The invisible bonds on Bear's arms and legs gave way, and he blinked in sudden light. He was standing in the corridor outside his sleeping room. Guardian Number Four was there waiting for him, that little smile on its round face.

"You look better," said the Guardian. "It's time for bed. I trust you will sleep well."

<hr>

Bear woke again in the middle of the night. Someone was snoring. The room seemed calm, reassuring, the same room he slept in every night. *His* room. He thought of the session in the dark place, the things Miss Sweet had said. He'd tried to please her, as he always did, and he would keep trying to please her. He would be good and make her proud.

He'd always trusted Miss Sweet. Why should he mistrust her and the other Janusians now? Because of things he'd thought? And it did seem possible, even reasonable, that there was something odd about his brain, like he'd heard the other woman say; and that the memories were false.

He shook his head, another part of him objecting. He'd heard the entire conversation between Miss Sweet and the other woman. He knew what they were doing. They'd tried to repress his memories and somehow failed. So, they were trying something else. They were trying to warn him away with the pain.

If his memories brought the pain, as Miss Sweet said, then there was one way to find out.

He conjured a memory. It was easy now. He thought of a day when he'd been playing with Tayor in the kitchen. Mum and Dad were making supper in their usual way, by sitting in chairs and somehow making cooking devices whiz and zip around the room, depositing food on the table. Mum came over to him and hugged him, and the dog had tried to get in between them. That was funny, that whenever Mum or Dad gave him a hug, the dog wanted one, too.

"Sorry, Tayor," said Mum, "we love you, but Bear is our special little boy."

And then she'd said, "Be true to yourself, to who you are, and that means being true to your thoughts and feelings."

Bear thought maybe he'd mixed that up, that Mum hadn't actually said that on the day when Tayor had tried to squeeze into their hug. It had been another time. He remembered her face, her voice, her words.

This was a good memory, a very good memory.

It brought no pain.

Bear could only conclude Miss Sweet and the other woman had brought the pain, and blamed it on his memories, as some form of treatment. Their "new approach".

He pounded and kicked against the sides of his sleeping bag, trying to tear it, to rip it to shreds. After a few minutes, he realized how stupid that was, that he needed his sleep bag, and he wasn't strong enough to damage it anyway, so he stopped. But the anger didn't go away.

"Bear, is that you?" whispered Aril. "What are you doing?"

"Nothing," Bear said. "I had an itchy spot."

"Oh. I didn't know what was going on there, you were making so much noise."

"Sorry. The spot was hard to get at."

"That's okay. Hey, where were you today?"

"I don't know," Bear said, which was true. Maybe he'd never left the corridor, although that seemed unlikely. The entire experience was so strange he didn't think he could explain it, so he just added, "I think I was sick again."

"Oh," Aril repeated. "Well, I hope you're better."

"Thanks, Aril. Goodnight."

"Goodnight, Bear."

Bear heard the real kindness in his friend's voice. Yes, there was still kindness to be had. He did have friends. He was not alone. He wondered if he should tell Aril about his memories. He had to tell someone.

A glimmer of light in the far corner of the room caught his eye. He looked.

The girl was there, floating in the air. She was dressed in the same clothes, the same shoes. She was looking at him.

"Aril," Bear whispered. "Aril!"

"What?" Aril said, sounding sleepy.

"Do you see her?"

"See who?"

"There, floating in the air. That girl."

The girl smiled, and then she disappeared.

"She's gone," Bear added. "Did you see her?"

"No, Bear," Aril said. "Are you dreaming again?"

Bear didn't answer. First the girl, then the memories. Or had it been the other way around?

He was tired, too tired to think. He shut his eyes and tried again to sleep.

Chapter 4

Despite his worries about his memories, about Miss Sweet's certain treachery, all Bear could think about the next morning was the golden girl. He'd seen her twice, maybe three times so far; and it couldn't be a coincidence that she'd first appeared the same time his memories of his family had started, so that must mean something, that there was a connection. Maybe she wanted to give him a message? Maybe she'd come to tell him where his family was, and how to get back to them. She'd come to help. Whoever and whatever she was.

That had to be it.

He wanted to see her again, to actually talk to her. He was sure she'd spoken to him before, asking him if he could see her. If he could just talk to her, she would give him answers.

That idea took hold and wouldn't let go. At breakfast, Bear ignored the chatter at the table and watched the room, surveyed the corners, in case the girl appeared again. Later, he looked for her in the classroom, then in the yard, and then in the dining hall.

She didn't appear.

The next day was the same. Bear's need to see the girl overrode every other thought, but her failure to return brought crushing disappointment.

The old routine continued, the days coming and going, the lessons, meals in the dining hall, free time. Miss Sweet was back to treating him like everyone else, and he did his best to pretend he was obeying her, that he was ignoring his memories. In a way, that was true, because he told no one else about them. He was afraid that, if he did, they would get in trouble, too.

Two days after the horrible session in the dark room, the Guardians led the children out of the classroom into the yard and opened a door in the outer wall.

This was a welcome distraction, a moment of freedom. Bear laughed as he followed Aril out into the meadows, into what seemed a vast open space. The pleasure of the moment was enough to make him forget his worries, to enjoy the sensation of the grass under his bare feet. The sun was warm on his face, and he felt happy, truly happy, for the first time in a long time.

Strong winds had blown some debris from the nearby forest into the meadow, and Bear and Aril found two stout sticks suitable for use as swords. They engaged in a running battle across the crest of the hill. Emmot soon joined in, fighting them both and roaring. The battle soon gave way to laughter and excited commentary from Emmot, who said this reminded him of one of Miss Sweet's stories, a Janusian tale that also featured a sword fight.

Bear stood back and just listened. He often just liked to listen.

Roma approached, saying, "What are you talking about?"

"Sword fights," Bear said.

These were his three best friends. He knew that he hadn't known them before the school, when he'd lived with his family, but now they were his closest companions. He only knew them because someone had taken them away from *their* lives and brought them to this place.

"Do you ever…?" he started to ask, then stopped himself.

"Ever what?" said Roma.

"Nothing." He turned and took a few steps away from the others. "I forget."

"There you go again!" said Roma.

Bear kept walking. He gazed toward the city, the buildings gleaming silver in the morning light. A black sphere was descending from the clouds to a landing pad somewhere in the city centre. Bear often saw the spheres taking off and landing, and wondered where they came from, where they went.

He glanced back at his friends. He'd been about to ask Roma if she, too, had memories of a previous life, of families and houses and friends. He didn't want her or the others to start thinking about it, and talking about it, because Miss Sweet might find out, and she would know he had started it. Then she might take him back to the dark room. He never wanted to go there again.

⁂

The Guardians herded the children back to the school, into the yard, and the door closed behind them. Bear was always sad when outside time ended, and this was no exception.

He glanced around, looking for any sign of the glowing girl.

"Look, Bear," Aril said.

He held up the stick he'd used as a sword. He'd hidden it from the Guardians, concealing it in a leg of his pants, and brought it with him. The school did not allow the children any personal belongings, not even an old stick, and Bear was alarmed, worried Aril could get in trouble, and would have to face the Snake and the dark room.

"What are you going to do with that?" he said. "You have to get rid of it!"

"I've always wanted to know what this stuff is made of," Aril said.

Aril was quiet, even quieter than Bear sometimes, smaller than the other boys, with a small sharp face and hair the colour of copper; but he also had a streak of mischief. He started poking the stick into the surface of the yard, which was not bare dirt but made of a smooth, hard, but yielding substance the same colour as the walls.

"Bear, I think I got it! Look, I made a hole."

Aril pulled the stick out of the jagged indentation he had made; but as they watched, the hole flattened and smoothed over, leaving no trace of any damage.

"Well, I thought I had it," Aril said, sounding dejected.

He stabbed the floor again. Bear moved closer to him, shielding him, looking out for Guardians. Roma came spinning by, her twin braids standing straight out from her head as she twirled.

"Hi, Aril, hi, Bear."

"Hi," they said in unison as she came to a dizzy stop, laughing and almost falling.

Bear motioned for her to be quiet, to not attract attention to Aril's experiment.

"I won't," she said. "I'm dizzy."

"Why do you do that?" Bear asked. "Spin around and dance and sing all the time?"

"Because it's fun," she said, her tone implying she thought his question foolish. She started spinning in the other direction, singing, "The sky, the sky."

"Hello, Aril," said Guardian Number Four, halting and holding out one smooth hand. "The stick, please."

Bear and Aril stood as stiff as statues. Aril gave the stick to the Guardian, who didn't stop smiling as he took it.

"It's time for class, boys," the Guardian said.

The chime sounded. The Guardian didn't detain them, and Bear and Aril joined the others. Bear slapped his friend on the back, relieved at surviving what seemed like a close call, but also a little triumphant they had pulled off something forbidden. At least until they'd been caught.

They filed into the school and down the corridor to the classroom, where they took their seats. Guardian Number Three strutted up and down the aisles before announcing, "Miss Sweet is coming."

Miss Sweet entered the room. Bear stifled a gasp and stared at her. She looked entirely human. Her skin was a creamy tan, her hair a plain dark-brown hanging to her shoulders. Her long dress was brown as well, and her hands were bare, without the usual gloves.

She smiled. Despite everything that had happened in the past few days, Bear's heart leapt.

He thought she'd never looked so lovely.

"Did you enjoy your time outside, my little birds?" Miss Sweet said.

"Yes, Miss Sweet," the children replied in unison.

"Good. This is a special day, and I mean to begin with a story. Would you like to hear a story?"

"Yes, Miss Sweet," the children said again.

Miss Sweet poked the air in front of her with one slender index finger, and the perfect image of an old-fashioned book, the kind with a thick leather cover and rough-cut paper pages, appeared before her, floating at eye level. Some of the children gasped.

Bear couldn't help grinning, and settled into his chair, ready for another welcome distraction. He loved Miss Sweet's stories, even the ones that were bizarre and incomprehensible, as they often were, for those were still interesting.

"This is the story about a young horse," said Miss Sweet. "Does anyone remember what a horse is?"

Bear knew that a horse was a semi-mythical animal from Earth. There'd never been any on Sturnus, at least not real ones.

Kanga answered the question.

"Most horses liked to run and carry people on their backs," Miss Sweet said, after praising Kanga's answer. "But not the one in this morning's story. No, he didn't like to carry anyone. He wanted his freedom! So, he broke out of his pen and ran away, far, far across the meadow."

After running for some time, Miss Sweet explained, the horse got his foot caught in a rabbit hole (a rabbit being another Earth animal that didn't live on Sturnus). Unable to get free, the horse asked a series of forest animals to help him, but none of them would or could. At last, as the horse grew more and more resigned to his imminent death, his human master found him, pulled his leg free, and took him home. There, the horse ran and ran in circles, happy to be back where he belonged.

31

Something about how the story turned out made Bear's stomach churn. He didn't like this story as much as Miss Sweet's other stories.

"I want to be a horse!" Roma called out.

Dead silence followed. Miss Sweet didn't allow the children to speak without permission, and her eyes locked on Roma. Coming out from behind her floating book, she advanced up the sloping aisle.

Bear was tense and worried for his friend, who didn't seem to understand her error. Roma was grinning.

Miss Sweet's words were not what Bear had expected.

"Someday, if you're good, you can be a horse," she said, gazing down at the tiny girl. "Don't you realize this? You can be a horse. It's true."

Roma gasped. "I can?"

"This is something that the power of Janus can provide. Today you are an ordinary little girl, Roma. Tomorrow you can be whatever you imagine. Would you like that?"

"Yes, Miss Sweet!"

"Good!"

Miss Sweet strode back to her book and snapped her fingers. The book disappeared with a ringing sound.

"It is true that we value reason above all else, is that not so, children?"

"Yes, Miss Sweet," the children said.

"But beauty is also important," their teacher continued. "There is beauty in perfection, like the magnificent figure of the horse. That sort of perfection is what we strive for. Perfection is what *you* will strive for." She pointed at the class with both hands, index fingers extended. "This afternoon, at second dawn, you will begin the next phase of your lessons. You are ready. Some of you will find this difficult, and some of you will fail. That is to be expected. But for those who succeed, the beauty of perfection will be one step closer."

She gazed at them in silence for a long moment, looking from pupil to pupil. When she met Bear's eye, she smiled.

He felt a burst of pleasure, followed by a burst of shame.

Then another memory came to him.

It was the smile that had brought the memory. Bear had seen that smile before, that smile in that beautiful oh-so-human face.

He was sitting in the greatroom, with Tayor at his feet. The house began to shake, the entire house bouncing and wiggling, the windows flexing and bending, things in the kitchen falling off their hooks. Electrical devices snapped and popped. Bear stopped what he was doing —he could not remember what. He only remembered the alarm, and Tayor barking.

After that there was a gap. It wasn't a blocked memory, because he had never known what happened.

He was buried in rubble, bits of wood and dust and stone and shattered hylar. A hard, cold mechanical hand took hold of his right arm and pulled him free. He thought the hand had come to rescue him, but it hurt where it gripped his bare flesh, and he complained… but it didn't let go, just held him up, forcing him to stand on his feet.

Wreckage was everywhere. People were running in all directions, some screaming and shouting. Bear looked around in bewilderment. The metal hand at last released him, and he saw now it was attached to a black metal creature like an enormous insect, with a rounded carapace and huge mechanical arms and legs. Several of these machines or creatures or whatever they were walked to and fro, and he saw one shoot twin yellow beams of fire or light from emitters that protruded from the front of its body.

The machine creature that had rescued Bear took hold of him again, this time gripping him around his belly and lifting him. He screamed as it tilted him toward a hatchway that opened in its top. Something smelled funny, like burned plastic. The interior of the machine creature was dark.

There was another gap.

Bear must have fallen asleep, awakening in what looked like a hospital. The hospital was not Doctor Kamra's hospital. Bear had never been here before.

"Tayor!" he called. "Tayor!"

Where were Mum and Dad? There were other children, in white beds to either side of him. They all wore gray tunics and gray trousers, their feet bare.

He drifted in and out of sleep, and then he saw a face looming over him, the face of a beautiful young woman with tan skin and a comforting smile.

The face of Miss Sweet.

"There, now," she said. "Are you awake? It's all right. Everything is going to be all right."

"Where's my mum and dad?" he asked. "Where's Tayor?"

Miss Sweet shook her head. "I think you must be imagining things. We rescued you from the slave pens. You're safe now."

That was what she'd said, and he'd stared at her in confusion. When had he been in slave pens? What had happened to his house, to the others in the neighborhood?

"Was there an earthquake?" he asked.

"Don't you worry," Miss Sweet said. "We'll explain everything later. You just rest now."

She left.

He hadn't known her as Miss Sweet at the time.

The memory stayed with him as he filed toward the dining hall. Miss Sweet had rescued him, she really had. How could he have forgotten something like that? Still, it was unclear what had happened. Had there been some kind of disaster? The machine creatures had been scary, but they'd taken him to the hospital. Maybe they really had been trying to help, rescuing people from the smashed houses.

What had happened to his mum and dad? Where were they?

The corridor smelled of something good. Really good, as good as the food in his old house.

"Mmm! What's that smell?" said Roma, turning to Bear with wide eyes and a crooked grin.

Bear's mouth began to water, and his stomach clenched. The hallway outside the dining room was filled with the delicious aroma; and he breathed it in, feeling his nostrils expand and wishing they could expand even further.

With glowing faces, the children crowded toward the door of the dining room, eager to see what this might be.

Inside, Bear took his seat at the white table with Emmot, Aril, Roma, and a tall girl named Kalla. His stomach was painful, and he didn't think he could bear to wait any longer. The memory of the disaster no longer preoccupied him. His hunger now ruled. He just wanted to eat whatever was making that incredible smell.

At last the table opened. A wide white bowl rose toward him, a bowl of steaming golden soup. White noodles floated in the broth alongside flaky white stuff—meat, maybe. On a plate next to the soup was a large oval slice of real bread, hot as if just out of the oven and covered in melted butter.

"Oh!" Emmot cried. He dove at his bowl, scooping the broth and noodles into his open mouth with his spoon.

Bear took a hesitant sip, worried the soup might be too hot. But it was just right; and as the rich flavour filled his mouth memories filled his mind, more memories of home and parents and the little dog at his feet. His chest felt tight, the emotions just held in check. He took another sip, and another, eyes squeezed shut.

When he was done, his bowl empty and his bread reduced to a few tiny crumbs, he looked up to see Miss Sweet come into the dining room. This was something she'd never done before, and all of the children stopped eating and stared at their teacher in sudden silence.

Miss Sweet placed herself at the head of the room, just as she did during her lessons.

"There is an old saying from Earth that is appropriate within the present context," she said. "This saying is 'leave room for dessert.' It is a warning not to overeat during the first courses of a meal. Your stomachs are not large, and though most of you would like to have a second serving of noodles and bread, that would fill you up and you would be unable to enjoy the next course."

Bear's empty bowl and plate disappeared into the table. Seconds later another bowl appeared. This bowl was smaller and contained two round-ed brown balls with rough surfaces. Bear took the small spoon that had arrived with the bowl and gave the brown stuff a poke. The spoon cut into it easily.

Bear looked at Aril with a broad grin. "Ice cream!"

He remembered the last time ice cream had been served here in the dining hall. It had been the anniversary of their rescue from slavery.

There were more howls and exclamations.

"I scream!" Emmot cried, proceeding to eat his in three enormous bites, which made him groan and hold his face, complaining about how cold it was.

Bear tried to savour his, taking tiny bites he let melt on his tongue.

Only Roma seemed a little unhappy.

"I don't like this flavour," she said.

"Children," Miss Sweet said, "your attention please!"

Bear looked up from his bowl to see that someone else had come into the room. He'd never seen this person before—a young man, thin but mus-cular, with light-brown skin and copper hair that glinted and sparkled. His clothes were simple close-fitting black trousers and a black square-cut jacket.

"Children," Miss Sweet repeated. "We have a visitor today from Janus. This is Mister Verren. He has come to inspect the school and to see how your lessons are progressing."

Verren grinned at the students and raised a hand in greeting.

"Are you enjoying yourselves, children?" he asked.

Cheers erupted, hands and spoons waving in the air. Verren's smile broadened, and he held up both hands for quiet.

"Good!" he cried. "That's very good. We want you to be happy. We have high hopes for you. High hopes. You represent a new beginning for both Janus and, indeed, for the entire human race. Did you know that? Do you know how important you are? And because of that, it's really impor-tant that you listen and work hard, especially for the next few weeks. Am I right?"

This was not part of Questions and Answers, so Bear was not certain of the correct response. No one else seemed to know, either, and only one voice replied. It was Kalla, who said, "Yes, Mister."

Most of the others then chimed in, saying, "Yes, Mister."

Bear remained silent.

"Good," Verren repeated. "That's really great. Well, it's about time you finished up here so we can get started. Right, Miss Sweet?"

Bear thought he saw the man's eyes sparkle—*really* sparkle with a glint of inner light. Which was strange, because human eyes didn't do that.

Chapter 5

F our Guardians led the children to the play yard, and there Guardian Number One told them to form one long line, elbow to elbow, facing the outer wall. Bear ended up standing between Aril on his left and Roma on his right.

He couldn't help being excited.

Miss Sweet and Mister Verren walked along the line, finally halting in the center and facing the assembled pupils. Miss Sweet stood a little closer to the kids than Mister Verren. She raised her hands in front of her, palms downward, then lowered them.

"Now, everyone sit," she said. "There are chairs provided."

Bear looked behind him. A chair had appeared where no chair had been before. It was white and shiny and didn't look very comfortable; but when he sat, he discovered it was made of a soft cushiony material, unlike the chairs in the dining hall.

The children gasped and giggled at this latest wonder.

"Quiet, please!" said Miss Sweet.

"Please, be quiet," Guardian Number One repeated.

The chatter ceased. The Guardians moved down the line of seated children, passing out tubes of gray plastic, each about twenty centimetres long. Bear examined his, turning it over, noticing a ridge or seam running along one side. He scraped at the seam, discovering it was actually the edge of a plastic sheet, rolled up inside the tube.

After the tubes had been distributed, the Guardians handed out what looked like toy animals, placing one at the feet of each child. Bear and most of the others laughed in surprise and delight. He thought the toy at his feet was an elephant, another animal that didn't live on Sturnus but that he recognized. It stood on its hind legs, like a human, about as tall as his knee, and was gray with a curling trunk and floppy ears.

Bear glanced from side to side and saw that every kid had received a different toy, all based on terrestrial animals—stuffed animals with fluffy fur, smiley faces, and bright yellow eyes.

"I got a horse, Bear!" Roma said, her smile bright. "Look!"

Aril's creature was a cat of some kind, light tan with brown spots.

Bear resisted the urge to pick up his elephant and hold it. They'd not yet been given permission, and he knew better than to do anything before he was told it was okay. At the same time, he sensed today was not a day for harsh reprisals. Something was going on. First, there'd been the good food, and now toys, all coinciding with the arrival of this Mister Verren.

Was he taking over?

No, Bear decided. Miss Sweet seemed to still be in control.

"Now, pay attention," Miss Sweet said. She held one of the rolled plastic tubes. "This is what you are to do."

She touched the tube to her forehead, just above and in line with her eyebrows. When she took her hands away, the tube stayed in place. It looked funny, and some of the children giggled. Miss Sweet then pulled the rolled plastic sheet out of the tube so that it covered her eyes, like a pair of goggles.

"Now, everyone do what I have just done. The tube is your controller."

Bear did as instructed. The tube stuck to his forehead with a faint tingling sensation, while the plastic sheet was so clear he barely noticed it.

"Now the moment you've all been waiting for," Miss Sweet continued. "You may pick up your animals."

With much shuffling and noises of delight and satisfaction, the kids took up their toys. Bear was surprised at how heavy his was.

"There is a mechanical switch on the back of each animal's head," Miss Sweet said. "Find the switch, turn it on, and hold your puppet animal in your lap."

Bear found the switch—a small black rectangle—and moved it, felt it click into place. A faint humming, almost like a musical note, emanated from somewhere. The sound didn't seem to be coming from the elephant, but from inside Bear's ears.

"Some of you may not be successful at what we are about to ask you to do," said Miss Sweet. "This is natural, and no one should be alarmed. Not everyone has an identical brain to everyone else. Some people are good at understanding some things, but not others. I urge you all not to worry, but at the same time, I also ask you to make a maximum effort."

Bear felt a sudden pang of nervousness, suddenly afraid he would be one of these kids who couldn't do the thing, whatever it was, they were about to be asked to do. It didn't matter that Miss Sweet told them not to worry.

"If you don't succeed the first time," Miss Sweet said, "there will be another time. It may take your brain a while to make the connection, but you all have the necessary machinery to do that. Every one of you has something in your head. Did you know that? You have something we have given you, a thing that will help you communicate with the animal puppet we have also given you. That thing we call a *nexus*. It will help you become entangled with your puppet, what we call a *proxy*. You and the animal will become one."

At the mention of the nexus, Bear's stomach did a flip. The last time he'd heard that word had been in the dark room, when the voice of the woman who was not Miss Sweet had said that his nexus was working properly.

He looked at his elephant, looked into its bright-yellow eyes, then pulled it toward his small chest, holding it in a tight embrace. That made him feel a little better.

"Have you all turned on your animals?" Miss Sweet asked.

A chorus of affirmatives.

"Good. Stand them on the floor in front of you, facing away. Once you have done that, we will take the next step. Quite literally!" She laughed a musical laugh. "These animals are robotic proxies. You can control them. When you do, you will become the animal, though you will also retain control of your own body. The controller device you have fixed to your forehead allows you to do this.

"Your brain produces electrical activity that is processed by the nexus. Your controller receives and amplifies those signals, filtering out the ones that are not useful and converting the useful ones to information your puppet understands. At the same time, your puppet emits signals that can be read by your controller. *If* you can sense them."

Miss Sweet paused. She held her hands clasped in front of her. The children waited, hushed. Miss Sweet seemed to look from child to child. When she met Bear's eye, she smiled, and the automatic pleasure that caused made him look away, embarrassed.

"Listen to the music," Miss Sweet said. "The music is all-important. It underpins everything. You may also sense colours and shapes, but the music is the most direct representation of what you need to see."

Bear listened to the humming in his ears, concentrating. To his surprise, the sound grew louder, more distinct, and changed, becoming higher in pitch. It sounded like someone drawing an endless bow across a violin string. Even more strange, it seemed to have a spatial origin, although not in the normal sense of something producing sound waves. The note still came from inside his head, but he could follow it with his mind, trace it to where it seemed *thicker*, and that was the elephant.

A translucent image appeared on the clear plastic sheet hanging over his eyes. It took him a moment to realize he was seeing from the elephant's perspective as it stared at the outer wall from its position at his feet.

"Do you have the link?" Miss Sweet said.

"Yes!" Bear shouted in his excitement, as did a few other voices.

"Well, I don't have it," Aril whined. "What's supposed to happen?"

"It's cool," Bear said. "You follow the music, and you can look with your puppet's eyes."

"Okay. But how?"

"If you have the link with your animal," Miss Sweet was saying, "you may control the dominance of each visual field. That means you can choose between what you see with *your* eyes and what your proxy's eyes see. This may be done with little effort, simply by concentrating on the view you want to dominate."

Bear discovered it was as simple as his teacher had described. If he wanted to just see with the elephant's eyes, he could. Or he could see with his own eyes only. It was a matter of engaging the musical tone, of bringing it closer or farther away, a sensation that was both pleasant and relaxing, especially when the strange tone seemed to fill him and recede into the background. He could sense it without really hearing it, like a wave through his body. This happened when he was the elephant, only the elephant, and it felt good.

He closed his eyes, his real eyes, for a few seconds, but could still see as the elephant. He hadn't realized how tensely he'd been holding his shoulders, how cramped they'd become, so he reached up to stretch his arms and back.

Bear's real body remained motionless in his chair, but the elephant moved, stretching *its* arms and back.

"Very good, Bear!" Miss Sweet said. "You are now a puppeteer. The rest of you! Do as Bear has done! Become the proxy in front of you and walk across the yard to the wall."

Bear felt like laughing. He wasn't the kid who failed, but the kid who took to the task like a natural!

In his excitement, he had let the elephant's view fade, but the musical tone was still there, still strong, so he followed it back to its source, riding it like a current in a wire; and he was the elephant. He took one hesitant step with what felt like his own leg. It was simple. He just walked, but he could feel the smooth floor under his elephant feet, and when he looked at his hands he saw fuzzy gray plush.

When he reached the wall and turned around, he saw himself sitting in the chair, hands on his lap, with Roma and Aril on either side of him.

Aril was one of only three children who had been unable to move their puppets.

"I can't do it," he said, sounding desperate and frustrated. "I just can't do it. What am I supposed to do?"

"Listen for the music, Aril," Miss Sweet said. "Can you hear it?"

"What music?" Aril cried, and he started to stomp the ground with his feet.

Bear pulled away from his elephant, dropping the music, letting it fall away until he'd returned to his own point of view.

"It's like a note, Aril," he said. "A note in your head. Can't you hear it?"

"No! That's what I've been trying to tell you!"

Mister Verren stepped forward.

"It's okay," he said, holding out his hands. "As Miss Sweet said, not all of you will hear it the first time. Why don't you and the other two who are having trouble go see Guardian Number Three? He has something for you to do. Don't forget to take your animal."

Aril let out one final exasperated sigh and rose from his chair. He and the two others who had failed went with Guardian Number Three, who led them back into the school.

Bear glanced at Aril's empty chair.

"Figures Aril would mess things up," said Roma.

Bear was a little worried about Aril, and sympathetic that he'd encountered the very problem Bear had feared; but there was no sense in dwelling on another person's problems. Aril would figure it out. For now, Bear had his own proxy elephant to play with, to walk around the yard and interact with the other proxies he encountered, waving at Roma's horse and punching Emmot's Hippopotamus on the arm.

Time passed too quickly. When the midday eclipse came, the session ended.

"Leave your proxies where they are, children," Miss Sweet said. "Just leave them be. You will see them again, don't worry."

The Guardians collected the tubular controllers, and the kids filed back into the school, disappointed but in good spirits.

Bear climbed the sloping classroom to his seat. When everyone had settled in, he noticed that neither Aril nor the other two kids who had failed had returned to class.

Miss Sweet went through a Question-and-Answer session, but Bear didn't answer with the usual enthusiasm. He started to worry Aril had been taken to the dark room, but that made no sense. For one thing, Miss Sweet was here. Plus, Aril hadn't done anything wrong.

He was probably getting extra instruction in how to use his proxy, that was all.

At supper, Aril's seat in the dining hall remained empty. Emmot looked at Bear and said, "Hey, where's Aril? You seen him?"

"He had to go for extra lessons with the puppets," Bear said, as if he knew for certain, but no one had ever skipped a meal for lessons. Except for Bear himself, when he'd been in the dark room.

Emmot seemed to accept Bear's explanation, but Bear was full of growing doubt.

"Miss Sweet said we'll get to use our puppets again tomorrow," Emmot said. "I can't wait! That was the most fun I've had in a long time. I wonder if we can fight them? I mean the puppets? Mine against yours."

"Stuffies don't fight, Emmot," Roma said.

Bear shrugged and poked at his food. No special soup and ice cream this time—they were back to a square of meat, one of grains, one of vegetables, and one of fruits. Bear had to force the food in and chewed with deliberate slowness.

Supper ended, and free time arrived. Bear went into the yard and climbed to the top of the playset, where he sat and gazed toward the forest. The sky above was already fading to deep mauve, with a few high cirrus clouds masking the face of Corvus. In the forest, a few birds fluttered and squabbled. For some reason, birds never came near the school, nor did flying insects.

Emmot joined Bear at the top of the playset.

"King of the Air?" he asked.

Bear ignored the question.

"Hey, Emmot, ever wonder what's on the other side of the woods?"

Emmot let out a single bark of laughter.

"All the time! Every day, I think. I'd love to find out. And you know what else?"

He pointed toward the city. Bear looked and saw a black ball rising from amid the distant gray towers. Another ship, probably going back to Janus.

"I wanna go where they're going," Emmot said. "They tell us all about Janus, but we never get to go there?"

"We never get to go anywhere," Bear said.

"Yeah," Emmot agreed, sounding plaintive.

Bear looked back toward the forest. He'd had a good day, a fun day, and for some reason that bothered him, as if he'd betrayed his growing sense that Miss Sweet and the Janusians were deceivers.

The problem was that he wasn't sure of anything.

What would happen if he just ran, just took off and ran into the woods some day during one of the play sessions in the field?

He'd be found and brought back pretty quickly, he supposed.

He thought of his parents, and his old home. He thought of the statue of Artemis. Was it still somewhere out there?

Resting his face in his hands, he closed his eyes. He needed answers and had no way of getting them.

He opened his eyes. Hovering in the air before him was the glowing girl.

He sat upright.

"Emmot," he said. "Hey, Emmot!"

"What?" Emmot said. He was now near the bottom of the playset, climbing on the lower layer of pipes. Bear hadn't noticed that he'd moved.

"Never mind," Bear said. He had been about to ask Emmot if he could see the girl; but she was hovering above the wall, outside its confines. Emmot couldn't have seen her from where he stood.

The girl floated closer. Now she was inside the wall. Her dangling feet in their buckled shoes looked funny.

Emmot didn't react, even though now she should have been well within his view.

Bear just stared.

"You can see me," the girl said.

"What?" Bear said.

"What do you mean, 'what?'" Emmot said.

"Nothing!" said Bear.

"You can see me," the girl repeated.

Emmot had climbed down to the ground and started running, away from the playset. All of the kids in the yard were doing their usual things. No one was staring and pointing at the glowing girl floating closer and closer to where Bear sat.

He looked back at the girl and nodded.

"I've been looking for someone who can see me," she said. "And hear me. You're the first."

"Who are you?" Bear asked.

The girl turned her head, her hair swinging as if it were real hair, with mass.

"I'm not sure," she said. "Things are coming to me slowly."

She was now so close that Bear could have touched her, but he didn't dare. Everything about her was golden and luminous, and he wondered if she'd burn his fingers. He thought she was very pretty—beautiful, in fact —and with the hair that spilled down past her shoulders, the shapeless dress that flowed around her, she was like a star that had come down from the night sky. For all that, he wasn't afraid. He was relieved to finally meet her, to talk to her.

"I think my name is Min," the girl continued. "That's the name I remember. Yes! My name is Min."

"I'm Bear."

Min had halted less than half a metre away. "Hello, Bear. That's a funny name."

Bear pulled himself up, finding a more comfortable position on top of the playset. "It is?"

The girl's smile vanished. "I'm sorry. I didn't mean to make fun of you. I was hoping we could be friends."

"We can," Bear answered. "And my name *is* kind of funny. It's a kind of animal. Don't worry about that."

The girl looked pleased.

"My first friend."

She hovered there, grinning. A few minutes passed as Bear searched for something to say. He wanted to ask whether she knew anything about his family, about what had happened, but he couldn't quite figure out how to start.

"Why are you floating?" he asked.

"Floating? Oh, that's because I'm not really here." The girl closed her eyes, and her face twisted in a series of rapid expressions. "I'm a projection," she said. "I think. From far away. One that only you've been able to see so far. To 'pick up'. I'm like…a signal." Suddenly, her eyes widened, her smile faded, and her face became serious. "I think I'm a prisoner. I think I'm trapped where I am. I need to be rescued."

"You're a prisoner?" Bear said, and his heart sank. This meant his hopes she had a special message for him, that she knew what had happened to his parents, probably weren't true. Maybe she had nothing to do with any of that.

"Yes. I'm stuck here. I've been looking for someone to help me. Can you help me?"

Bear shook his head.

"I'm sorry, Min. But…how?"

Min had begun to rise, floating into the air like an ember from a fire.

"Where are you going?" Bear cried, careless of who might hear him. "Where are you a prisoner?"

"I have to think about it," Min said, rising higher and higher. "I'll come back. I think I can figure it out. Then you can come and help me."

She started to fade, her light dimming, her form becoming less substantial. She raised one hand and waved, and then winked out of existence.

Bear stared after her, hoping she would come back but knowing she wouldn't. Not tonight.

A few stars had appeared in the sky, and a faint breeze stirred. The chime sounded. It was time to go in, time for bed.

Bear climbed down from the playset in a daze, disappointment and soaring excitement mingling, but the excitement was gaining ground. Min said she would come back. He would see her again.

He had too much to think about and felt like he understood nothing.

He followed the other children inside, through the Washroom and into his bedroom. There he discovered Aril, safe and sound and already asleep. That was a huge relief, but now Bear was too tired and too distracted to think about it. His sleeping sack opened, and he climbed in.

Chapter 6

"T hey took us to another classroom and made us practice," Aril told Bear the next day in the yellow breakfast room. "I started to get it—I could hear the music, like you said, just a little. But I kept losing it, and my cat kept falling down." He sighed, a long dramatic breath of dissatisfaction. "It's really hard!"

"You just need to practice," Bear said, happy that he had been right after all. "Everything is easier with practice."

"I hope so," Aril said. He leaned on his elbow and prodded his wheat cake, and didn't look his usual enthusiastic self.

"You gotta learn how to do this," Emmot said, "so we can have battles."

"It's fun," said Roma. "I got to be a horse. It wasn't like a real horse that runs on four legs, but it was still a horse. I can't wait to try it again! You'll get it, Aril. You'll see."

After breakfast, the Guardians herded the children into the yard and told them to line up in four files of ten children each facing the outer wall. Bear stood in the rightmost file behind Emmot. He knew they were going to get to play with the animals again, and that was exciting.

The outer wall split, its sides folding back like curtains to reveal the grassy hills outside and the woods beyond. A collective gasp went up from the children, and Bear felt his mouth drop open. He'd never seen the wall do that before.

Miss Sweet was waiting for them, standing in the grass. She was dressed in tight green leggings and a slender coat of a deep rich brown made from a very fine material. Her face was also brown, although her eyelids were coral pink; and her hair looked like green leaves.

46

Bear looked for Mister Verren, but there was no sign of him.

The meadow seemed wider than usual, a vast sea of grass; and the morning air was still, and smelled of green and growing things, and the passing of the colder season on Sturnus. Bear thought it must be a warm day, but it was hard to tell, since his clothes kept him warm no matter the air temperature.

He wiggled his bare toes in the yielding turf. The grass and soil always felt so strange after the smooth surfaces of the school floors. Birds twittered in the distant woods, and they drew his attention.

The woods had always fascinated him. In among the yellowpines were scattered fire maples, glowing with new yellow-green leaves, luminous in the sunshine; and sight of them reminded him of Min. The anticipation of seeing her again, of learning more of her secrets, filled him with warmth of a different kind.

"So, my little birds," Miss Sweet said, "we will build on what you learned yesterday. Today, you will study the signal that your proxy emits."

The Guardians were walking along the files of children, passing a tubular controller to each one, and also a band made from some stretchy black cloth.

"We are giving you blindfolds," Miss Sweet explained. "When you receive your blindfold, pull it over your head and place it over your eyes. When you have done that, fit your controller in place. Does everyone understand?"

"Yes, Miss Sweet," Bear said with the rest.

"Once you have done that, reach out and try to sense your proxy. The signal will appear in a few minutes if you are patient."

Bear pulled the elastic cloth band over his face, and the beautiful meadow disappeared, the world going dark. For a few seconds he panicked, because it reminded him of the dark room; but he could still sense the environment and the people around him—small noises from the other kids, the breeze, the chattering of the distant birds. Footsteps sounded on the soft ground, moving here and there, probably the Guardians. Bear's fear subsided.

Now he could hear another sound, a faint fluting. This must be the tone of his proxy, except it was different from before. This wasn't the elephant's tone he'd heard yesterday. Maybe the Guardians had placed a different toy in front of him. He couldn't see it, so how was he to know?

He followed the tone as he'd done before. It grew stronger, but something seemed wrong, seemed off. The tone was coming from behind him. That didn't make sense. He must have done something wrong.

Alarmed, he dropped the signal, letting it go with a snap. He shook his head. It was strange, because now he could hear multiple signals, all faint but distinguishable, similar but with different tones, different textures, some smooth, some warbling, some with undertones or overtones. It was confusing, and again he panicked. He couldn't find his proxy signal, and realized that, despite his success yesterday, he was failing after all, only unlike Aril, he could hear too many signals instead of none. Where were they all coming from?

They must have been from all of the other proxies. For some reason he could hear them all.

He took a deep breath and tried again. His signal had to be there. He just had to find it, to sort it from all the others.

He listened, and his heart leapt, because there it was, close to him, just as it should have been! How had he missed it before? Maybe the Guardians hadn't placed his elephant in front of him yet, or maybe they hadn't turned it on.

Relieved, he followed the signal, and his world was once again filled with light as he opened his eyes. The *elephant's* eyes. He was in control of his puppet again.

"Once you find your proxy," Miss Sweet's voice said, although Bear was sure he was hearing it with the elephant's ears, "you must practice. Walk about. See how well you can control a machine that you cannot see."

Bear spun around on short elephant legs and saw that he was just a few yards from his file. There he stood, with Aril and Emmot and Roma, all of them with their eyes covered by the black bands. It was a little unsettling to see himself from the outside, so he turned away, walking a few paces through the grass. It seemed to take a long time to get anywhere, the puppet's legs were so stubby, so he started to run. Wind rushed in his floppy ears. He *was* the elephant!

He ran for the forest.

The yellowpines drew closer. They looked taller than he remembered, seen from the elephant's perspective. He wondered what would happen if he just ran into the woods. Would the Guardians chase his proxy and bring it back? Or would they just let him go? After all, his real body was still back inside the school wall.

He ducked under the trees. He'd never run so far without feeling out of breath, without gasping, his chest heaving and the blood thudding in his ears. He didn't feel any pain or discomfort at all, just the prickly pine needles under his elephant feet. The trees were fragrant, and he took a breath, felt the air come in through his little elephant trunk. A few insects buzzed, but they didn't bother him. The forest lay calm and golden in the morning sunlight.

This was his chance to find out what was on the other side of these woods.

"Now, bring your proxies back from wherever you have taken them," Miss Sweet said, and Bear knew he was hearing her with his own ears, not the elephant's. "Bring them back."

He hesitated. He didn't want to leave the forest so soon. He toyed with the idea of running just a little farther, just a few more metres. But he could not disobey Miss Sweet.

With one forlorn glance over his elephant shoulder, he made his way back into the meadow. Again he ran, relishing the sense of power and control. He could feel his breathing, if he thought about it, but it was just his own lungs at rest. He ran right back to where his body stood and halted at his feet.

"After some time," Miss Sweet said, "your proxy will become matched to your brain pattern. It will be imprinted. For some of you this will already have happened. After that, no one else will be able to use your proxy but you."

Bear walked his proxy toward Aril and stood it on one leg, elephant arms in the air.

"Aril," he said in his own voice (he wasn't sure the elephant had a voice), "can you see me? Where's your cat?"

Aril was sweating, his hands clenching and unclenching.

"I don't know where it is, Bear." He sounded exasperated. "I haven't been able to find it."

Bear looked. The cat puppet was sitting on the ground half a metre away.

They practiced again later that day, after second dawn. It was clear some of the children were better at controlling their proxies than others, and Bear seemed to be among the best. At one point, he challenged a boy named Puck, whose proxy was a spotted cat, and a girl named Mella, whose proxy was an odd thing with spines and a long nose, to a race. Bear won the race. His stride was more natural and efficient than the others, who wobbled and even fell down a few times. Puck challenged him to a second race, and Bear won that one, too. And a third.

Aril continued to have trouble. He could only use his proxy if he could see it, and then he kept losing contact. When he was able to control it, his steps were awkward and hesitant, and he fell often.

"You'll get it," Bear assured him. "You were better today than yesterday. You just have to keep doing it."

Roma stayed with Aril and tried to coach him, but Bear couldn't watch for long. Aril's clumsy efforts were making him anxious.

When the instructional day ended, and the children sat down in the dining hall, Bear felt how tired he was, almost as tired as he would have

49

been if he'd been running all day for real. He'd been impressed by his elephant's stamina, but its actions had drained his strength after all. Maybe thinking made him tired, and it seemed that thinking was really the way he controlled his proxy. He hoped he would get stronger over time, just as he'd told Aril that *he* would improve. It seemed an important goal, although he had no idea why Miss Sweet and the other Janusians were teaching them how to remote-control toy animals.

An image appeared in his head, of his father sitting in a chair with a chappie maker whirling around his head. His father had been controlling the chappie maker with his thoughts, just like Bear controlled his elephant. That meant his parents had known about this sort of thing. That gave him comfort. He was doing something his father had wanted to teach him.

That night his sleep was more relaxed and deeper than it had been in days.

In the morning, his sleep bag opened, and he followed the crowd to the privy and Washroom, going through the usual motions with a little more enthusiasm than even before his memories of home and parents had surfaced. He was looking forward to finishing his breakfast and getting back to playing with his proxy, maybe even returning to the woods, maybe exploring a little farther.

When he got to the breakfast room, something seemed different. It took only a moment's examination, of looking around, to see what had changed. The four rows of ten children had shrunk. At his table there were eight children on one side, six on the other. At the other long table, there were seven and six. The chairs had been spaced at even intervals, but this did nothing to hide the smaller numbers.

Thirteen children were missing.

"Where's Aril?" he said, half-rising from his seat. He realized he hadn't seen Aril come out of his sleep bag that morning, that his sleep bag hadn't even been there. Someone had removed it.

Roma and Emmot remained at his table. Aril was gone. There wasn't even an empty chair.

"There's a whole bunch of people missing," Roma said.

Guardian Number Four stepped forward from his place near the door. He loomed over Roma, his little round face looking stern, almost angry. Bear had never seen the Guardian look like that before.

Roma shrank from the tall man's presence.

"Now, Roma," he said, "this is not something you should worry about, or alarm the others. Everything is as it should be. You must refrain from speculation."

The Guardian's tone was so stern that Bear froze with his spoon halfway to his mouth. Roma was cringing, as if she thought she could squeeze herself into the table.

"Eat your breakfast," the Guardian added, and then he paused, staring across the room. After a few seconds, his smile returned. "It's all right. You mustn't feel bad. Some of the children, those who were having trouble with the next step, have been sent to a different school. Do not worry about them."

He walked away, and Bear was surprised to see him leave the room. Guardian Number Three came in to take his place. He stood by the door, smiling and not speaking.

"A different school?" Roma whispered. "What does he mean, a different school?"

Bear could see that she was trying not to cry.

Emmot looked around with wide eyes as he ate his porridge. Bear lifted his spoon to his mouth again, but his breakfast tasted like dry dirt, and his stomach felt sick and heavy. Aril was one of his best friends, and now he was gone. He'd simply disappeared.

Miss Sweet had said that some of them would fail. Aril had failed.

Chapter 7

B ear left most of his breakfast on the table when the Guardians led the remaining children to the large classroom. It seemed there was to be no practice with the proxies this morning. That added further disappointment to an already distressing day.

"Miss Sweet is on her way," said Guardian Number Two. "Miss Sweet is on her way."

Bear was quiet. He held his hands folded in his lap. The atmosphere in the classroom was solemn.

Miss Sweet swept in, arms outstretched, looking magnificent, some hybrid between human and dragon, a mythical beast that populated Janusian tales. Her face was green and scaled, her eyes cold blue, her hair a scaled crest that ran across the top of her skull and down her back; and her flowing green dress gave the impression of wings.

Bear found it a little frightening.

"Good morning, my little birds! And congratulations to you all. You are the children who have passed the first test, who have taken the next step. The lesson is over, and you all did very well, very well, indeed. Give yourselves some applause."

She started clapping her hands. A few kids joined, and then the whole class was clapping, Bear included. He couldn't help feeling a little proud that he'd performed so well with the proxies. He'd achieved something, and his fears hadn't come to pass. But that pride wasn't enough to counter his upset at losing his friend.

"So, for the next few hours we will have a break," said Miss Sweet. "A story, I think, about travelling in space."

Bear loved Miss Sweet's stories, but this time he found it hard to listen. Too many strange things had happened in the past few days, some wonderful and some terrible. If he added them all together, the terrible outweighed the wonderful. At least, the confusion and uncertainty and suspicion outweighed the fun of playing with a puppet.

He thought of Min. He hadn't seen her yesterday. He wanted to see her again. Even after what she'd told him, he still sensed she could help him figure out what was going on, that there was some connection. There had to be.

The story was ending, and the children were clapping again, and Roma was grinning. There'd been a dragon in the story, a bad dragon that had somehow turned good, but Bear hadn't really been paying attention.

In the yard after class, Bear lingered in the southwest corner of the wall. The yard was not as noisy as usual, so many kids were missing.

"Why are you moping again?" Roma asked him.

Bear shrugged. "Because Aril's not around?"

Roma looked panicked for a second and turned away without saying anything more. Bear could see he wasn't the only one who was upset.

He spied Guardian Number Three strolling among the scattered children, hands clasped behind his back. Bear had always found the Guardians a little intimidating—strange adults who did nothing but issue instructions—but they were also helpful sometimes.

Bear walked toward the Guardian.

"Excuse me, Guardian?" he said.

"Yes, Bear?" said the Guardian, crouching to bring his odd face level with Bear's.

"I just wanted to know," Bear said, but his throat tried to close over with sudden anxiety, so he cleared it and started again. "I just wondered if you could tell me where the other kids went? The ones who needed more instruction?"

"To another school," said the Guardian. "As I believe you have been told?"

"I know," Bear said. "But where is it?"

The Guardian continued to smile, but to Bear his eyes seemed empty, like the eyes of a bad drawing.

"It is in the city," the Guardian said. "On the other side. You should be happy for them. They are receiving the instruction that they require."

Bear sighed.

"Will I ever see them again?"

The Guardian rose to his full height.

"You may someday. When your instruction has concluded."

That brought a faint glimmer of hope.

"When will that be?"

It had never occurred to Bear that his time here would conclude, but of course it would.

"That is for Miss Sweet to decide," the Guardian said. "Now, I'm afraid those are all the answers I have for you on this subject, Bear. Why don't you go and play?"

The Guardian resumed his stroll. Bear stared after him, feeling small and unimportant.

Second dawn came. The Guardians led the children through the wall and back into the meadow for more practice with their proxies. Bear waited with Roma and Emmot, but he wasn't as excited as he'd been the day before. Instead, he felt bored and impatient and dissatisfied.

Miss Sweet appeared, and now she was no longer a dragon but her ordinary self, with tan skin and black hair piled on top of her head, and a dark-mauve coat that hung below her knees.

The Guardians distributed the controllers and placed each child's proxy on the ground in front of them. Bear looked at his elephant. His stomach felt bloated and heavy. He didn't feel like playing.

"There has been much talk and speculation," Miss Sweet began, "about what has happened to your former companions, those who have not achieved what you have achieved. Yes, I do listen to you when you speak amongst yourselves."

Bear felt a stirring of hope. The Guardian had told him that Miss Sweet would answer his concerns, and here it looked like she was about to do so.

"You need not think of them anymore," Miss Sweet said, and now she looked stern, and that was alarming. "They were your friends, but you have moved past them. They failed to do what you can do, and so do not deserve the standing that you will have, as you grow and develop. Does that sound strange to you? That you are the future of the human race? The future of Sturnus?"

She paused and looked from child to child. Bear's heart was pounding, and his face felt flushed. Miss Sweet had just dismissed his friend as a failure.

"You may feel sad for a while," she added, "but this will pass, and is unnecessary. Remember that negative thoughts and feelings are unproductive!"

The Guardians had formed a dispersed line behind her. Bear knew they were here to look after the children, to make sure none of them wandered away or got lost; but suddenly they didn't look like protectors at all. They looked like soldiers from the stories. Enemy soldiers.

"This afternoon, we will practice," said Miss Sweet. "Simple practice. No blindfolds and no new lessons. Take your proxies and have some fun!"

The children began to play with their proxies, but Bear hesitated. Picking up his elephant, he studied it, looked at its funny smile and curled trunk. Around him, the others were finding their tones, and some were already walking their proxies across the grass.

"What am I going to do, elephant?" said Bear.

He flipped the switch in the puppet's head, put it down and closed his eyes, searching for the tone. He found it at once, followed it in and became the elephant. He walked past Roma's horse, through a patch of yellow starflowers, and toward one of the Guardians. Bear wondered if he could walk up to the Guardian and stomp on his foot, or climb up his leg and hit him in the face.

That was a negative thought, one that Miss Sweet wouldn't like, but it made Bear smile. So many of the heroes in the Janusian tales took matters into their own hands, fought the monster or the enemy, and triumphed.

Bear was unsure now whether the Janusians were his friends or his enemies. If it was the latter, how could he fight them? He was just a boy. And he didn't want to have to fight Miss Sweet. He didn't want to upset her in any way.

He wandered about in the grass, aimless, looking at the other proxies around him, some moving alone, some walking together or racing as he'd done yesterday. After a few minutes, he grew bored, so he stopped in the middle of the meadow.

The elephant's tone was there in his head, and he started playing with it, experimenting, discovering that he could let it fade and slip into the background. He could also pull away from it and have partial awareness of his real body. When he did this, he saw through two sets of eyes—two images, superimposed. He began toying with the strength of each image, making one dominate, then the other. After a while, he discovered he could pay attention to one while letting the other just sit there, even if they were the same strength.

All of the other tones were still there as well, a mosaic of sound in the background. Bear found them a bit annoying, but with a little experimentation, he found he could follow them just as easily as he could his own.

What would happen, he wondered, if he followed someone else's tone all the way to its source?

Picking a tone at random, he held onto his elephant but followed the third one, like sliding along a rope or cord, all the way across the meadow to a point near the edge of the woods. The new tone grew loud in his head, almost drowning out the elephant's. It was so strong Bear wondered if he could actually jump into someone else's proxy. Miss Sweet had said the proxies would imprint on their owners, and other people wouldn't be able to control them after a while. Had that already happened?

Expecting to be repulsed, or for the signal to simply block him or stop, Bear took the final step.

He found himself looking through a third set of eyes. He could see with his real eyes, through his elephant's eyes, and now through the other proxy's eyes, too. Three images, superimposed.

Where was this new proxy's owner? Was Bear just along for the ride? If he concentrated, he could feel the body, feel the arms and legs. He could see his surroundings, smell the warm yellowpines and hear the buzzing of insects. Looking down at his hands, he saw they were stubby hooves. He was a purple donkey or horse. Puck's proxy. But where was Puck? Had he dropped his signal?

Bear let his elephant fade a bit and took a few steps with the donkey puppet. It seemed to work for him fine, as if Puck had given up control.

He'd taken over Puck's proxy.

He knew he shouldn't be doing this, that it wasn't fair, that he wouldn't like it if someone else took over his elephant; but he was so amazed at this new ability that he just kept walking, taking one step after another, moving away from the woods, back toward where he and the other children stood in their line.

He saw Miss Sweet. She was looking at him, the real him. Did she know what he'd done?

That seemed possible, so in sudden panic he dropped the donkey with a snap. He was back where he'd started, half inside the elephant and half in his own head. He could still sense the multiple signals, the multiple tones, and could see Miss Sweet, looking away from him now. She had her arms folded across her chest. She didn't seem upset or suspicious.

So, she hadn't discovered that Bear had been using two proxies at once.

Relieved, Bear decided to try to see if he could do it again. Choosing another signal, a deep bass tone, he followed it, and within a few seconds he was in control of a yellow giraffe with purple polka-dots. It was strange to have such a long neck, with his hands and feet so far below.

"Bring your proxies in," Miss Sweet commanded.

Bear dropped the giraffe and returned to full command of his elephant. As he walked it back across the meadow, he regretted not having tried to walk two proxies at once, his elephant and the donkey or the giraffe. That led him to wonder if he could also control his body and a proxy at the same time, or if he had to choose one or the other. That would have to wait for next lesson.

He pulled his controller from his forehead and glanced along the line of children until he spied Puck. Puck was holding the purple donkey and frowning.

"Mine stopped working for a few minutes," Puck complained.

Bear felt a small pang of remorse. So, he'd knocked Puck out of his puppet and taken over completely. He thought he shouldn't have been able to do that, and that it was strange he could. His instinct was to tell Miss Sweet about this new development. Maybe it was normal. But no, he was sure it wasn't. He'd stumbled on another mystery. And if this was something he wasn't supposed to be able to do, something he shouldn't do, there was the threat of the dark room again, and of the pain.

He would keep this to himself. This was his secret, another secret in an increasingly long list.

⚜

It was hard to keep secrets. It made Bear lonely, and he missed Aril all the more. Aril had been easy to talk to.

In the yard after supper, Bear watched as Emmot and Puck climbed after each other on the playset. This made him a little angry. Emmot had just scooped up another playmate as if Aril had never existed. They'd never played with Puck before. Not much, anyway.

Maybe Emmot had the right idea. Why dwell on all the missing people that you couldn't bring back? What was the point?

But Bear missed them. He missed them already, just like he missed his mum and dad. Just like he missed his dog.

His surroundings seemed to close in on him, the walls of the yard looking less and less like they were there for his protection and more like those of a prison. He'd had a home once, a real home filled with sunlight and music, not this terrible gray place; but someone had taken it from him. Someone had reduced it to rubble.

Miss Sweet had rescued him. The bug machines had rescued him.

They hadn't rescued his parents.

Tears pooled in his eyes. His parents had been under that rubble. The bugs hadn't pulled them out. And Tayor, too. They'd left him in there. That meant his dog was dead, that his parents had been killed. Why hadn't the bugs rescued them, too?

Bear turned his face to the wall so no one would see him cry, but his shoulders began to shake. They were dead. He would never see them again.

An image came to him, another flash of memory, of the mechanical bugs like the one that had saved him. He gasped. Yellow beams projected from the front of the bugs. The beams had been hitting people, knocking them down. Killing them. He remembered it now. The bug machines had been shooting people, survivors of the wreckage, down in the street.

That meant the bugs hadn't rescued him. They'd *captured* him.

"Bear," a voice said from above. "Bear, are you there?"

He rubbed his eyes and looked up. Min was just at the top of the wall, making a slow descent toward him. Sight of her was a relief. Maybe he could talk to her. Maybe she would listen. He could tell her things he couldn't tell the other kids. She would never reveal his secrets. She *was* a secret.

"They took a bunch of us away today!" he whispered. "They took away my friend Aril, and I think they may have killed my family."

His voice broke, and he stifled a sob. Min stopped her descent and hovered just above the level of his eyes. She clasped her luminous hands to her mouth.

"Who did?"

"They told us that they saved us from slavery, Min," he murmured, "but they lied. They destroyed our town and captured us. I know that's what happened. I remember. They killed all the adults, and now half of the kids are missing."

"Who did this?" Min said.

Bear glanced around, but no one was paying attention. He hadn't been overheard.

"The Janusians," he said. "The people that look after us here at the school."

"That's terrible," said Min. "What are you going to do?"

Bear shook his head. There was nothing he *could* do.

"I have to escape," he said, even though that seemed ridiculous. "I'll figure out a way, if you can help me, Min."

Min brightened.

"If you escape, then you can come and rescue me. Remember? I'm a prisoner, too."

"I will, if I can find out where you are."

Min frowned.

"I still don't know where I am, but I almost have it. I'm still collecting…information. I'm still finding things out. Wait." She glanced to one side, as if listening for something. "I'm sorry. I have to go. I have to go, but I'll come back."

"What? You can't go yet!"

Bear took a step forward, but she was already gone, having winked out of existence.

He stared at the empty space where she'd hovered a second before.

"Come back," he said. "Min!"

He kicked at the spongy floor, the floor Aril had tried to tear up with a stick. Someday, he vowed, he would tear the whole thing up, the stupid floor and the school, too, and even the city if he could.

"Who were you speaking to a moment ago?" said Miss Sweet.

Bear whirled. He hadn't heard her approach, but there she was, tall and thin, her face dark-maroon, her hair waves of auburn. She'd changed since the morning.

"No one," he told her. "I was playing a game."

She nodded.

"I believe you," she said. "However, some of the things you said, as you played this game, concern me, Bear. You mentioned a family again. And that someone had killed them. Was this part of a game as well?"

Bear felt a stab of something like lightning through his heart. She'd heard everything. How had she heard him?

"I...I," he stammered. "Yes, it was the game."

Miss Sweet now shook her head and looked sad. She bent forward at the waist, bringing her face, her strange maroon face, close to Bear's.

"Bear," she said. "Bear, do you remember your parents?"

Her expression was unreadable, but her soft voice told Bear that she knew, she knew he remembered, that his memory repression, whatever that was, hadn't worked. And because she knew, there was no point in pretending, because she would still know, and she would still do the same thing.

"Why are we here?" Bear said, his voice trembling. "What did you do? Did you invade and kill everybody? Why did you take us away from our parents?"

There would be no escaping the dark room now, but he had to know.

"I am trying to help you, Bear," Miss Sweet said, straightening. "I want you to understand that."

"Maybe you didn't do any of those things yourself," Bear said, and suddenly he was angry, so angry he felt the pressure building in his head, his face, "but Janus did! Janus invaded and killed everyone and took us prisoner!"

Miss Sweet extended her right arm. Her face remained expressionless, but there was a dangerous light in her eyes.

"Bear, oh, Bear, must we go through this again?"

The Snake uncoiled from her wrist, the black cable twisting toward Bear's forehead.

"No!" he shouted, charging forward and shoving at her side with both hands, hoping to push her out of the way, but her body was solid, and he bounced off, almost falling backwards and just managing to regain his balance.

Then he ran.

He ran past the playset and the gaping faces of the other children. He wished he could climb the wall, just leap up and over it, and rush across the meadows and run into the forest. And that was the problem—he was trapped. There was nowhere to go.

The Guardians were fast. They seized him by the upper arms, deathly white hands squeezing his flesh so hard that he howled. They lifted him between them, high off the ground, letting his feet dangle. Miss Sweet was striding toward him, children leaping out of her way, and when she reached him she looked at Guardian Number Four.

"Bring him, please," she said. "I want to try something different."

The Guardians carried Bear toward the school.

Chapter 8

The Guardians didn't take Bear toward the usual entrance to the school, but toward what looked like a solid wall. He was so afraid that the strength had gone out of his body, and he hung limp in the Guardians' arms. Tears streamed down his face.

As they neared the wall, a doorway opened. Beyond was a gray corridor like the others in the building, although this one was longer, stretching away into distant shadow.

The Guardians did not take Bear far along the corridor. About five metres in, a flat table top emerged from the wall on the left, sliding from an unseen slot. The Guardians hefted Bear up onto the table, laying him on his back. A faint humming seemed to fill his head, not so much a sound as a sensation, similar to a proxy tone; and his limbs froze. It was just like the dark room. He was staring at the gray ceiling, able to blink his eyes but unable to move his arms or legs. He tried to shout, to speak, but nothing came out but a gurgle.

"This way," said the hushed voice of Miss Sweet.

The table or stretcher or whatever it was broke away from the wall and started to move. Bear tried again to break free of his bonds, so similar to those that had held him in the dark room, but his muscles wouldn't respond.

The ceiling twirled to the left as the table turned and entered another space, which felt like a small room or closet. The sense of motion ceased for a moment, then Bear's stomach seemed to rise, as if the floor had dropped. He was falling, and realized he was on a lift, and it was taking him down.

The sensation lasted only a few seconds, and then Bear's body was pushed down onto the stretcher as he decelerated. He hoped this was the end; but after a moment the room moved again, now sideways, suggesting that it wasn't just a lift but some kind of transportation system, a vehicle that ran inside vertical and horizontal passages, like the subways Miss Sweet had talked about in some of her stories.

The two Guardians remained on either side of the table, visible in Bear's peripheral vision. He couldn't see Miss Sweet, but assumed she was there. No one spoke.

The journey seemed to go on and on. Fatigue, probably the result of his fear, crushed down on him, and his eyes drooped and finally closed.

He awoke, eyes snapping open, to the sound of voices. Above him was a new type of ceiling, a high white dome crisscrossed by pale blue buttresses or rafters. He'd never seen a ceiling like that in the school, a ceiling with decoration. He was in another building, and the only other buildings that existed were in the city. There were several domes there. He knew them well, from gazing at them day after day.

"So, this is your primary?" one voice said, the voice of a young man. "He does not look like anything special."

"What should he look like?" said a second voice—Miss Sweet.

The first speaker snorted. "I don't know. What does a traitor look like?"

"That is not a useful way of thinking," Miss Sweet said. "There is no question of this boy's abilities. And there's something else, some other variable at play. No doubt, if you had not destroyed all of the records, we would have something to go on, but we don't."

"We don't want their technology," the first voice said, and Bear thought now it was familiar. "We don't want them at all."

"If you don't believe in my project, then you should not be here."

"I'm curious about your project, but I still need to be convinced."

Bear at last realized he was listening to the voice of Mister Verran, although he wasn't talking the way he had before. He sounded mean, and angry.

"We need an influx of genetic material," Miss Sweet said. "All of the remaining children have the ability to assimilate, this one more than the rest. But he is secretive and defiant, in a quiet way."

"He's willful and he's sneaky," said Verran.

Bear wanted to shout that he wasn't sneaky, but of course he still couldn't speak. And, anyway, he actually was sneaky, he supposed. Having secrets made you sneaky.

"He can be convinced to join us," said Miss Sweet. "To make his own decision. Maybe he can't be forced or coerced. Maybe he has to understand, to learn for himself that our way is the only way."

"Almost no one agrees with you," said Verran. "No one else thinks these kids are worth even a second of our time."

62

"I will make them see."

There was a pause. Verren said, "So, what next?"

Bear heard Miss Sweet draw in a long breath and let it out as a sigh.

"As you say, almost no one, including El-Ann, agrees with me, and I'm running out of time and resources. I have to show real results soon. The animal experiments were helpful, but we have to go further, and I believe this boy can help me."

There was a shuffling of feet.

"Allright," said Verran, now sounding farther away. "I'll defer to you, and support what you think is best. For now."

The dome above him started to rotate. Bear was moving again. Footsteps accompanied the table, although he could not see who made them. The Guardians, he assumed. He passed into another corridor, but this one was different, its ceiling arched and decorated with golden bands at even intervals. All sound became softer, muted, the footsteps less ringing.

From the arched corridor, they entered another room with a domed ceiling, this one oval, painted white with gold orbs and stars. The sense of movement ceased. The table tilted forward, raising Bear to a standing position.

The feeling came back into his body, and he slid a few inches to a carpeted floor. He cried out in surprise and almost fell, but by throwing out his arms managed to keep his balance.

Behind him, the table righted itself, then floated away in silence, back the way it had come. Bear watched it glide toward an open doorway on his left. The doorway was wide and framed with gold mouldings; and when the table had passed through it, an ornate door patterned with luminous gold diamonds slid into place.

Bear glanced around the room. It was the biggest room he'd ever seen. Two massive windows in one wall filled it with light. Under one of the windows, a woman sat in a golden chair.

Bear started. He hadn't noticed her at first, she'd been so quiet. He recognized Miss Sweet, although he had never seen her like this. Her face was a medium tan, long and thin, the skin a little lined and spotted, her hair plain and black, sprinkled with copper and gray and tied back in a single tail. She looked old to him, although not quite grandma-old. She looked like somebody's mom—and pretty, even striking. Her dress was plain, amber in colour, and fell past her knees, just covering the tops of her tan boots. She seemed small.

Bear had assumed he'd seen Miss Sweet as she truly was before, but realized he hadn't. Not until now.

"Bear," she said, rising from the chair. She was small, not much taller than he was. This was not the stately Miss Sweet who appeared in the classroom every day but a different woman, one less perfect. One more human.

It seemed she really could change her body parts.

Coming toward him, she halted, her eyes almost level with his. When she reached for him with one hand, he recoiled.

Her brows knit.

"I'm not going to hurt you, Bear. Why would you pull away?"

Bear looked at her arm. The sleeve of her dress came halfway to her wrist. There was no sign of the Snake.

"I didn't like being held on that table," Bear said. He was still tired, and he was also angry, and the anger gave him the nerve to respond with honesty.

Miss Sweet nodded.

"No, but you were not being cooperative, so we had to restrain you. I'm sorry."

"Okay," said Bear. He liked that she'd apologized. That meant she was going to treat him with a little more kindness, at least for now. "Where am I?"

"You are in another facility, outside our school. This one is more advanced. It is a facility for the most advanced students. Such as yourself."

Bear looked at his feet. Her praise could still make him feel proud, and a little embarrassed.

"You are very shrewd for a boy your age," Miss Sweet went on. "You understand things the others do not."

Her mouth curved in a smile, just a tiny crimp at the corners of her lips.

"I do understand things," Bear said. "Like that you lied to us about our being slaves. You lied because of what you did."

Miss Sweet frowned.

"We had to tell you a simple story…" she said, and Bear was a little shocked to hear this admission. "…because the truth is too complicated. It's not as bad as you think it may be. I don't wish for you to begin to hate us, to blame us for the loss of your old life. However, you must believe me when I tell you it was not all our fault. It was the fault of history. Some things must happen."

He shrugged. That sounded foolish. "Why? Why did you have to attack our town?"

"Because of things that happened before, things of which you are not aware. This is a step in our evolution, Bear. New and better systems supersede old systems. Do you know what that means?"

He didn't feel like playing the Question-and-Answer game, but knew he had no choice, so he shook his head.

"It means that, within history just as within organisms, new responses to new problems will arise as natural processes. Someone will formulate a method for doing something better. Other people will then use that method, or they will not. If it's a good method, more than half the time they will use it, and then they will stop doing things the old way and just use the new way after a while. Do you see?"

This sounded like so much nonsense, what Emmot would call "yak-yak," but Bear just said, "I get it," because he wanted her to stop. It sounded like she was making an excuse.

She reached out and touched his arm, actually held his left arm in her hand and gave it a squeeze. At one time he would have been over-joyed, overwhelmed with pleasure, to have her do that, but not anymore. Nevertheless, her spell had not entirely diminished, and her hand was warm where it gripped his flesh.

"Now," she said, voice softer still, "that's not the reason we brought you here, to talk of these things. We brought you here to test you further, to see if you can go to the next level. Because there is a next level. Can you turn around, please?"

He did as she asked, turning to face the wall behind him. His eyes widened in amazement.

The wall was curved, and on it was a series of shelves rising from floor to ceiling. On the shelves were lifesized figures of people and animals and other things—fanciful things, like armoured knights with swords, a fairy princess with luminous green hair and gossamer wings, a full-sized grizzly bear. There were realistic people, too—boys and girls, men and women, some very ordinary looking, others with outlandish clothes and skin that was turquoise or pink or blue.

"Are they...are they puppets?" he asked.

"Yes. They are proxies. Better ones than your little elephant."

He felt her hand again, this time on his shoulder. A flash of memory came to him of his mother, of the garden with the statue of the woman with the bow. His mother's hand on his shoulder. He wanted the hand to stay there, and he wanted it to go away. It was not his mother's hand. It was Miss Sweet's.

But he was sorry when she took it away and walked toward the shelves.

"You may choose one," she said. "Any one that you like. These are fully functioning models."

His eyes fell upon one of the knights. Emmot would have loved it. It was a gleaming fantasy figure, its armour of chrome plate, the helmet sport-ing sleek wings on either side of the eye slits.

"Can I be the knight?"

Miss Sweet leaned toward him and smiled again, a broader smile this time.

"As I said, you can be whatever you wish to be. It was true what I said to your friend Roma. She can be a horse, if she wishes. Not a little play horse, but a real horse. And today you can be a knight."

Excitement, anticipation, warred with Bear's other emotions. For a fleeting moment, he thought of Miss Sweet's words to Mister Verran just minutes before that she would make him learn her way was the only way. This, he supposed, was how she intended to do that.

And it didn't matter, because he really wanted to play with the knight.

Miss Sweet touched a spot on the side wall, and a little drawer opened beneath her hand. From the drawer she took a black strip.

"This is your controller," she said, passing him the strip. "It works the same way as the others."

The controller was a simple tube, with no extendable eye shield. Bear hesitantly placed it on his forehead and felt it adhere to his skin. At once, he could sense the signals emanating—from all directions, it seemed, from every one of the proxies on the shelves—a blare of musical notes, buzzing and humming. He took a few steps toward the knight, hoping its signal would stand out, become more obvious if he got closer, and it worked. The tone seemed to hover just in front of the shining figure. It was complex, an overlay of several notes in harmony, but it was clear.

"So, I…can just use it?" he asked.

"Of course," she said. "Try it, Bear."

Just like with his elephant, and like with the proxies he'd hijacked, Bear followed the combined tones along a line, an arc, sliding in toward their source.

He became the knight.

It was simple. Suddenly, he was looking down on both himself and Miss Sweet from his place on the shelf, from within the knight's visor. Moving his hands and flexing his arms, he felt the straps for the armour, their weight against his artificial skin. The sensation was natural, much more realistic than with the elephant. This was like being someone else. He *was* the knight.

He took a careful step, climbing down from the shelf, landing on the carpet and bending his knees to absorb the force of the drop. The armour clashed and rattled, the helmet tilting forward over his eyes. He pushed it back and started strutting up and down the large room. He was so big, his legs and arms so long, but somehow they didn't seem awkward or alien. This body understood itself, and it was his.

Going to one of the large windows, he gazed out over the rooftops of the other buildings in the city. He seemed to be inside the tallest one, looking down on all the others, and at the empty streets below, free of any kind of traffic. In the distance, beyond the buildings, he could also see a green hill, fields, the yellowpine forest, and the compound of the school.

Reaching down, he found his sword and drew it from its leather scabbard. The chrome blade flashed, and he slashed the air a few times before holding it up in front of his face.

He looked at Miss Sweet.

He could chop her into bits with this.

The thought horrified him, and it horrified him even more that he had thought it at all. He didn't hate Miss Sweet. He would never hate her, even though she was one of these people.

But what if he wanted to escape. Could he do so as this knight? Where would he go, and would he have to carry his real body? Would he go to the school and chop up the Guardians and lead the other children through the wall? He had no idea how the doors in the wall even worked.

He marched back toward the shelf and stopped, sheathing the sword. He dropped the knight's signal and was just himself again.

"Can I try another one?"

Miss Sweet gave him her crinkly smile. "As many as you like."

Bear ran his eyes over the selection on the shelves. "Is it possible to control more than one at the same time?"

Miss Sweet stroked her chin with one slender hand.

"In theory it is, but only a very few have succeeded. It would take too much energy. You're not quite ready to try something like that."

"Okay," he said, and it was good to know that Miss Sweet had not figured out everything about him. He still had some of his secrets. Did he have a special ability? Or maybe these bigger proxies were just harder to control than the little ones.

The knight hadn't seemed any more difficult than the elephant.

He thought of another question.

"Miss Sweet, what if someone else with a controller came along? Could they steal my proxy and kick me out?"

Miss Sweet shook her head.

"Once you have imprinted on your proxy, you set up what we call an entanglement. Your nexus alters the tones you hear ever so slightly, so slightly you would not even notice the difference, but it creates a connection. The proxy becomes locked to the spin—to the vibrations—that your nexus produces. All of these proxies here..." She indicated the shelves. "...are here for you, for practice. Once you have used them once, no one else can until they're reset. Their signal will be matched to you."

"So, our little puppets were all signal-matched?"

"They were from the first time you used them."

"The first time?"

He'd taken control of Puck's proxy on their third time.

"You must not concern yourself with these things," Miss Sweet said. "You have done very well, Bear. Very well! You easily connected to the knight and moved as if it were your own body. It would be rare for even a Janusian child of your age to have as much skill as you."

He looked at her. "Why is that? I mean, why do some people find it so hard?"

Like Aril.

She shrugged. "It is difficult. Your brain must develop. On Janus, we have evolved to where our brains have greater ability to work with artificial enhancements, and allow us to communicate with a variety of machines, like these proxy bodies. We become entangled. The people of Sturnus didn't have that processing power, not in the same way. But it seems that you do."

She touched him again, this time placing both of her hands on his shoulders. It was the third time she'd touched him.

"Do you know why I work with children?"

He shook his head.

"Because teaching is a form of creation," she told him. "That is my calling. To find those who are useful and to create heroes of them. You are my little hero, Bear."

He looked at her, at her smiling face, the gray in her hair. "Don't you... don't you have a little boy of your own?"

Her smile flickered, just a little.

"My children are grown. Not so small anymore."

He looked down. "Oh."

She squeezed, once, twice. "Now, try a few more of these proxies. Then, I will take you back to the school, and you can have supper with your friends."

⚓

Bear had wondered if he would ever see the school again, but two Guardians took him back, the return trip very different from his journey into the city. The Guardians guided him to the travel tube, allowing him to walk, then rode in it with him. He sensed the sideways motion again, then the vertical motion, until it stopped and one side opened. He was back in the gray corridors he knew so well.

When he entered the dining hall, the other children were already there. Roma saw him, leapt up from her chair, and threw her arms around him.

"Bear, Bear! You're back!" she cried.

Her show of affection embarrassed him.

"Yeah, I'm back."

Emmot was behind Roma, grinning. "Hey, where did you go?"

Bear saw no reason to be evasive or keep secrets from his friends.

"I went into the city to play with some bigger proxies."

Emmot's eyes seemed to double in size. "No way! Really?"

Bear told them more after they sat down—about the knight, the sword, the other proxies he'd used. The one thing he didn't tell them was what Miss Sweet had said to him—that he was her top pupil. He didn't want them to feel like he thought he was better than they were.

When supper ended, the dirty plates dropping away, Roma leaned in close and said, "I knew you'd be back. I knew it wasn't like when Aril disappeared. You know why?"

Bear frowned. "No. Why?"

She giggled. "Because they didn't take away your chair."

⁂

During free time, Bear climbed to the top of the playset and sat there, gazing at the city. Emmot and Puck were with him, chattering and swinging on the bars. Bear tried to identify the domed buildings where he'd been earlier that day and pointed these out to the others.

"I want to go there, too!" Emmot said, and Puck agreed.

Bear played like he hadn't played in many days. He swung on the bars and chased the other boys. He felt easy in his mind, with nothing to weigh him down, as if all the things he'd worried about were gone, even though they were still there, lurking.

What would tomorrow bring?

Bear climbed into his sleep bag and closed his eyes. The room went dark.

A light gleamed, and Bear's eyes opened. Min had come. She was floating between the rows of sleep bags, grinning at him.

"Min," he said, rubbing groggy sleep from his eyes. He had almost forgotten about her. "Min, hi…"

"You're doing it," she said. She seemed excited. "It's working."

"What? I'm doing what?"

"Getting closer. You were in the city."

It took his sleepy brain a moment to understand what she meant. "Wait, how do you know that? How do you know I went to the city?"

Min's smile broadened. "I'm learning more and more, getting stronger and stronger. I can't leave my prison, but I can send my mind out everywhere. I can understand things. I can see things."

69

"What—so you saw me in the city?"

She shook her head. "No, I saw it in their computers. A record of it. I can see into computers, into machines. It's wonderful!"

"So, you can…find out things?"

Min nodded.

Bear's mind was still too sleepy, but this struck him as important.

"Wait," he said. "What do you mean I'm getting closer?"

Min floated toward him until her face was just centimetres from his.

"To finding out how everything works," she said, "and escaping."

Bear's heart was pounding now. "How can I escape? If you can see things in computers, you can find out how things work yourself, and tell me."

"Bear!" came Roma's voice. "Stop talking in your sleep! Bear!"

He clamped his jaw shut. Min glanced toward Roma's sleep bag, then grinned again at Bear.

"I'll come back later," she whispered, waving with the fingers of one hand. "Look for me."

And she was gone again.

Chapter 9

The day after Bear's first visit to the city unfolded like every other day at the school. Following breakfast, he sat in his seat in the classroom as Guardian Number Two heralded the arrival of Miss Sweet, who swept in to take her place in front, tall, regal, face golden and hair platinum, her figure too thin, her fingers long and silver and dangling at her sides.

Bear knew this wasn't what Miss Sweet really looked like, and he finally realized, much later than he thought it probably should have dawned on him, that Miss Sweet had never set foot in the school. She hadn't simply been wearing masks, makeup, wigs and clothing to change her appearance. All this time, she'd been changing bodies. When she arrived with a green face or a red face or even a normal brown or tan face, it was a new proxy.

Miss Sweet was probably sitting in the domed room in the city, controlling her proxy from there. And she'd been doing that all long.

How far away was the city from the school? It looked pretty far. How far away did a proxy have to get before it went out of range and you couldn't control it anymore?

"Questions and Answers," Miss Sweet said, raising her arms.

Bear sat up straight, as he usually did, but it was an automatic response, a learned behavior. He didn't feel any enthusiasm for this exercise anymore. The thought of it bored him.

He glanced at Guardian Number Two, where he stood like a sentry. He probably *was* a sentry, keeping watch in case one of the children decided to try and run or something. That was another thing Bear had never understood before.

The Guardian looked back at him with his strange artificial smile. They were proxies, too, Bear realized, controlled by people in the city. That was why they all looked the same, with those odd round faces.

He looked away, but the Guardian was already coming toward him, strolling with his arms behind his back. Bear concentrated on his answers to Miss Sweet's questions, trying to ignore the Guardian as he came closer.

A faint, high-pitched whining accompanied the Guardian, growing louder as he approached. It reminded Bear of a proxy signal, but that was impossible, because he wasn't wearing a controller.

The Guardian didn't stop at his seat, just strolled past. The tone went with him. If Bear concentrated, if he listened behind the voices of the students, he could hear other signals. One was definitely coming from Miss Sweet's direction, and the more Bear concentrated on it, the stronger it became. He shouldn't have been able to detect the signals from Miss Sweet and the other Guardians.

Except that he could.

Maybe this was the nexus, this thing in his head. Maybe it was all he needed to hear the signals. Maybe the controller was just a teaching tool.

He squinted at his teacher. He'd always thought she looked beautiful, but now she seemed bizarre, only half-human, and he wondered why she did this, wore these funny costume-bodies, living life through the eyes of a doll. Why did all the Janusians do this? Were they afraid of getting hurt? Were they playing, always changing the way they looked for fun?

They must use the proxies all the time. That was why he and the other children were being taught how to use them.

So they could become Janusians.

Except that it wasn't just the Janusians who used robot or machine proxies. He remembered his dad playing with the lawnmower.

See my latest magic trick? Dad had said, pretending to move the lawnmower by waving his hands. The lawnmower must have been similar to a proxy. All of Dad's magic tricks had involved mental control of machines and devices.

It had to be for fun. That was the only reason Bear could understand. And using a proxy *was* fun. As Miss Sweet had said, he could be whatever he wanted.

"That is all for now," Miss Sweet was saying. "Now, we will go outside to practice. Today is another important day. Try to do well."

❦

The sky was dull gray, and a steady breeze blew across the meadow. Bear felt a chill in the air, a dampness on his cheeks and hands. He thought it might rain, a prospect he found uninviting; but at least the heavier air held the wonderful scent of growing grass.

As before, the children lined up and the Guardians distributed the controllers and proxies.

"The first thing you are to do," said Miss Sweet, her golden lips smiling, "is choose a partner. Form pairs! After you have done that, find your own patch of ground. We're going to have races!"

This sounded like fun, and some consolation after getting to work with bigger, more complex proxies yesterday. Bear looked at Miss Sweet and gave her a weak smile. He found it impossible to hate her and wanted to believe she'd had nothing to do with the destruction of his old home, that she really was trying to help. It was complicated, she'd said, but that meant there were still villains somewhere, bad people who had done a terrible thing.

It still meant Bear and his friends were really prisoners.

When he'd last seen her, Min had told Bear he was getting closer to escaping. He wasn't even sure what that meant, and still had no idea where he could go. Back to the destroyed town where he'd lived, maybe, if he could find out where it was.

He wished Min would come more often and stay longer. Her short visits were becoming frustrating. He wished she would give him more answers.

He missed his parents, and felt their loss as a deep sorrow, growing deeper as his memories of them grew stronger. He wanted to find out what exactly had happened to them. He had no memory of that, maybe because he had never known.

For now, he would continue to learn how to control proxy devices. What else could he do?

Picking up his elephant, he wandered a little way toward the trees, stopping and looking back just as a break in the clouds appeared, the blue showing through, promising sunlight after all. It was the kind of weather that made him want to run, to just run and shout and play.

For a moment, he wished things were still simple, like they'd been before the memories, before Min. He'd known what was expected of him. He didn't have to plan and make decisions.

The elephant was in his hands. He pulled it close and hugged it tight and closed his eyes. He didn't want to think about any of those things just now.

"Bear, do you have a partner yet?" said Guardian Number Four, approaching.

Bear hadn't yet donned his controller, but he could still hear the Guardian's faint signal.

"Not yet."

The Guardian pointed. "Your friends Roma and Emmot have formed a pair, but Kanga is in need of a partner."

Bear made his way toward Kanga, a thin girl with copper skin and hair that stood out in an even ball around her head. Kanga's proxy was a white rabbit with enormous teeth. Bear thought the teeth looked funny, and he laughed.

"I call him Chomper," Kanga stated with pride.

"I don't have a name for mine," Bear admitted. "I just call him elephant. Maybe I should call him Elly."

"That's a little obvious," Kanga said, then added, "but it's still a good name."

Guardian Number Four hovered a few paces away.

"You should race," he shouted.

Bear gave the Guardian an uneasy glance. It seemed like the tall figure was watching only him and none of the other kids. That had never happened before.

"Okay," he said, sticking his controller in place and pressing the switch on the back of Elly's head.

For the next thirty minutes, he walked Elly back and forth across the grass, noticing how constricted the little puppet felt compared to the full-sized knight. Chomper trailed after him, unable to keep up. After five races, all victories, Bear had grown a little bored, and Kanga seemed frustrated and was growing sulky.

Bear didn't want Kanga to feel bad, so decided to try something new.

"Hey, watch this," he said.

So far, he and the others had controlled their proxies while standing still with their real bodies. What if it was possible to control a proxy while also moving?

Bear superimposed Elly's view over his own and tried to walk while also moving the elephant. It wasn't easy, but he could do it to some degree. The two images weren't so different that he couldn't tell where he was going, but he had to keep stopping and letting one image dominate, then the other, walking a few paces himself, then with Elly, and so on. It was just too strange a feeling to move two bodies at the same time.

Kanga hadn't been paying attention to what Bear's real body was doing and had continued to race her proxy against his. Thanks to Bear's frequent pauses as he switched from body to body, this time she won.

"Finally!" she said.

"Guess Elly's tired," said Bear.

"Chomper never gets tired, do you, Chomper?"

Chomper had one ear that stood up and one that flopped over. Bear could sense the rabbit's signal, clear and strong, a sound like a mosquito's wings, right next to his own. He could take over Chomper right now if he wanted to, jump in and make the rabbit run in circles, make Kanga chase him. But that would be mean, and he didn't want to upset Kanga further after winning all those races.

Could he ride along with Chomper, he wondered, if Kanga was still in control? Could he just take partial control of a proxy?

There was only one way to find out.

He gave Chomper's tone a little push, just to see if he could follow it in, finding that he could. Soon, he was looking through the rabbit's eyes, with a view of both Elly and of Kanga's ankles. It was his third view, since he still controlled Elly and his real body's eyes were open.

"Walk over there, Kanga," he said, pointing with his real arm to a spot about three metres away. "We can start another race from there."

"Okay," Kanga said, and Chomper strutted across the grass.

The sense of motion, coupled with multiple views, made Bear's stomach lurch, and he closed his real body's eyes and took a deep breath. Chomper's view remained, and Kanga didn't seem to notice that anything was amiss. Bear could feel Chomper's body, and the urge to move it was strong, so strong that he just couldn't resist and moved Chomper's arm, just a little bit.

The rabbit stopped walking. Bear could still feel its body, but Kanga was no longer in control.

He dropped Chomper's signal and opened his eyes. Kanga was next to him, frowning.

"Hey, what's the matter?" he said, pretending not to know.

"I lost it," Kanga said, and then she smiled. "No, I have him again."

Bear nodded. He stole a glance to where Guardian Number Four was still standing, still watching him. It didn't look as if the Guardian had noticed anything strange.

Bear had discovered it was possible to go for a ride in someone else's proxy, as long as he didn't try to exert any control. Why, he wondered, could he do this and no one else?

"Hey, Kanga," he said, speaking in a murmur. "See if you can use Elly."

Kanga opened her eyes and looked at him, wrinkling her nose. "Miss Sweet said we couldn't do that."

Bear shrugged. "Just try it."

Kanga looked down at the elephant, but after a minute she shook her head.

"I can kind of feel the signal, but it stops after a while. I can't follow it."

"Okay, I just wondered."

On the other side of the meadow, a kid let out a wail and started crying. It was a boy named Deej. He was kicking at his motionless proxy while Guardian Number Three tried to console him.

Bear and Kanga both stared. All of the children were staring, eyes open, proxies abandoned.

Miss Sweet strode across the grass toward the boy. Deej had fallen to his knees and was shaking. Guardian Number Three stood still, raising his hands as if in surrender.

"I want my mom," the boy sobbed. "I want my mom! Where is she?"

Bear felt as if someone had kicked him in the stomach. His face went cold.

When Miss Sweet reached Deej's side, she reached forward, the black cord of the Snake coiling from her right arm, its end striking Deej in the forehead. The Snake then recoiled as Deej collapsed in the grass.

Guardian Number Three picked up the boy, threw him over his shoulder like a sack of grass seed, and started carrying him toward the school.

"Gosh, what happened to him?" Kanga said. "Did he say his mom? His *what?*"

Bear was unable to speak, and struggled to control his breathing, his heart hammering.

Deej had remembered his family. Just like him.

⁂

Deej was not at lunch, but his chair was still there. That meant he hadn't been sent away to another school, but Bear figured he was certainly being punished. Miss Sweet had probably taken him to the dark room. The room with the pain and the pleasure.

How could Miss Sweet be so kind and lovely sometimes, and so horrible and cruel at other times? For the first time, remembering how she'd struck Deej down with the Snake, Bear felt true anger at Miss Sweet, because she was responsible for the dark room and what happened there. And that was mean, and wrong.

Bear couldn't speak to Emmot or Roma about this, about his anger and his fear, his suspicions and his confusion. If he did, there was a chance they wouldn't understand, or that the Guardians would hear, that he would be punished again.

He thought about Min. Maybe he could talk to her, but she'd made so few appearances, and he knew so little about her. He wondered if he could call her, summon her, and suddenly his need to do so seemed urgent. He had a strange feeling something bad was about to happen.

Free time came. The gray skies had completely cleared, and it was a fine afternoon with the sun heading into the side of Corvus. In the yard, Roma spun circles while Emmot and Puck tried to get Bear to join them in a game of imaginary combat, but Bear was too distracted. He was determined to try and contact Min. He just needed a diversion so the Guardians wouldn't notice.

Emmot had climbed the playset and was hanging upside down from the top bars. Bear grinned up at him and said, "Hey, Emmot. Can you make a lot of noise?"

"Ha! I can make more noise than anyone here!" Emmot boasted.

"Well, can you, then? I mean for real."

Emmot swung up, grabbing the bar with his hands and pulling himself into a seated position.

"How come?"

Bear shrugged. "Just…can you do it?"

Emmot glanced toward the closest Guardian, then back at Bear. His grin broadened. Jumping down from the playset, he cried, "Puck!"

"What?" Puck shouted back.

Screaming, Emmot charged him, arms outstretched. Puck did nothing for a few seconds, perhaps rooted in indecision; but then he bolted, racing around one side of the playset with Emmot at his heels, still screaming.

Bear wasted no time. Backing into the southeast corner of the wall, he looked up and said, "Min! Min, are you there? Can you hear me? I want to talk to you."

Nothing happened. Puck had turned the tables and was now chasing Emmot.

"Min, I need to talk to you. Please!"

A door in the side of the school opened, and Miss Sweet stepped out. She looked around for a moment, spied Bear and started toward him. She ignored the two noisy boys.

Bear pressed his lips shut and watched her come closer. It seemed impossible that Miss Sweet had overheard him.

Miss Sweet stopped and looked at him. She smiled.

That was when Min appeared, hovering in the air just above Miss Sweet's left shoulder.

Bear's mouth dropped open in astonishment. Despite the strength of his need, his hope, he hadn't really expected his call to work.

"I heard you," said Min. "I heard you, Bear! That's new, another thing I've learned."

Bear gave his head a vigorous shake. He couldn't speak to Min with Miss Sweet so close. Miss Sweet was bending down, still smiling at him, that strange crinkled smile, even on her proxy face. Her arrival must have been a coincidence, and nothing to do with overhearing him. She didn't show any sign of knowing Min was there.

"It's time for another special lesson, Bear," she said. "What do you say to that?"

She held out her strange long-fingered hand. Bear glanced at Min. She just smiled and did not speak.

"Okay," he said, taking Miss Sweet's hand. The artificial flesh of the proxy was as warm and yielding as real flesh.

She led him across the yard, toward the door to the school. Just before he entered it, he looked back.

Min was two paces behind them, following.

Chapter 10

Miss Sweet took Bear to the travel tube he'd used before to get to and from the city. The doors opened at some unseen command, revealing the small white room; and Miss Sweet took Bear's hand, guiding him inside. The doors closed behind them, but not before Min also entered the tiny room.

Bear felt the room drop, then stop and begin to move left.

"I apologize for the sensation of motion, Bear," Miss Sweet said. "We could have dampened it, but find it useful as an indicator. It reminds us that the travel tubes provide us with real movement."

"That's okay," Bear said, wondering why this mattered, unless it had something to do with living through a series of proxy puppets. Maybe after a while nothing seemed quite real.

Bear glanced at Min. She was staring at him, smiling, then stuck out her tongue. He had to clench his jaw tight and take a deep breath to keep from laughing.

The travel tube stopped, and one side of it opened, revealing a large room with warm golden lighting. Miss Sweet took long strides as she exited, almost dragging Bear. He stumbled after her, glancing around and trying to get his bearings based on his previous visit.

He didn't recognize this room. It seemed to be a library, the kind that only existed in stories and legends, a large square chamber tall enough to have a balcony or gallery running along three of its four walls. Bookshelves lined both levels on those walls, bookshelves filled with what looked like real books, the kind with covers and pages, or at least representations of real books.

The fourth wall, opposite the door, had no shelves, but featured a large fireplace surrounded by a stone hearth carved with a combination of real and fanciful creatures, including a unicorn, a dragon, a lion, an octopus, and a pair of dogs or wolves. Above the fireplace floated a massive video-window, the largest Bear had ever seen, displaying shifting images of stars and planets, forests and mountains.

The room was an overwhelming place of wonder, and Bear stood and stared. A circular display table sat in the center of the room, while smaller tables and chairs floated here and there, just above a floor that appeared to be made of polished wood.

The floor in the house where he had lived with Mom and Dad had looked like that.

A sudden pain in his stomach made him grimace.

"There you two are," said the cheerful voice of Mister Verren, speaking from the gallery. As Bear came farther into the room, Verren stepped onto a small levitator pad and descended to the floor.

"Hello, Bear, welcome," he added.

"Hi," Bear said, still fighting the results of his memory of home by trying to mask his upset with waving and grinning.

Verren wore the same black clothing he'd worn the last time Bear had seen him, at the school, but otherwise he looked different. His hair was longer, sticking out in places, and gray at the temples, while his face was fuller, heavier, with lines around the eyes and mouth. This was the real man, Bear presumed. He had only met a proxy before, and the proxy had made Verren appear much younger.

"I must leave you here," Miss Sweet said. "But I will be back."

She gave Bear a little pat on the shoulder.

"I'll leave you for now with Verren," she said.

"Okay," Bear said.

She returned to the travel tube. When the door closed behind her, it looked like nothing more than a varnished wooden panel in the library wall.

Min had been hovering next to the door, but now she moved in close and floated at Bear's side. He had almost forgotten her presence, and the sight of her was both a surprise and a comfort. She remained an enigma, but she made him feel less alone.

He didn't trust Mister Verren, not after their last encounter, when Verren had been nothing but a voice—a much less friendly voice than the one he was using now.

"This is a wonderful place," Min said. "I like places like this."

Mister Verren smiled as he approached, showing no indication he could see or hear Min, nor acknowledging that he knew Bear had heard the things he had said before.

"Do you like to read, Bear?" he asked.

Bear had always enjoyed the chance to read during free time. He knew that he'd even owned books once, both virtual and real, in his old house. He remembered them, remembered the feel of the real books in his hands.

"Yes," he said.

"Well, there are lots of books here. This is our main library, and a place I like to visit rather often when I come to Sturnus. You can come here when you want. Just let Miss Sweet know, and you can come over here during your free time."

"I can?" Bear said, gazing up at the shelves of books. He liked that idea. "What kind of books do you have?"

Verren showed his teeth when he grinned.

"Any book known to the human race. Not that they're all here on the shelves. Those are just for show, really, like this classic library setting. People like it. The presence of so many real books, we've found, helps you relax and absorb whatever text you choose. They have a certain scent, as well, that people associate with reading, that also helps. However, you can have a real book made for you, by an assembler. You just have to ask the computer. It's right here."

He went to the display table, which looked like it was made of dark wood.

Bear considered what he might want to read, whether a story or something that gave him information. He decided on the latter.

"Can I get a book about the mammals that were brought to Sturnus?" he said.

"No problem."

A flat display appeared in the air above the table, with the images of a dozen books in two rows. Verren pointed at one, and the display disappeared. The book, in hard copy, appeared on the table. Verren picked up the book and passed it to Bear.

"Here's an example."

The book was solid and real in Bear's hand, the cover slick and showing images of a bear, a wolf, a porcupine, a sloth, a leopard. All animals he knew, animals that had originated on Earth. The examples pictured on the cover were of the subspecies now found on Sturnus, which differed in subtle ways from their Terran ancestors.

Min was still hovering at Bear's shoulder.

"That's fantastic," she said. "And there's so much more! I can read all of these."

"This table is quite versatile," Verran said to Bear, then raised his voice to say, "Show the present planetary system."

A tiny three-dimensional rendition of a solar system appeared above the table, little coloured planets set amidst the inky blackness of space with its sprinkling of tiny stars. At the centre of the system was a yellow dwarf star with one massive gas giant planet orbiting very close and two more gas giants orbiting at more comfortable distances. Verren reached into the image, waving his hand over the third gas giant, causing the image to zoom in. Now the big planet became the focus of the image. With its several massive moons, it looked like a little solar system itself.

"Here is the Upsilon Andromedae system," Mister Verren said. "And here is Corvus, and this moon, a rocky moon almost as large as old Earth, is Sturnus. The world we're on right now."

Bear nodded. Miss Sweet had taught them these things, but he'd never seen a representation quite like this. Reaching into the image cloud, he cupped the little rocky moon in his hand, as if he could hold it, although he knew he could pass his hand right through it if he wanted.

Above him, Min had started floating in a slow circle around the upper circumference of the great room, level with the gallery.

"I can't read these paper books," she said, her voice seeming to echo in the large chamber, "but there are other books here. Books made just of data. So many things to know, Bear!"

He looked up, wishing he could answer her, but he kept his attention focused on Mister Verren.

"I know you can't talk to me, Bear," Min said, as if sensing his thoughts. "You'll look crazy, since no one else can see me. And we don't want them to find out about me!"

"Now show Janus," Mister Verren said to the table.

The image pulled away from Sturnus, bringing the yellow dwarf back into view, together with its three large companions. The view held there for a second, then again zoomed in, a little farther away from the sun than Corvus. A rocky planet appeared, gray and blue with a sky full of swirling white clouds. Orbiting the planet were two moons, one quite large and gray and spherical, the other lumpy and small, a massive chunk of rock.

"It's the only rocky planet with an atmosphere in the system," Verran said. "The rest are moons, like Sturnus, orbiting those gas giants. Janus is also slightly larger than old Earth. Do you know about Earth?"

Bear nodded. Of course he knew about Earth. Maybe Miss Sweet had not explained to Verran how much she'd taught the children?

"Janus is the heir to Earth," Mister Verren said. "It's the most advanced civilization that has ever existed. Would you like to go there someday?"

Min descended from the gallery and again hovered at Bear's shoulder.

"There's lots of information here about Janus," she said. "I'm learning so much, Bear! And so many other subjects! Things about Earth, things about this world, too."

Bear had been hearing about Janus since first awakening in the school, and he'd always wanted to go there. He still did, even though it was the home world of his enemies.

"Yes," he said. "I'd love to go there."

Mister Verren chuckled and tousled Bear's sandy hair. "Good. That's what we're working on, then. To get you to Janus."

Bear's smile was genuine. His dad had always tousled his hair like that. The attention was pleasant, but it also made his stomach feel a little sick. The two feelings happened at the same time. It was just like how he could still like Miss Sweet, and have fun at the school, and think this library was wonderful, and even start to like Mister Verran a little, when he was being nice, all the while knowing these same people sometimes did horrible things. They had destroyed his family and home and taken him against his will.

He could never let them make him forget. Mister Verren could never take his dad's place, no matter how he tried.

They didn't spend much more time in the library. Mister Verren went toward a section of the lower bookcase, and it swung open to reveal another door with a short passage beyond. Bear followed Mister Verren into the passage, and a moment later they emerged into the reddish daylight of second dawn. They were outside, standing on the edge of what looked to Bear like a wide open playing field, flat and green with short-cropped grass. High gray walls rose on both sides, like the walls of the school, and another building stood at the far end, a gray cube with black rectangular windows.

"Come on," Mister Verren said, striding across the field to where two motionless figures stood, one human and one an animal. When they drew nearer, Bear recognized the figures as two unoccupied proxies. One was the chrome knight he had used before. The other was a shaggy black-and-yellow Sturnusian yellow wolf, fullsized and looking very real, standing almost waist high to the large armoured human figure.

Bear went to the wolf and stroked the thick fur behind its ears. His mother had worked with animals. He'd forgotten that, until this moment. The memory was another shock, another distraction.

"What do you think of this, huh?" said Verren. "There's the proxy you imprinted yesterday, and this other one is free and open. You can try them both if you want. This is your main lesson for today. We have a couple of hours, so you can take your time. What do you say to that?"

Bear could not speak for a moment, the memory of his mother still too strong. He continued to stroke the yellow wolf's shaggy coat, buying time to recover by admiring the thick black bands around the robotic animal's neck and shoulders, the bright, pure yellow on its legs and hindquarters.

"I think it's great," he said at last.

He forced a grin, beaming at Mister Verren, but that brought a sudden stab of shame; and he jerked his head down, pretending to be more interested in petting the motionless wolf than was actually the case. He didn't want to like these people, to be delighted by what they offered, but he couldn't help it.

Min appeared at his elbow. He hadn't seen her come with them through the doorway in the bookcase and had assumed she'd stayed in the library. She was looking at the two proxies.

"These are more robotic devices," she said, "but mostly made of organic materials. Though it would seem they were fabricated at the molecular level. Very clever." She looked pleased with her discovery. "I can see things like that now! I can look into things, like computers and databases and electronic machinery!"

Bear could only respond with a smile and a nod.

"Good," said Mister Verren. From a pocket in his black jacket, he produced a controller, the same kind Bear had used yesterday. "It's all yours."

Bear took the controller and fastened it to his forehead, then searched through the fur on the back of the wolf's head for a switch, but couldn't find one.

"These don't have physical switches," Mister Verren explained. "Just listen for their signals."

Bear remembered then he hadn't needed to switch on the knight yesterday. He listened for the signals, and found many, all around him, a confusing symphony; but the wolf's harmony was close, and soon he found it. It grew stronger the more he concentrated, all of the other signals fading into the background. The wolf's tone was complex, the most complex signal he'd yet heard, but he followed it, slid along its imaginary line, and suddenly, he was standing on all fours.

His mother had once told him that wolves could only see in shades of gray with limited colour, but the proxy's vision was sharp and clear and very human. The sense of smell was also extremely sharp, almost overpowering, and gave him the dank aroma of the dirt at his feet, the rich scent of grass, plus other things he could pick out but not identify. There were scents hanging in the air, including that of the nearby human beings, himself and Mister Verren. Verren's scent was unusual, somehow too clean.

And there were other strange sensations. Although he stood on all fours, the urge to use his front paws as hands was strong. He could also feel his long shaggy tail, could wag it back and forth, and could feel the long rows of sharp teeth in his large mouth.

"Understanding what it might be like to be someone who's not like us, even another form of life," Mister Verren said, "is one of the many things a proxy can give us."

He scratched Bear's proxy on the side of its neck. That felt good.

"I feel like a real wolf," Bear tried to say, but what came out was a mix of a bark and a howl.

Verren laughed.

"The eyes have been augmented on this one, but the vocal chords have been left natural. No one could mistake you for anything but a yellow wolf."

Bear tried a few steps on four legs. At first it was a little awkward, but soon he got the hang of it and was able to run, and run faster than he'd ever run before. The proxy must have had some inbuilt systems, like artificial instincts, to help reduce the amount of learning required for use. It seemed to have been designed to let anyone jump in and become a wolf without the need for hours of physical practice.

Bear ran and ran in the field, with the wind blowing in his face. The many scents in that wind were glorious.

After about a dozen laps, he started to feel tired, something that had never happened with Elly the elephant. So, realistic fatigue was a feature of this proxy.

Dropping to the ground, Bear lay half on his side and half on his back, like he'd seen dogs do, dogs like Tayor, and stared at the sky and the edge of the field. Mister Verren was standing to one side, looking at a card or tablet computer he held in his hands. There were a few other people about, maybe proxies, ones that looked like Guardians wearing black clothes and little helmets, but without the numbers on their chests. One was a woman, the first woman Guardian Bear had seen. She made her way along the edge of the field toward the big building at the end. The black door opened, and she went inside, just as a massive gray-and-black sphere rose from beyond the railing that edged the flat roof.

Bear sat up and watched the sphere ascend. He'd seen it dozens of times, but never from this close; and it looked enormous.

Releasing the wolf proxy, he pulled back to his own body and said, "Mister Verren? What's that big ball?"

Mister Verren glanced at the sphere.

"That's a ship, of course. Bound for Janus, or maybe somewhere else."

Bear nodded. As suspected. "Where else?"

"Oh, one of the other moons. Would you like to ride it someday?"

"Yes, I sure would."

He watched the ship until it was nothing but a black speck, wondering all the while where the launch pad was located. Was it really on the roof, or somewhere inside the building at the end of the field? Maybe the roof opened, like the doors in the outer wall of the school.

He wanted to get a look at it.

An idea came to him. A bold, daring, crazy idea. What if he rode a proxy into the building to see what was in there?

No, it was too crazy, too soon, too risky. But he was sure he could do it. Just for a few minutes. It was dangerous, it was foolish, and could give away his secrets if he was caught. But he felt sure it would work.

He looked at Min. She was hovering there, watching him with a blank look on her face.

He would try it. If things went wrong, he would drop out.

Connecting to the wolf again, he got up and ran a few more laps, his wolf tongue lolling, trying to rid himself of some of his nervous energy. He grew tired again, and that was perfect. It gave him another idea.

He let the wolf body flop to the grass. Mister Verren would assume he was just having a rest. He would not suspect Bear had abandoned the wolf proxy to send his awareness elsewhere.

One of the unnumbered Guardians was making his way across the field toward the building at the end. Bear dropped his wolf head onto his paws and reached out, looking for the signal. It was easy to locate. It featured a pulsing sensation, a repeated pattern; but it was clear, and Bear followed it to its end, closing his wolf eyes and pretending to rest.

The Guardian's perspective came into focus. It was just like riding Chomper the rabbit. Bear remained still, letting the body carry him, feeling the feet strike the ground, the arms swing, the pressure of the little helmet on his scalp. The Guardian kept walking, showing no sign he'd noticed someone else had accessed his proxy.

Bear struggled to stay calm, to resist the urge to move, to do anything, even to blink the proxy's eyes. It was hard, for some reason; the proxy didn't need to blink, but it was a strange compulsion, maybe because he was just so used to doing it with his real eyes. His agitation was growing worse by the second, a burning frustration; but if he moved, he would take over the proxy, and that, he was sure, would make everyone suspicious.

The building drew closer, the black doors slid open. Beyond lay a wide gray corridor with a series of what seemed to be identical black objects along one wall. Bear couldn't determine what the objects were because the Guardian didn't look at them. He just had to let the images flow past. It was imperative that he didn't move.

The corridor narrowed at the back, and there were more black things; and now Bear could tell they were vehicles of some kind stacked side-by-side, black with rounded bodies. He was only able to catch a glimpse of them from the corner of the proxy's eyes before the corridor curved to the right.

The corridor ended at another door. The door opened. The Guardian walked into a cavernous room that was open to the sky. In the center of the room was a circular hole with red lights at intervals along its circumference. This was it. Bear was sure of it. It was the launch and landing pad for the ships.

Another Guardian approached, and the head of Bear's Guardian turned to face her. It was the woman he'd seen earlier. Her face was pure white, her eyes a strange yellow.

"Return shuttle in twenty-five," she said.

Behind her were more of the black vehicles. Now Bear had a clear view of them.

He knew what they were. They were the bug machines that had captured him, that had shot yellow beams at people from his neighborhood.

With a jerk, he dropped the Guardian and opened the wolf's eyes. He could feel his real heart beating wildly, although the wolf remained calm.

Until this moment, the bug machines had existed only in his memory.

The wolf was rested, so Bear jumped to his four feet and started running again. His shock at discovering the bug machines was nothing compared to his triumph at the victory he'd just won. He'd done it! He'd ridden in another proxy in secret. He'd found the landing pad, found the bug machines. They were real! That meant his memories were real. He had not realized that he'd still harboured some doubts, but no longer.

Verren was studying his device and didn't appear to have noticed anything odd.

After another lap, Bear took another rest. He didn't want to wear out the wolf, harm it or break it, and had noticed it was getting more difficult to run fast, that the muscles were starting to ache with real pain. Walking the wolf toward the knight, he sat on his haunches as he had seen dogs do and dropped the signal, returning to himself.

Min was floating next to him.

"What did you do there?" she asked. "There was something going on, wasn't there? The electrical activity in your wolf proxy went down to almost zero for a few minutes."

"You could see that?" he whispered.

"Yes, I'm learning to see a lot of things! So, what happened?"

"I'll tell you later," Bear told her.

"Of course, you can't talk out loud," Min said, eyes widening. "I forgot! You'll give me away."

She rose into the air just as Verren put away his device and came toward Bear.

"Having fun?" he asked.

Bear nodded, not needing to pretend. He *had* been having fun.

"I've never been able to run so fast." He reached up and rubbed the controller where it was stuck to his forehead. "This itches, though."

Mister Verren looked thoughtful. "You know, Bear, I was going to wait to suggest this next thing, but you're the fastest proxy learner I've ever seen. You're ready if anyone is."

"Ready for what?"

"For the next step. Janusians don't use these itchy controllers, you see. We have a device installed under our scalp, with the nexus. A built-in controller. It's made of organic material and grows with you as you age." He put his hand on Bear's shoulder. "Do you think you're ready for that? To have your own controller implant?"

Bear didn't think he liked the idea of having something placed under his skin. That sounded like cybernetics. He remembered his dad saying that no one on Sturnus approved of cybernetics. Then again, he already had the nexus, and did an organic implant qualify as a cybernetic thing or not?

Mister Verren frowned and squeezed Bear's shoulder. "It's okay, I know it's scary. But it doesn't hurt. You won't even notice it."

"It won't hurt?" Bear repeated.

"Of course not. You think about it. We can talk again later." He straightened. "Well, I think it's time to get back. It'll be supper soon, and you'll want to see your friends. Tomorrow maybe you can spend some time with the knight, since you spent all of today as a canine!"

Chapter 11

For the first time, Min didn't leave. She stayed with Bear for the remainder of the day. In the dining hall, she hovered by his side, a silent companion. During free time, while Emmot and Puck again created a diversion, she floated at Bear's shoulder while he tried to look inconspicuous in the southeast corner of the yard. Her glowing feet almost touched the floor.

"I think I can stay with you all the time now," she said. "I think I can do that. Our connection is stronger."

"Not at night. You'll keep me awake with your glowing."

"Do I really glow?" she asked, looking at her arms.

"Don't you see it?"

Min seemed to stare into the distance for a moment. "I see things differently from you. Yes, I understand what you mean when you say 'glowing'. Emitting light. I wouldn't have thought of it unless you taught me how to interpret it."

Bear smiled. "Then I've helped you already."

"Yes! And today most of all. Going to that library. I discovered so much."

"I did, too," Bear said. "I can control other people's proxies, Min. Everyone's. Not just the animal puppets here."

"The proxies are all these robotic devices?"

"Yes. Everyone here who isn't a kid rides in them. Even Miss Sweet."

Min's eyes again seemed to go blank for a moment; then she blinked and looked at Bear.

"Yes, there are five of those devices here right now. I never noticed that before. Well, I think I did, but I didn't look at them, or didn't know what they were. I'm learning things every day, every hour, every minute, every second."

Bear made a quick survey of the yard nearby, checking to see if any Guardians were watching him. Guardian Number Two was not far away, about five meters, and seemed to be looking in his direction. Maybe he had seen Bear talking, but it was plausible Bear was talking to himself as part of an imaginary game. That wasn't unusual.

Bear raised his arms and spun around, throwing out a few random words and phrases. "Look at the sky! Blow with the wind!"

"I…What are you saying?" said Min.

"I'm pretending to be pretending," Bear said, his back now to the Guardian. "To throw off anyone watching."

Min grinned and nodded.

"Oh, I understand."

"I was about to say," Bear added, spinning again, "that all of the real people are somewhere else, back in the city." He raised his arms and rocked on his feet. "They just ride around in the proxy bodies. The thing is, Min, that Miss Sweet said only one person can control each proxy. If you own one, you imprint on it, and no one else can use it until you reset its code or something. But it's not true, because I can use everyone's."

Min's smile was full of pride. "I knew you could do things, Bear! Special things. You see? That's why you're the only person who can see me. The only one who can read my signal. That's why you have to rescue me."

Bear's stomach did a flip at Min's talk of rescue. He was just a boy, and still hadn't figured out how to rescue *himself*. He still wasn't sure if he *could* be rescued.

"Do you know where you are yet?" he said. "Is it a jail or a dungeon somewhere?"

Min looked unhappy. "I'm still not sure. But I don't think it's a dungeon."

"Do you even know who you are? Why can you send out a projection, and why can you figure out things?"

"I don't know yet. I don't remember, but I wonder if I can talk to computers and machines in the same way that you talk to your proxies."

That made sense. Min was almost certainly another girl taken prisoner, but held somewhere else, maybe being taught other ways to use different kinds of proxy machines. Like Bear's dad with the chappie maker.

Bear leaned against the wall with a sigh. Emmot and Puck had stopped shouting and were sitting on the playset along with a dozen other children. Guardian Number Two no longer stared at Bear, and had joined the other Guardians in their usual stroll back and forth across the yard, hands behind their backs.

He had to make a decision, plan a course of action. He'd learned a lot about controlling proxies. He'd also learned much about his situation and that of his friends. The time had come to actually do something. He enjoyed his special sessions with Miss Sweet and Mister Verren, but that enjoyment wasn't enough to make him forget what he had learned about them.

A wave seemed to rise up from his stomach, continuing to his head, and his lips quivered as tears started in his eyes. He tried to push the wave down, to stop the sobs he knew weren't far behind. He couldn't lose control. Not here, not now.

"I need to ask you something, Min," he said, and his voice came out as a hoarse croak. "I...I think it's not just you I need to rescue. I think I need to rescue everyone."

Min rose into the air, spun, and looked down on Bear from above the wall.

"I think I need to get all of these kids out of here," Bear murmured. "I need to do that first. Then we can come and look for you, rescue you, too."

"That sounds difficult, but I agree it's the right thing to do, Bear."

He gazed up at her. He'd been worried that she'd insist on being rescued first, and it was a relief to have her agree with him.

"It's only fair," he added. "I can't leave them here. We're all prisoners."

"I knew you were the type of person to value fairness."

Not for the first time, Bear noticed that Min did not speak like a girl who was only nine or ten e-years old. She was precise, matter-of-fact.

"There's something else I need to tell you," he said. "Did you hear it when Mister Verren asked me to get an implant? A controller, like all the Janusians have to control their proxies?"

"Yes," Min said. "Would it help us? Wouldn't it mean you could always control one of the robots, all the time? Then maybe you could find a great big one that could smash the wall down or something!"

"I guess so," he said, but suddenly he was uncertain. He needed a controller, but what if Miss Sweet and the Guardians could also watch him or see where he was all the time because of it?

Of course, they could probably already do that, through the nexus. Maybe this idea of escape was just impossible, because they were watching right now, suspecting that he was secretly communicating with someone but just not caring enough to stop him because he could never escape this school or the city anyway.

That thought hung like a heavy weight.

The chime sounded.

"You'd better go," he told Min, despondent. She was floating higher and higher, her light seeming to grow brighter in contrast to the darkening sky. "If I call you later, will you come?"

"Yes," she said, her voice still strong despite her increasing distance. "I'll find you whenever you call me. It's getting easier. Just call!"

The other children had already lined up to enter the school. Bear ran to catch up and followed them in as the evening ritual went on as always—return to the sleep room, climb into his hanging sleep bag, try to get comfortable.

But he couldn't sleep.

It didn't matter if they were watching. He had to try something. He had to be brave. And he knew a way he could do it, a way he could get everyone out of here, if he could just figure out a few more things. Such as where they could go, where they could hide, where they could live and be safe.

At last he fell asleep, dreaming a dream in which he was sitting in his favourite chair, his dog Tayor snoring at his feet.

His subsequent dreams were fitful and confused, a series of twisted images—his old home, the school and the city all melding into one; and he woke several times during the night, sweat pooling under his clothing faster than the fabric could wick it away, stomach buzzing with a mixture of fear and excitement, doubt and certainty.

In the morning he felt sick and groggy. Dropping out of his sleep bag, he let his feet carry him through the privy and Washroom, almost like riding a proxy, and then to breakfast, where he took his seat without noticing much about his surroundings. He ate slowly and without any interest in the food that rose up to greet him, but after a few mouthfuls he started to come awake. The room was much quieter than usual. Even Emmot was silent, his round face red and unhappy.

"Where's Puck?" Bear said.

Emmot shrugged, but Bear had already realized his mistake. All of the other children must have seen it, and that was why they were so subdued.

There were only eighteen of them left. Ten more kids had gone missing, their chairs gone, their existence erased.

Bear froze in the act of chewing his grain stick. Roma and Emmot were still there. Kanga was gone. Puck was gone. Kalla was still there. Eight others had vanished. Sent to another school, Bear guessed.

That felt like a lie.

He put his grain stick on the table, his appetite having also disappeared.

After breakfast, when Miss Sweet arrived, he couldn't look at her. He was angry again, and she became the focus.

"Questions and Answers," she announced in her usual cheerful tone. She was blue-and-silver today, like ice and lightning. "Where did the human race come from?"

"The planet Earth," the children answered, but their collective voice was weaker than when there'd been forty of them, and Bear didn't respond at all. He saw what this was now, this ridiculous morning ritual. This was just to get them to think a certain way, to think the Janusian way.

"Oh, I think you can all show more spirit," Miss Sweet said. "Let's see how loud you can shout. Question! Where did the human race come from?"

"The planet Earth!" the children screamed.

"Let's stand up. Everyone stand up. It will be fun!"

The children all sprang from their chairs, taking stiff poses worthy of the Guardians. Bear did his best to pretend to be enthusiastic, just to avoid drawing unwanted attention.

"Why did humans leave Earth?"

"Earth was corrupt and overcrowded!"

"What is the most advanced planet in the known galaxy?"

"Janus!"

This continued until Miss Sweet had exhausted her standard questions, but then she repeated them, although not in the usual order. Some children, so used to shouting certain answers at a certain place in the rote, made mistakes, which meant the entire class had to repeat the entire sequence until everyone got it right.

Bear was growing frustrated and annoyed, but still he did his best to follow along.

Finally, it ended. Bear's limbs were leaden and his eyes were heavy as he followed the file of children, so much smaller now, out of the classroom and into the yard for their break.

In the yard, Guardian Number Three stopped Bear with an upraised hand.

"Miss Sweet will see you," the Guardian said. "Please wait here."

Bear waited. He yawned. Another special lesson, he assumed.

"Bear," Miss Sweet said from behind him. "Look at me, Bear."

He turned, alarmed at her stern tone. Could he be in trouble? Could she have found out about Min? Or his ability to travel inside another proxy?

Miss Sweet didn't look angry.

"Come closer to me, Bear."

He did as he was told. She took him by the chin, her touch gentle, and tilted his face to peer into hers.

"You mustn't let the discipline bother you," she told him, her tone now soft, soothing. "I know you find it tedious, that you are far beyond that sort of thing. You have made great progress in a few short days. You do know you are special to me, do you not?"

His mum had told him he was special. An image of her face flashed in his mind.

He shrugged. "I don't know."

Miss Sweet laughed and pulled him to her, held him, her arms encircling, for a few moments before backing away again, although she maintained a gentle grip on his shoulders.

"You are, Bear. You are special to me."

A mix of emotions boiled and struggled to find dominance in Bear's weary form. It had felt good to be held, to be spoken to in such a way, with such kindness, such love. But he still saw his mother's face.

"Mister Verren told me he offered you a prime controller," Miss Sweet said. She gazed at him as if she expected him to answer.

He nodded.

"Good. Have you thought about it? About having one installed?"

"I've...I've thought about it," he said in a tiny voice, his throat tight.

"Good. You must understand, Bear, if you get the implant, it cannot be removed. It is a complex organic machine that fuses to your nervous system and becomes self-regenerating. Yet it will change things for you in many ways.

"You will become one of us. That is the whole purpose of this school, you understand. To help you become one of us. And you are our star pupil, despite some of the trouble you sometimes get into, hmm?" She caressed his upper left arm. "You have had great success, and if you receive the prime controller then you can leave this place, this school, this planet, and go to Janus and become a pupil at a nicer school, a school surrounded by gardens with many children like yourself, talented children. Would you like that?"

He couldn't reply. He didn't know what to say. Of course that sounded nice, a way out, an escape he wouldn't have to plan himself. Its pull was like a gas giant, sucking him into its gravity well. And there'd been a time when all he'd wanted to do was go to Janus, before the memories had come back. He'd dreamed of it, and echoes of that dream still remained.

Miss Sweet really seemed proud of him, hopeful for him. He had been angry with her earlier, but now she was being nice; and it was still hard not to want to please her. But if he agreed to what she wanted, he would not really be escaping, and he would have to leave his friends behind.

"I don't know," was all he could say.

Miss Sweet's smile became tight, and he could see that his answer, his failure to leap at what she must have considered an unrefusable offer, had disappointed her.

"You must think about it more," she said. "Think about it, and tell me tomorrow, in the morning. So you will have one full day. Is that fair?"

Bear nodded. Yes, he would think about it.

"That's fair, Miss Sweet."

She twirled away from him, her long proxy legs carrying her into the school. Bear went back to where his few remaining companions were doing their best to play as if nothing had changed. He climbed to the top of the playset, joining Emmot, who was quiet for once, just sitting and staring at Corvus. That was so unlike Emmot. Bear didn't like it. At least Roma was below them, spinning and humming to herself as usual.

Bear touched his head, just above his eyebrows. They wanted to put a thing there, another thing. It would change him.

Miss Sweet had given him a choice. What if he said no?

They would make him do it anyway. They wanted him to be one of them.

Or he would disappear, like Puck, like Aril.

They would put this thing in his brain...

Another memory came.

He gasped.

He was in the hospital, with Doctor Kamra. Mum and Dad were there in the examination room, but Tayor had stayed home. The pup had grown too big to sit in Bear's lap and would have been a bit of a nuisance.

"After this," Doctor Kamra said, "we don't need to do any more tests, I think. You're old enough that we expect you to continue to grow and develop normally. And everything looks good."

"Why do you look at my brain?" Bear asked. He was nine e-years old. He knew that because now he also remembered his ninth birthday party. He'd thought he deserved an answer, that he was smart enough and old enough to understand.

"To make sure it's growing properly, which is the same reason that I check your heart and your lungs and your muscles. Except that you're right, and your brain is much more special than your muscles. You have a very special brain, just like your parents have special brains." He chuckled. "But yours is even more special! It's specially special."

Bear felt a little bit of personal pride at this assessment, but it still didn't give him much information.

"What does that mean?"

Doctor Kamra leaned back in his chair, glanced at Mum and Dad, and said, "It means you're ready to learn how to do your own magic tricks."

Bear liked the sound of that. "How?"

"You just can," Doctor Kamra said, clapping his hands. "You and many of the children of your generation, who all have special brains. I believe my daughter would have, too, had she lived. Did you know I had a daughter?"

Bear shook his head.

"Yes. She would have been your age, just about. Unfortunately, she is no longer with us, due to an accident. These things happen."

He was silent for a moment.

"That's sad," said Bear, because it seemed an appropriate thing to say, and he liked Doctor Kamra and didn't want him to feel bad.

Doctor Kamra smiled.

"Yes, yes, but what I'm telling you is not sad. Things have been getting better, ever since we all came here from another world. Did you know that we moved here from another planet?"

"Earth?"

"Well, yes, Earth originally, but after that, we were on a harsh colony world. It was our technology, our ability to control our machinery with mental commands, that helped us survive. We couldn't even breathe the air, so we used little machines in our brains to talk to other machines, to even seem to become those machines. So, if we wanted to go outside, we would link to a machine that could do that, and it felt like we were outside, that we were the machine."

"That's neat."

"Yes, isn't it? It certainly helped. Anyhow, we learned how to talk to these machines by studying how our brains worked in the first place. Do you know why you can think and react so fast sometimes? Because parts of your brain communicate with other parts using something we call 'entanglement'. They can communicate, or talk, instantaneously."

"I know what 'communicate' means," Bear said, with pride.

"Of course you do! So, we decided that if one part of your brain could become entangled with another, we could also make a part of your brain entangle with something outside. Like a computer. And it worked, which was good, because we could move around and seem to live in places where our bodies could not go.

"But even with that ability, life on that planet was still too hard for some people, so we spent a long time trying to get this planet, this moon, ready, to make it nice to live on, and when it was ready, we moved."

"When you say we used little machines in our brains to talk to other machines, do you mean like Dad's chappie maker? Or the statue in the park?"

"Ha, yes. Your dad's chappie maker is a good example. He is one with his chappie maker."

Doctor Kamra and Bear's dad shared a chuckle for a few minutes.

"But," Doctor Kamra continued, holding up one hand, "using little machines in the brain is not a perfect system, because sometimes the little machines break, and so we have looked to another way, a better way. The machines can only talk to one thing at a time, and they wear out. So it was that we decided to change our brains themselves instead of using machines.

"We created a virus that can alter DNA, which is the plan for how every cell in your body grows. Your grandparents would have been the first to receive that virus, and that altered certain parts of their brains so they worked like those little machines."

"So we don't need machines in our head?" Bear said, which was a relief. He didn't like the idea of having something metal or ceramic stuck in his head.

"Not at all. And now we have the virus and others like it working much better, so that you, Bear, and the other kids are something special, something beyond what we once were, something that has been emerging with each successive generation here on Sturnus. You can use your brain, when you learn how, to communicate with any number of toys and machines and devices that have been made to work with this system. And the truth is, most things are made that way these days. Every device has a brain of its own, and your brain has the ability to become linked to that brain."

"How?" Bear asked.

Doctor Kamra leaned forward.

"You just have to listen. You see, very tiny particles in your brain and in the machine brains have something that we call 'spin.' Your brain's particles can match the spin of the particles in those machines. To you, it sounds like music. All you have to do is find the music, and your brain does the rest.

"And unlike the old machines that we used to put in people's heads, you can talk to and take control of many things, not just one or two. Once you hear the music of a machine, your brain can repeat it, and so you can become linked. The wonderful thing is that you can do this no matter how far away the machine is. So, your dad's chappie maker can be miles away, and as long as he can sense its music, he can make chappies."

"So now I can make chappies, too!"

Doctor Kamra chuckled.

"Yes. Just listen for the music. The music everywhere."

Chapter 12

The rest of the day was a struggle. The memory had answered one of Bear's key questions, which was why he could use more than one proxy at a time; but it also led to other questions and didn't help at all when it came to answering Miss Sweet's offer. He had no idea what to tell her. He didn't want to go to Janus, not anymore. He wanted to go home.

His belly felt full of snakes as he wandered in the yard, walking among the various playsets, trying to work off the terrible energy. One of the playsets was unoccupied, something that had never happened before, but there were so few kids now. Bear climbed to the top and gazed over the wall at the forest.

If his memory of the session with Doctor Kamra was correct, then the children of Sturnus already had an ability to communicate with proxies or similar machines. Some were better at this than others, but that wasn't the most important detail. The thing of real significance was that Bear shouldn't have needed a controller at all, or a nexus. But it seemed that the Janusians still used machines to talk to machines.

Bear had already discovered he didn't need a controller to hear proxy signals, but he'd never taken the next logical step and attempted to follow one of those signals to its source, to connect and take control without a controller.

He would try that now.

Guardian Number One was strolling through the yard about ten metres away. Bear listened, identified a low hum that grew louder as he concentrated. Closing his eyes, he followed the signal to its source.

Nothing stopped him, no barrier, no resistance at all; and then he was inside the Guardian, looking through his eyes at the scattered children in the yard.

He dropped the signal after a few seconds. He didn't want to risk being found out, and his experiment had been a success. He'd never needed a controller. Maybe he'd never even used one when he'd had it. It had been a useless and irritating object stuck to his forehead.

That meant he didn't need the implant Miss Sweet was offering.

What now? Did he tell Miss Sweet about this? Admit to more memories, or keep this a secret?

He would keep it a secret. His secrets were his only power, his only advantage. Those memories belonged to him and him alone, all he had left of his family.

Resting his head on his arms, he recalled a time when he and Mum and Dad had walked on the beach, laughing as Tayor ran through the waves; and another time when they'd had a picnic in the garden with the statue of Artemis. The sense of homesickness, the longing for another time and place, became unbearable, and he wanted to scream. He wanted that world back, and didn't want to believe it was completely gone.

What if some of it had survived? He only had the one coherent memory of the attack by the bug machines. What if they hadn't destroyed everything?

He lifted his head. He remembered some houses still standing. Maybe the people of Sturnus had fought back, like in some of the stories he'd read, stories where an evil king had invaded a country, but the people had rallied and formed a resistance.

The school was just a prison somewhere on the moon. Somewhere else, the battle could still be raging.

He sat up straight, hope giving him strength. He'd believed Janus had completely destroyed his whole world, that no one was left, but that was just an assumption. It had never occurred to him that Sturnus might still have forces out there, that there was still some kind of fight going on.

That people were looking for their lost children.

Second sunset was approaching. It was time for bed, but Bear knew he wouldn't be able to sleep. His plan of escape had been granted new life. He just needed Min's help, and he needed it now.

The sleeping room was almost empty, and it was quiet. Bear waited until Roma and the other two remaining occupants besides himself seemed to be asleep, their breathing heavy and even.

"Min," he whispered. "Min, I need to talk to you."

Light filled the corner of the room near the door.

"I'm here," she said, in a voice that should have been loud enough to wake the room. "I thought you wanted me to stay away at night."

"I have to whisper," Bear said, pleased and relieved Min had responded so quickly. "I have to ask you something, and it's important. When you were looking around for me—I mean, before you met me—you said you were looking for someone who could see you. Where did you look? Where did you go?"

She frowned and held her chin between the thumb and forefinger of her left hand. Her hair seemed to flow out from her head, as if she floated underwater.

"I don't know. I don't remember that much. There's minimal…data from that time, as if my mind didn't work that well. I didn't know anything. I just looked for someone who could see me. I didn't even know my name."

"So, you didn't see if there were still towns and cities and people on the planet?"

"I know I encountered people, but none of them could see me."

"But you saw other people?" he said, speaking a little too loudly in his sudden excitement. "What about now? Can you fly outside the school, way past the forest, and see if there are any people? Any cities?"

Her smile was bright. "I can do that!"

She was gone. Bear was left in sudden darkness, a little bewildered.

Within seconds, Min was back.

"I went out past the forest," she said. "I didn't see anyone. No lights or people."

His heart sank. He'd been so sure.

"No buildings?"

"Oh, yes, I found buildings. Houses. Streets, and an ocean!"

"An ocean?" he almost shouted.

Roma stirred in her sleep bag.

"Bear," she groaned. "Are you talking in your sleep again?"

Min began to rise toward the ceiling. "I'm waking people up, like you said I would. I'll come back tomorrow. Goodnight!"

Bear needed her to stay, to go back for a second look. He needed to know this now. There was no time left. But now Emmot was awake, coughing and clearing his throat. Bear watched Min rise through the ceiling, wave once, and disappear.

He stared at the ceiling for some time, his mind churning. Min's words stayed with him. She'd found houses, and an ocean. That was something, at least.

His town.

And there would be a beach, he thought, and a row of houses, some in ruins, along the cliffs.

Bear was becoming accustomed to feeling miserable in the morning from lack of sleep, his muscles aching from the constant tension and worry; and the next morning was no better. Breakfast revived him a little, and he was able to resume formulating his plan. At least Min had given him some information, and it would have to be enough. If he was going to act, it had to be now.

Immediately after breakfast, the Guardians announced that the children would all have a break and could go to the yard. This was unusual, but Bear welcomed the extra freedom before having to face Miss Sweet. He was nervous, and tried to distract himself by chasing Emmot, wearing himself out by running, until they both ended up on their favourite perch atop the playset. Emmot was not as cheerful as usual and gazed at the distant woods.

"It's pretty boring here now," he said.

Roma also seemed subdued. She climbed to the top of the playset to join them, something Bear didn't remember her ever doing before.

"Maybe we'll all get to go somewhere else soon," she said. "Are we almost finished here? I hope so. Why didn't we have a class this morning? We must be done."

The chime sounded. Bear formed in file, but he saw Miss Sweet waiting beside the door. His stomach did its usual growl and dance.

The children went inside, but Miss Sweet, as expected, stopped Bear. Her face and hands were bone-white today, her lips and hair bright red. Bear found the look unsettling.

"The time has come," she said brightly. "You don't need to follow the rest, Bear. Not if you don't want to."

Bear couldn't look her in the eye. He took several deep breaths. He knew he couldn't refuse, that he at least needed to appear to agree to her offer.

"What do you say, Bear?" she murmured.

"I've made up my mind," he told her. "I'd like to get the implant and go to Janus."

She clapped her hands, and he saw that her fingernails were also red, like blood.

"That's wonderful! Then, there's no reason to delay. You may come with me now to the city, where you will complete your education. Your school days here are over."

His stomach did another flip. This was too soon. He wasn't ready.

"Do I have to go right now?" he said. "Can I have one more day?"

Miss Sweet smiled and frowned at the same time. "Why would you want one more day? Soon you will be leaving for Janus."

"I just want to say goodbye to my friends. Can I go tomorrow? Tomorrow morning?"

Miss Sweet crouched so her face was below Bear's eye level. Her hair flattened back on her head.

"I understand that you might be afraid. This is a big step. However, you have nothing to fear. You are evolving beyond this place. You don't owe the remaining pupils anything."

"But they're my friends, Miss Sweet. I just can't disappear."

She said nothing, and he saw she was considering his proposal.

"Just one more day. Please?"

She rose to her full height. "Allright, Bear. One more day. Consider it a day of rest. I want you to get a good night's sleep. You have seemed tired for the past few days."

"I am," he admitted. "I've been nervous, thinking about this. Thanks, Miss Sweet."

She nodded.

"Good. Come and join the class, then. We'll have one more ordinary day, and tomorrow a new chapter of your life begins."

In class, Miss Sweet didn't do Question-and-Answer. Instead, she produced her magic floating book and told stories about funny animals, fluffy and pointless stories that made the children laugh. Bear could not recall another class in which Miss Sweet had not taught a lesson of some sort. Today's session had just been fun.

It was as if her lessons no longer mattered, the school no longer mattered.

After that, there was lunch in the dining hall, a good lunch of real food —noodles in a sweet red sauce, followed by a square of cake with pink and yellow frosting. There was jam in the middle of the cake.

Bear remembered jam from home, his real home, and also eating noodles in red sauce. Tomato sauce. And having jam. He'd never had jam here at the school before.

After lunch, the children went out into the yard to play before the midday eclipse. Bear noticed that everyone seemed happy again, like they'd always seemed when there were still forty of them, before the memories and the disappearances. He watched them playing the same games and doing the same things they did every day. He had a feeling that, whatever *he* did, whatever choices he made, this was all about to end, that the school was done.

This was his time to say goodbye to everyone, but that had never been his intention.

"There you are, my little bird," Miss Sweet said. She was strolling the yard as she always did, watching over her kids, and stopped at Bear's side. "Are you having a good day?"

"Yes, Miss Sweet," he said, and because he thought he should seem to be friendly, he added, "I liked your stories."

She gave a soft chuckle. "Thank you. It seemed the best way to pass our morning." She placed one long hand on his shoulder. "Now I have some things to do. I'll see you later in the afternoon, after eclipse."

All Bear could do was give her a crimped smile.

"Okay."

She squeezed his arm once, then turned and left the yard, going back into the school.

When the door had closed behind her, Bear ran to the playset and sat on one of the lower rungs. This was an unexpected opportunity to start his plan early. He had not meant to start until the night.

Making sure he was comfortable and well-braced on the playset, he closed his eyes and listened. His nerves flared, a sudden wave of unexpected terror or excitement in anticipation of what he was about to do. It was so overpowering he took deep breaths until it passed. He feared he was on the verge of losing his nerve. This was going to be hard. It was going to be really hard, but he couldn't fail. He had to do this.

Taking several more breaths, he tried to clear his thoughts, to listen. He searched for the music of the proxies. In seconds he'd found the signals for the Guardians who still patrolled the yard. That wasn't what he was looking for. He was looking for the fifth signal.

He found it. It emanated from the school, and was different from the others, having an odd smoothness, a more complex harmony, and it was moving deeper into the building, and growing fainter.

He concentrated, and the signal again grew strong, so strong it made him wince, forcing him to pull back.

"Come on, Bear," he muttered to himself. "Just do it. Just follow it in."

He took the last step, following the signal to its source.

White walls surrounded him, and he was moving. He was in the travel tube, heading into the city.

He dropped the signal, snapping back into his own mind and awareness. His hands were slick with sweat and trembling, but this was no time to let his nervousness get the better of him. It was now or never.

Returning to the signal, he again followed it all the way. Again he was looking through Miss Sweet's eyes, still facing the walls of the travel tube. All he had to do was nothing, to just relax and not exert any control. That was all. But it seemed harder than usual.

The travel tube stopped, and then something odd happened. Bear felt and heard Miss Sweet's proxy emit a series of shrill notes—three the same and one of a higher pitch—and the travel tube door opened.

Bear hadn't suspected there would be other types of signals, other types of communication between people and machines, but of course he realized he'd known this for a long time. This was the sort of signal that had allowed his dad to use a chappie maker.

Miss Sweet stepped into a corridor like the one he had travelled through on that first day, the first time he'd gone to the city. The dominant colour in the corridor was white, with walls and ceiling banded with gold. Miss Sweet followed the passage to a door set in one wall, where her proxy again emitted a shrill note followed by a series of dashes. The door slid open with a hiss.

Miss Sweet walked through the doorway, and Bear had to use every bit of his strength of will not to move, not to close his eyes, not to gasp or cry out in surprise.

The room was lined with deep shelves from floor to ceiling, and on every shelf stood a silent, motionless version of Miss Sweet.

Bear recognized many of them. Here were the many Miss Sweets he'd encountered in the classroom, the ones with the pink faces, the turquoise faces, the big heads, the strange hair and fingers. Some wore clothes, but some were naked, which Bear found embarrassing, although he couldn't look away, could only let the eyes through which he gazed go where Miss Sweet sent them. And right now, Miss Sweet was looking at her many proxies, perhaps in admiration, or maybe just searching for an empty space on the shelf.

She found it—a gap on the bottom tier. As she made for it her eyes swept across the back of the room, falling upon, just for a second, the form of the real Miss Sweet where she sat in a chair, facing the door, her eyes closed.

The proxy stepped into the space on the shelf, turned, and became motionless. Bear could still see through the open eyes, but he didn't dare move or look around. He stared at the shelf opposite, at more versions of Miss Sweet, like a collection of life-sized dolls.

The real Miss Sweet had risen to her feet. She came into view and looked straight at Bear. He almost dropped the proxy's signal, fled back to himself, but rallied his courage at the last second to hold his ground. She couldn't know he was there.

After a moment, she turned away.

Back in the schoolyard, Bear felt his real body sigh, his real heart pounding. But the proxy remained still.

"Personal log entry," he heard Miss Sweet say from somewhere to his right. "Project Newbrood, Sturnus, local day two-hundred and twenty-three.

104

Child known as Bear agreed to receive primary controller. First Sturnus subject to do so. Comments: This indicates my efforts here have not been in vain, despite over fifty percent of child subjects proving unfit.

"Child known as Bear has proven an unexpected success, given his occasional defiance and the failure of his memory suppression protocol. How much he remembers of his past is unknown. Whether he understands that Janus perpetrated an aggression against Sturnus is unknown. However, as it currently stands, I consider these questions not of significant importance, given Bear's apparent acceptance of his place in Janusian society."

There was a pause, footsteps on the carpeted floor. Miss Sweet was pacing, now walking straight past Bear's line of sight, to his left.

"Several other subjects have shown glimpses of ability in proxy control," she continued. "I believe that, with sufficient time, every subject would achieve the same level of success as Bear. Given the continued resistance I have received in the upper chamber, this is now impossible. This may, in fact, be the final personal log entry as this project nears its terminus.

"I have applied for several extensions and have been rejected every time. The school may continue for a few days, months, or weeks, but I think it likely that Bear will be the only successful result of an e-year of work."

Bear listened with growing dismay approaching horror. He hadn't understood everything Miss Sweet had said, but two things were clear. First, she'd just admitted that Janus had attacked Sturnus. There was no more room for doubt. Second, the school was some kind of experiment, using the captive children, and now it was about to end.

What would happen to the unwanted kids?

At last, his nerve gave out, and Bear dropped the signal of his hijacked proxy. He gasped for breath back in the yard, clutching his head, which had started to ache.

After a few minutes, he started to feel better, calmer. His mission had been a success, a brilliant success, and he'd learned several important things. The discovery of the place where Miss Sweet stored her many robotic bodies presented a new opportunity, a modification of his plans. He could go back there as long as he could find his way, as long as he could sense the proxy signals in the city. If Miss Sweet and the Guardians could do it, staying in the city while their proxies came to the school, then he could. If not, he would just fall back on his original plan.

Now that he knew what it sounded like, he had to try to get Miss Sweet's signal back, no matter the distance. He had to find it in the city.

He listened. The nearby Guardians were loud to him now, almost deafening. He tried to screen them out, to hear what was behind them, toward the distant cluster of buildings. Before too long he heard it, like the buzzing of insects. The Guardians' signals faded, and the buzzing grew louder. He was in the city now, in its cluster of proxy signals, but it was difficult to isolate specific tones. There seemed to be hundreds, a symphonic blare making a growing noise in his head.

Then, he noticed that the wall of signals had a shape—a shape, and a colour that jumped out at him, resolving in his mind to form a real image emerging from darkness. The tones had always had visible textures, but this was a combination of those textures, forming a twisted ribbon, a kind of road. For a moment, he let himself be swept along, mesmerized by this discovery, passing through subsets of note clusters. One group made a sort of metallic ringing, and another a burbling, like water flowing; and then there was a group of melodious signals that reminded him very much of Miss Sweet.

He followed this last in closer, and became convinced that he'd found her, although what he'd located wasn't the single signal from before but many—the many signals of her many proxies as they stood there on the shelves.

He grabbed one at random and followed it all the way.

He'd found her.

The proxy he now inhabited was on the other side of the room from the first. Miss Sweet was still pacing the room, still speaking, but now he had a clear view of her.

"I still maintain that the destruction of all data relevant to organic quant-comm technology on Sturnus was a terrible, shortsighted mistake," Miss Sweet was saying. "They should not have destroyed the records. But the hatred of the Sturnus system, the belief that they are descended from traitors, the desire to obliterate what is seen as an almost heretical departure from Janusian technology, has been the driving force behind this entire endeavour."

She stopped pacing for a moment and stood looking toward the shelf where Bear's proxy was, just to his right.

"And yet now I find myself faced with a question I cannot answer," she continued, speaking slowly. "Bear exhibits unusual brain activity, which seems at least partly responsible for the failure of his memory suppression. We don't know why, and cannot consult his medical records because they were destroyed by those who opposed my project, who despised that data and saw no use for it. If he finds acceptance on Janus, then we will need to study him further. Or would my superiors also consider that heretical? Some would, at least."

She resumed her pacing, rubbing her hands together as she took one careful step after another.

"His acceptance by Janus is our next step. He has accepted us, so will we accept him."

She sighed.

"End log entry."

Bear dropped out again, and the room with its many proxies disappeared. His arms and legs were trembling, and he wasn't sure if that was from nerves or fatigue from all the energy he'd used trying to stay still and absorb what he'd heard. Whatever the case, he had to rest for a few minutes, had to conserve what strength he had left.

A curved shadow appeared on the wall across from him. Midday eclipse was here. Bear looked up as Corvus began to engulf the sun. He had a few minutes before the children would all go back inside.

He got up and crossed the yard to speak to his friends, to tell them important things they needed to know.

Chapter 13

Bear's feet felt heavy as he approached Roma. How was he going to explain? He should have said something before. It was too much at once.

Roma and Ralla were both spinning and laughing; Ralla became dizzy and staggered.

"You have to spin the other way!" Roma said.

"Roma," Bear said, "can I talk to you?"

Roma spun past him, stopped, and started spinning back to him, her braids standing out from her head as usual.

"I'm right here," she said.

"I'm sorry," Bear said, giving Ralla an apologetic look. "But I need to talk to you by yourself."

Roma looked irritated, her brow crinkling; but she stopped her dance, glanced at Ralla, and said, "Just a minute," then dragged Bear over to the far side of their favourite playset.

"Okay, what is it now?" she said, as if Bear did this often.

"Um…I have to tell you something. Something important."

Roma put her little fists on her hips. "What is it?"

Guardian Number Four strolled past, glancing at them and saying, "Almost time to go in, children."

Bear nodded, and the Guardian continued on his way. Bear waited until he thought the Guardian was out of earshot, and said, "I need your help."

Now Roma gave him a smug grin and cocked her head to one side.

"Help with what?"

Bear leaned in close to her. "Roma, tonight, after we go to bed, we're all going to escape from the school. Every one of us."

She stared at him a moment before bursting out laughing, hands to her mouth.

"You sound so serious."

Bear balled his fists in frustration.

"Really, Roma, listen! Tonight Miss Sweet will come and take us all out of our sleeping rooms, then outside, and we'll escape into the woods. We're never coming back."

Roma shook her head. "You're making up a story, Bear."

He sighed. "Roma, you don't need to believe me, but it'll happen. And when it does, I'm going to need you and Emmot to lead me along, because I won't be able to walk very well. I'll be slow and trip a lot. I'll need you to guide me or pull me along, because I'm going to look like I'm asleep. Just don't leave me behind, because we'll be heading into the woods, and then we're going to go and find out what happened to our parents."

A shadow passed over Roma's face, and she backed away.

"You're not supposed to talk about that," she murmured. "I know you're not. You'll get us in trouble."

She whirled away from him, and he reached out to grab her shirt; but she was already five meters away. He didn't call after her. That would have just attracted attention, and he would have to make up a story for the Guardians, and he didn't want that, didn't have the energy for it. He wanted to convince Roma to help him.

He just had to hope she would understand and help when the time came.

Next was Emmot. Bear found him on his perch atop the playset. This was his place of comfort, like Bear's corner, or Roma's twirling.

Bear told Emmot the same things he'd told Roma, that there would be an escape, all of the kids, and Miss Sweet would lead it. She would take them away, and then they'd see their parents again; but Emmot had to guide Bear along and make sure he was not left behind.

Emmot didn't say much the entire time Bear was speaking, just stared at him with round eyes. He made no reaction to Bear's reference to their parents.

"How do you know all this?" he said.

"I planned it," Bear said, "with Miss Sweet. That's what I've been doing when I haven't been around."

Emmot narrowed his eyes, then gazed toward the yellowpine forest.

"I've always wanted to see what was behind those trees," he said. He turned to Bear, a fierceness in his eyes. "You better not be lying, Bear."

Bear had never seen him like this. His face had gone a deep red, as if he were burning inside.

"I'm not," Bear assured him. "I promise I'm not."

Corvus had swallowed the sun, and it was dark. It was time for class, Bear's final class at Miss Sweet's school, maybe everyone's final class.

Just like in the morning, there was no actual lesson. Miss Sweet was green, like a large plant. All green—her hair, her face, her dress, and her hands, with darker green spots on her face.

"Take out your cards," she said. "It's a reading period! I've prepared some stories for you all to enjoy."

She waved her hand, and a series of titles appeared in the air above Bear's card. The titles were bright and cheery, and Bear was happy not to have to concentrate on math problems or something similar, and even happier that his stomach was not a coil of snakes. Ever since talking to Roma and Emmot, he'd been calm, decision made. He was pleased to pass some time reading stories, and went through five in a few minutes, skimming.

The stories were strange, just silly things about people from Janus—people and animals. There was one about a girl who climbed a mountain to steal an egg from a bird's nest. There was another one about a boy who found an ancient steam engine, and how he and his friend the scientist fixed it up and got it working. The stories were odd because they didn't put Bear in mind of Janus at all. None of them even mentioned proxies.

Then he realized that none of the Janusian tales they'd ever read, or that Miss Sweet had read to them, had ever mentioned proxies.

At last the period ended. Bear gazed about the classroom and felt a pang of regret, something he hadn't expected. It was strange to realize he'd some good memories of this place, of many warm experiences, with Miss Sweet in charge. When Aril and all of the other kids had been here.

At supper, Emmot kept giving him knowing looks and winking. This wasn't unusual behavior for him, so Bear didn't worry it might alert the Guardians to his plan. Roma, on the other hand, scowled at them both.

There was one more bit of preparation to make, and thinking about it made Bear's stomach snakes reappear. During free time, he retreated to his place in the southeast corner of the yard. It was an exposed position, but it had worked for him thus far, so worrying about discovery seemed pointless.

"Min," he whispered. "Min. Can you hear me?"

Someone on the far side of the yard burst into laughter, and Bear started. It was Ralla, doubled over at something Roma had said. The laughter sounded too loud, too wild. There was something wrong with it, an edge of hysteria, as if she sensed that today was not a normal day, that the normal days were over.

"Min," Bear repeated, his sense of urgency building. She should have appeared by now. "Oh, please, Min, where are you?"

"I'm here, silly," she said, descending from behind him, doing a pirouette to come face-to-face, although her arms remained straight at her sides, her feet dangling in their buckled shoes.

He breathed a sigh of relief. Everything was going well so far, but the next part hinged on what Min would do.

"Bear, I've been learning things," she said. "I've found out so much! Things about me, things about my location, and things about Janus and Sturnus."

That was interesting, and Bear wanted to ask her what she'd learned; but it would have to wait.

"Min, please," he said. "I need you to stay with me. Can you stay with me from now on? I mean, unless you have to go and check on something. I think I need you to stay with me all the time, or I won't be able to do this, which means I won't be able to rescue you."

She looked at him with concern and sympathy. Reaching out with one hand, she tried to touch his cheek, but her hand passed through him. He felt nothing.

"Of course I'll stay with you," she said, dropping her hand to her side. "I owe you a lot, Bear. Without you, I think...I think I wouldn't be alive. I was fading just before I found you. I think I'd be gone now. Just having you here to believe in me has made me stronger."

Her glow increased as she spoke, the details of her face and clothing becoming less distinct, buried in light. Bear could only stare at her, and for a moment he was struck with wonder how he could have taken this creature for granted, like any one of his friends, this glowing, flying image of a beautiful girl about his age.

What was she?

"Are you an angel, Min?"

Some of Miss Sweet's Janusian tales had been about angels, creatures of great beauty who arrived from some other world or universe to help people in need.

Min looked thoughtful. "I'm just checking to see what that is. I think I read about them in the library. Yes, I have it, and no, I don't think I'm one. They're beings from mythology, and I'm real."

"Okay. Well, to me you're an angel, Min. Or like one."

This was going to be scary and difficult, but with Min to keep him company, he could do it. If her existence was possible, then anything was possible.

He climbed to the top of the playset, and Min followed him. He gazed toward the yellowpine forest, which glowed like Min in the golden light of evening.

"That's where we're going tonight, Min," Bear whispered. "Through the woods and out the other side."

"But I didn't find any people there, Bear," she reminded him.

"I don't think you went far enough or looked long enough."

"I could go now. It won't take long."

Bear didn't like that idea. He didn't want her to leave him, and he didn't need her to look for people. None of that mattered. He and the others had no choice but to get away from here, to find another place, and he was certain the town where he'd lived was still there.

"Just stay with me here," he said. "Please."

"Allright, I will."

"We should go over the plan. Just to be sure."

"Okay," she said. "Tell me what I have to do."

He told her. Saying it out loud made it seem more real and gave him a chance to look for flaws.

"Are you sure you know how to open the door?" she asked him.

"Yes," he insisted, although he knew this was the one flaw in his plan. He knew how to open the door in theory but was ignorant of the details. He thought he could figure it out, but what if it was harder than it looked?

Then he would fail. He had to face the possibility this wouldn't work. What was his backup plan?

"What happens if you can't open the doors?" Min asked, as if she had read his thoughts.

He looked at her in silence for a moment; then an alternate plan occurred to him.

"I'll look for another proxy to inhabit," he said, "on the other side of the door. Then I'll jump into it."

"What if there's no proxy there?"

"Then we'll just wait for one to come along."

Other problems with this solution tried to push into his awareness, but he turned away from them. He would solve problems as they occurred. It was the best he could do.

The chime sounded. Bear filed into the school, filed into the Washroom, and then to his sleeping room. The gray walls and rows of sleep bags seemed meaningless now, vestiges of another time. As promised, Min stayed at his side, hovering above his left shoulder. Sleep was impossible, so Min's brightness wasn't a problem.

Bear hung in his sleep bag, listening to the sounds of the children around him. He had to stay awake and wait for the proper hour. How late did Miss Sweet stay awake? He had no idea. He would just have to wait until it was very late. It was essential that he didn't fall asleep. If he fell asleep and didn't wake until morning, he would have missed his chance.

There were so many ways his plan could fail; but at least he had Min to help, and her bright light and chatter to help him stay alert.

He wiggled his feet, and that made him remember his old bed. It had been a long soft mattress on a wooden frame standing about a metre above the floor. He had slept on it by lying down, and it had been comfortable, much more comfortable than hanging from the wall like a bat.

He remembered what a bat was.

This was the first time he'd thought of his old bed in detail, and suddenly the sleep bags seemed completely ridiculous. Why did the Janusians make them sleep this way? What was their purpose? They made no sense.

They seemed so bizarre he started to giggle.

"Why are you laughing, Bear?" said Min.

"Sleep bags are stupid" was all he could say.

It occurred to him that, if this plan did fail, and he was forced to accompany Miss Sweet to Janus, that he would probably have to sleep in a sleep bag for the rest of his life. That alone would have been enough to convince him escape was the only option, but he hadn't considered it before, because he hadn't remembered his bed.

Min turned away from him and hovered at his side where Aril's sleep bag had once hung. Her face resumed a blank expression, and Bear suspected she was searching or learning or doing whatever it was she did. Her mind could roam just like his did when it grabbed a proxy signal.

Time passed, although Bear had no idea how much. He had to pee, and pee badly, so he just went in his sleep bag, which was designed to absorb urine and other wastes. He tossed back and forth, unable to get comfortable, unable to rest. There were no snakes in his stomach, but his skin and muscles seemed to buzz.

At last he decided there was no sense in waiting any longer. If he found Miss Sweet awake, he would just have to wait in silence in one of her proxies until she went to bed.

Opening his sleep bag, he dropped to the soft gray floor, making no effort to be quiet. He had to wake the others soon anyway.

"Bear?" Roma called. "Bear, is that you?"

Bear braced his back against the wall under where Min was floating. Min's eyes fluttered, and awareness returned to her face, her eyes.

"Who is that?" she said.

"Roma," Bear said. "Just give me a minute, Roma."

"You mean you weren't just making it up?" Roma said. She sounded a little annoyed.

"No. Just give me a minute. Min, will you come with me?"

"Of course," Min said.

"Who's Min?" Roma said.

"Never mind, Roma," Bear hissed. "Just give me a minute! Please! I need a minute."

Squeezing his eyes shut, he took a few breaths and struggled to concentrate. For a few seconds, he worried Miss Sweet or the Guardians were watching him, and had always been watching him, in which case he should have stayed in his sleep bag while he searched for the proxy signals. But he hadn't wanted to.

All he had to do was cast about for the proper signals. That was easy. He could do that.

He tried again, and now he encountered a chaos of fluting and trumpeting, high and low tones, buzzing and whirring, just like he'd felt before. With his eyes closed, all external distractions neutralized, he felt like he was in another world, a world of colours and lines and glowing ribbons, bright in his mind, real and solid.

He travelled the coloured highway, searching for the harmony of Miss Sweet.

It didn't take long to find it, a single massive chord amid the noise, and follow it, all of it together like he'd done before, until the mess of other signals faded into the background. Choosing a single strand of that vast array, a single harmonious tone, he traced it to its source. It didn't matter which one of Miss Sweet's bodies he chose, and he found himself inhabiting a tall form. At first he saw nothing but darkness, and with a jolt of alarm he worried something was wrong, but then he realized the proxy's eyes were closed.

A faint voice, sounding in his own ears, said, "Well, hurry up."

It was Roma.

He opened the proxy body's eyes. The room around him was dim, a faint glow coming from the floor. The glow reminded him of the nightlight in his old room, the bedroom he had only just remembered. Mum and Dad had always left a faint light on for him.

The room he was in now was quiet.

"Min," he whispered in the proxy's voice. "Min, are you here?"

It was strange to hear his teacher's own voice coming from his mouth.

"I'm right here, Bear," Min said. She was at his side.

"I can't see very well," he told her. "Can you tell me where the door is?"

Min floated to his left and returned.

"There's a blank wall over here with a hidden door. You wouldn't be able to see the door, even if it was light, but I can. There's a corridor outside."

"Okay."

Bear looked down at the floor. He was standing on a shelf—the bottom shelf, in fact, which was lucky, although he still had to step down about fifteen centimeters. He almost stumbled in Miss Sweet's funny high-heeled shoes, but the proxy must have had some body memory, like the wolf, and once he was settled on two feet, he was able to walk without any difficulty.

Facing the wall where Min had said the door was located, he looked for a way to open it. He couldn't feel or sense any door signal, and for a second he panicked. Here was the moment of extreme danger. He'd assumed the doors worked just like the proxies, that they gave out a signal someone could track, to send a command to open or something; but there was nothing there.

He rubbed his eyes with one of Miss Sweet's long-fingered hands. It was too soon to go to his backup plan, but here he was, just starting, and his greatest fear was staring him in the face.

He hadn't thought this through properly. He should have figured out how the doors worked.

"Min, how do I open the door?" he said. "Miss Sweet used a signal before, but there's nothing coming from the wall? What did she do?"

Min floated in front of him, looking at him with brows knit. "Well, we should have realized this, but I can see it. The robot that you're riding has the capability of sending signals, too. I can read its software and see its hardware. You have to send a signal to the door."

"Okay," he said.

So, he had to send, not receive, a signal. But what signal?

Maybe the proxy itself could tell him. They were built to help the user, built so that anyone who understood the basics of their operation could hop in and know what to do. The wolf had been like that. Bear hadn't known how to be a wolf, but the wolf proxy had shown him. So, the way to open a door should have been easy to understand, like having a tail and four paws. The method for sending signals to doors should be there somewhere, in his mind.

A dozen green spinning boxes appeared in the air in front of him. He flinched backwards, but the boxes didn't move. They hovered there in a line, like a dozen Mins, spinning.

These were the door signals. Thinking about them had brought them into existence. To release a signal, some innate programming told him, he just had to open the appropriate box. This new puzzle tempered his relief. Which box?

He tried the first, giving it a mental command to open, and its virtual lid swung back. A high-pitched and unpleasant tone emerged, but the door remained closed.

Closing the box, he tried the next one. Again, nothing happened.

On the third attempt, the door opened.

Triumph. Victory. Elation. His prize was in his grasp.

He stepped through the doorway.

The corridor beyond was also lit by a faint glow from the floor. Min floated ahead of him.

"There's no one here, Bear," she said. "Don't worry. I can't sense anybody. They all must be asleep."

Bear looked to the left and right. Empty, as Min had said.

"There's a travel tube this way," Min added, floating down the corridor and stopping at a spot near the wall on Bear's left. "Right here."

Bear approached the spot, and again called forth the spinning boxes and opened the same one, which he assumed was the signal to open all doors. A section of wall slid away, and there was one of the little white rooms.

"Does this go to the school?" he said, stepping inside and closing the door behind him.

"It can connect to the school," said Min. "Yes."

As she spoke, he realized one of the other signal boxes in his head was an instruction for the travel tube, an instruction for it to start moving. He sent the signal, and a list of destinations appeared in the air (or inside his eyes—he couldn't tell). Most of the words meant nothing to him, but one stood out because he recognized it. It simply said *School.*

Bear chose it.

The room seemed to drop, like an elevator; then it changed direction and moved sideways for several minutes. Bear found himself tapping his proxy foot.

The travel tube changed direction again, rising, and at last the sense of motion stopped.

Bear told the door to open.

They were in the school, in the long corridor. He'd done it. He'd stolen one of Miss Sweet's proxies, and now all he had to do was lead the children to freedom.

Chapter 14

W hen he walked into the sleep room, the first thing Bear saw was himself—his real body, leaning against the wall. He stopped and stared, then switched points of view, opening his real eyes so he could look across the room and see what version of Miss Sweet he'd chosen. It was the one dressed in a flowing turquoise gown, with the turquoise face bisected by a coral line.

It was lucky he'd chosen a proxy that had clothes.

Closing his real eyes again, he let the proxy view dominate. The other children were still in their sleep bags. He would have to wake them and get them out quickly, hopefully with Roma's and Emmot's help. He had to assume it wouldn't take the Janusians long to discover what was happening, and that they'd come after them as soon as they could.

"Children." He spoke through the proxy in Miss Sweet's voice, trying to think of the kind of words she would use. "You have to...you must wake up, and get up. Leave your sleep bags and come with me at once...my little birds."

There were a few stirrings, a whine and a moan, and someone said, "What?"

"Children, you must wake up," Bear tried again. "Roma and Emmot, please help to wake up the children."

Miss Sweet would probably have said "wake" the children, not "wake up." He had to try harder to imitate her.

Roma's sleep bag opened, and as she emerged she took one look at Miss Sweet's proxy and turned to the room, clapping her hands.

"Come on, everyone. Wake up! Wake up now! Emmot!"

"Do you believe me now, Roma?" Bear asked in Miss Sweet's voice.

Roma flashed him a look that was half-horror and half-annoyance; but she continued to help, running from sleep bag to sleep bag, shaking them and even opening Emmot's for him. Emmot dropped out, bare feet slapping the floor as he rubbed his eyes.

Bear just watched. Roma herded the others into a short file, like a Guardian in training. Now Bear had four followers. They were groggy and cranky, snuffling and whining, staring with stupid, wide eyes, but it was a start.

"Come, then," he said, and led them out of the room.

Once in the corridor, he paused, letting Miss Sweet's body wait while he caught up with his real body. This would be the thing that could slow them down, because he would have to move in stages, walking a few steps himself, then stopping and walking Miss Sweet for a few steps. He wished there were a way to walk both bodies at the same time, but he'd never quite figured that out.

"Please wait here," he said as Miss Sweet. "Emmot, you're in charge. Please look after the others. Roma, come with me."

Leaving his own body with Emmot, he and Roma went into the next sleep room, where four more children hung in their sleep bags. Bear told them to wake up, and Roma shook them, as she had before. A moment later, this second group was shuffling, bleary-eyed and groggy, into the corridor to join the first.

Bear and Roma entered the third sleep room, and there they ran into a glitch. None of the five children would respond to any attempt to wake them.

"Open their sleep bags so they fall out," Bear said.

Roma did as he commanded, while he stood back, playing the role of Miss Sweet. The first child spilled onto the floor, putting his hands out at the last second to break his fall, then gaping around with wide sleepy eyes. The second child, a girl named Petra, screamed and started to cry.

"Quiet!" Bear snapped, taking a step forward. "You must be quiet!"

Petra shook her head and kept crying, cramming herself into a ball against the wall.

Bear looked at Roma. "If she won't get moving, she'll have to catch up or something. We have to go now."

He and Roma woke the last children. Believing him to be Miss Sweet, they obeyed his commands, although with sluggish reluctance. Even Petra, maybe thinking better of defying her teacher, joined them. Soon, there was a shapeless clump of tired and cranky kids in the corridor, gathered around Bear's body.

Bear, as Miss Sweet, turned to Emmot.

"Emmot," he said, "please guide Bear, because he can't see well. Roma, bring them all and follow me."

He led them down the corridor, taking ten paces as Miss Sweet, then ten paces as himself. The whole time he could feel both sets of legs, but kept about two-thirds of his awareness in the proxy, allowing the view from its eyes to dominate, allowing Emmot to guide his real body.

When he reached the end of the corridor, he retrieved the box to send the door-opening signal. The wall slid aside.

Min was waiting in the yard. She was a beautiful sight, and just for a fleeting second, Bear allowed himself a burst of excitement. His plan was working, and they were almost free from the school. There was the old yard, its silvery walls, the playset, all bathed in the bright light from Corvus, its great striped ball hanging high in the sky behind a few wisps of luminous cloud. This was a night for great things.

"There's nobody coming," Min told him. "You can make it, Bear!"

Roma was leading the shuffling mob of barefoot children, encouraging them, speaking in soft, kind words. "Come on, you can do it. It's not far now, just a little nighttime walk."

"Where are we going, Miss Sweet?" he heard Kalla say.

"Home," said Bear. "We're going home."

That would probably make no sense to her, since they all thought of the school as home; but he heard a few gasps and one plaintive cry, and he wondered if a few more of them had started to remember their old lives.

"We have to be quiet," he said, "so the Guardians don't hear. They don't want us to leave, but I'm in charge. We're leaving the school forever."

He turned and strode toward the wall on the proxy's long legs, walking as he'd seen Miss Sweet walk so many times. With his own body, he took a few slow steps, Emmot at his elbow. The yard wall had no obvious doors, but Bear sent the signal anyway.

Three doors opened at the same time. There must have been other signals, more specific ones for each door, but that didn't matter. The way was clear. Through the massive doorways, the meadow shone in the light of Corvus, and beyond was the dark line of forest, like a gate into the unknown.

Choosing the doorway in the centre, Bear went through, taking three strides into the meadow and halting. He paused and gazed at the sky, which was a deep velvet blue and bright with stars, and for a moment he just stared. The night was warm. Far to his right, he could see a few lights in the city.

The children shuffled out, still confused, still nervous. Bear jumped back into his own body and dashed forward, then returned to the proxy and walked Miss Sweet a few paces, then did the same—his body, then Miss Sweet, alternating until he'd crossed the meadow and was at the edge of the forest. Turning, he looked back toward the school with Miss Sweet's eyes, at the squat, dull grayness of the wall and its single convoluted building. This was the last time he would ever look at it.

Stooping to avoid low-hanging limbs, he plunged into the woods, into almost complete darkness, but the trees held no fear for him.

Min appeared on his right, a serene smile on her face. "Well, what now?"

Bear took a few more steps, his hands outstretched, halting when he came to a large yellowpine. He dropped out of Miss Sweet's body completely. It had done its job, and he no longer wanted it.

"Can you lead us through to the other side?" he asked Min in his own voice, coming up behind her from the edge of the trees. "We don't have any light."

Min turned and nodded. "I will guide you."

As she floated ahead, Bear turned and said, "Allright, everyone, join hands! Join hands and follow me."

He took the hand of the first child in the line. Min glanced back before carrying on, dodging between the trees. Bear went after her, the forest floor soft with needles under his bare feet. He left Miss Sweet standing alone, one long arm outstretched, the index finger pointing the way.

Soon, the tree trunks began to thicken, growing larger, older; but there was little undergrowth, and the going was easy. The children formed a long chain of pale-gray figures, like a string of paper dolls, their footsteps muffled by the spongy duff. Some of them complained, but Roma continued to offer encouragement, as did Emmot.

Time passed—ten minutes, twenty. Roma and Emmot grew quiet, and now there was just the sound of shuffling feet and breathing. Bear was starting to tire, the nervous excitement having worn off and his lack of sleep finally beginning to tell. His breathing grew loud in his ears, and Min's image faded in and out of focus.

At last, the trees thinned, and the sight of this gave him a burst of energy.

"Look!" he said. "We're almost through."

It wasn't so. They emerged into an open area filled with tall sword grass. The forest continued on the other side. It was just a clearing, a momentary gap in the trees.

Bear stopped. His exhaustion weighed on him, and he sat down, pulling the nearest children with him.

"Min!" he cried. "Min, come back!"

She snapped into existence above him, floating in a circle around the clearing.

"Do you think it's safe here?" she said.

"I don't know," Bear whined, "but I have to sleep. Roma! Emmot! Let's all just clump together and sleep here in the grass."

Neither Roma nor Emmot objected. No doubt they were too tired.

"Everyone bunch up," Roma said. "Let's all bunch up like a group of rabbits."

They formed a rough circle and lay down to sleep. The night was still warm, but they huddled like puppies, their special clothing protecting them, their closeness providing a sense of security. Bear rested his head on his arms, the ground soft beneath him. Someone's head was against his side, someone else's legs thrown over his. He hadn't felt this comfortable in a long time, this warm, this peaceful. He seemed to sink down into the ground, the earth swallowing him, embracing him. The last thing he saw was Min, still circling, keeping watch.

"I'll try to wake you if anyone comes," she said.

Then he was asleep, his anxiety gone and his mind free.

Bear's hair was wet when he awoke, opening his eyes to see white mist hanging in long tendrils in the clearing. Thicker batches of mist hung still and silent among the dark pillars of the trees along one side of the clearing, like a line of watchful ghosts. The air smelled like something he had forgotten, something he once knew; and for a moment his heart swelled and he sat up. He was home! That was the smell of home, the smell of the world outside.

Then the last shreds of sleep fell away, and he remembered he was in the woods with the children from the school. They were stirring, sitting up and rubbing their eyes, various once-perfect hair styles now frayed and askew, scraps of hair sticking this way and that. Some of them had smudges on their faces and clothes. Dirt, something they hadn't seen or had to deal with since they'd been taken, clung to them—dirt and sweat. All of them looked about with confusion or fear.

All save Emmot, who sat up and stretched both arms out to his sides, gazing at the towering yellowpines, his ruddy face beaming, showing his teeth as he smiled.

"Where can we go pee?" a very small boy named Nang whined. "Where's the privy and the Washroom?"

Emmot struggled to his feet, brushing away bits of bark and fallen needles. "Just go behind a tree. I think…I think I've done that before."

"Where's Miss Sweet?" someone asked, a question several others repeated. Bear realized they might not have noticed her disappearance in the darkness. They'd just assumed they were still following her.

"Did Miss Sweet leave?" Kalla said. "Is she coming back?"

Bear struggled to his feet and faced them.

"Miss Sweet isn't coming back," he told them. "We have to make it the rest of the way on our own."

They stared at him, and Kalla said, "How do you know?"

Bear wasn't sure what to say. He had to be careful here. He was pretty sure that if he told them the whole truth, some would want to go back.

"Miss Sweet told me she had to stay with the school," Bear said. "She can't leave it. But we have to keep going. She told me where to go."

"It's true," Roma said, and she grinned. "She told me, too. We have to follow Bear."

Bear looked at her, and she looked back. He hadn't been sure of Roma, but she'd proven a staunch ally. There must be something she wasn't telling him. Maybe memories of home she'd kept to herself.

He nodded to her.

"So, we keep going," he said.

The others were all staring at him, and he saw a few frowns and looks of incredulity, but no one openly objected. They were still with him, at least for now.

His stomach growled, hunger pangs squeezing. He'd forgotten all about bringing food in case they had to walk a long way, and hadn't thought the forest would go on for so long. But where would he have gotten it? Why did he even think he should have brought food? As if they were going to a picnic?

Min was still hovering high amongst the tall narrow trunks of the yellowpines. Bear spied her, and she slowly descended.

"Min," he said, "is there anywhere to get food around here?"

Min shook her golden head. "There's nothing around here, Bear. You'll have to wait. The forest ends just a little way over there."

"Who's Min?" Roma asked. "I heard you talking to 'Min' last night, too."

Bear considered making up an explanation, but Roma's help had been key to the success of the adventure so far. She deserved to know what was really going on.

He told her the whole story.

"She's a kind of guide. Only I can see her."

Roma screwed up her face. "That's really weird, Bear."

Bear gave her what he thought was his most serious look. "Roma, everything I've told you would happen has happened so far, right? Miss Sweet did lead us into these woods, like I said she would, right?"

Roma nodded. Emmot had come to stand next to her and was watching with bright eyes.

"Right," Roma said.

"Well, Min told me that right over there the forest ends. So I think everyone should pee, and then we should go over there and see if I'm right."

"I'm hungry," Emmot asked. "Real hungry, Bear."

"We have to walk a ways first," Bear said. "Come on, we can do it."

Min drifted ahead, and Bear followed. The others trailed behind him. He tried to imagine what they would find once they came out of the forest.

So many times he'd stared at that line of trees from the top of the playset, wondering what lay beyond, and now he was about to discover that very thing. Maybe there would be farms, or maybe there would be soldiers, something he'd heard about in stories but had never seen—soldiers on Sturnus. Good soldiers who were fighting the Janusian invaders, like in stories of old Earth. They would feed the starving children, give them proper clothes to replace these ugly gray pajamas.

All of that seemed unlikely, but he enjoyed thinking about it.

The dark tree trunks grew closer together. Bear's feet were sore, the sides and tops scratched and bleeding in places. He stared ahead at Min's back. Just in front of her, a patch of different light appeared, bright blue light through the trees.

"There it is!" he shouted, pointing.

Despite his sore feet, he started to run. Emmot ran with him, laughing. The rest tried to keep up.

The edge of the forest opened like the big door in the yard wall of the school. Bear stumbled to a halt, as did Emmot. The whole company piled in behind them, stopping and staring, wide-eyed and uncertain.

The land fell away in rolling, sweeping hills, ending at a crest about a thousand meters distant. The ground was black, as if burned, covered in ashes; and everywhere new spring plants were growing from that fertile mix, bright-green sprouts contrasting the dark surface. Not a tree stood, not a house, although it was clear houses and buildings had once been here, for there were remnants—shattered fragments of walls and foundations. Bear saw piles of bricks, a clump of twisted pipe, the back of something that had wheels and may have been a ground car.

About two dozen paces away stood a crooked statue, its surface as black as the scorched earth.

Something seemed to fall away inside him. Bear took a few steps into the ash, then started running again, running toward the statue. His heart was racing, his mind focused on that one thing, that one object, an object he'd seen in his memories. Those memories had not lied, had not been false, for there it was.

When he reached it, he skidded to a stop, ash rising in little clouds around his feet, blackening his skin and the hem of his light-gray pants.

The statue stood on a square base of pale stone, but one corner had sunken into the ground, and the whole thing was canted at a steep angle. On top of the pedestal was the figure of the girl with the bow. With her was a small deer. Both of the deer's antlers had snapped off, as had the top and bottom of the bow.

All around was desolation. The statue was real, but everything else was gone. The park was just more flat ground covered in ash and spots of fresh green.

Bear's legs felt weak, and he slid down until he sat with his back to the crooked pedestal. Roma came up behind him, trailed by the others, their shambling feet kicking up ash and disturbing the new green plants. Someone sneezed.

"Bear, we can't stay here," she said. "We have to find something to eat."

"I remember this," someone whispered. "Hey, I've been here before."

"Mummy and Daddy," someone else said.

They were remembering. Bear blinked away tears, pushed himself to his feet, brushing at the clinging ash. He had been wrong to think some of the town still stood, but maybe there were intact structures farther on. He had to keep going.

He saw the faces of his fellow pupils, his fellow orphans. They looked as if they'd just awakened from a dream and found that reality was worse than a nightmare.

Min drifted down to hover in front of Bear's face, between him and Roma.

"Bear, is this where you lived?" she asked.

He nodded. If this was the garden, he was close to home. Miss Sweet's school hadn't been so far away after all. And although he knew his house had not survived, he recalled some houses had, at least before the bug thing had grabbed him. Some of his old neighborhood—all the wooden houses with the big windows, the little roads and the yards and trees and gardens—might all still be there. And the beach. The cliffs and the beach.

Shading his eyes, he looked toward the distant ridge, beyond the rolling charred hills. Just over the horizon. That's where they'd be.

"Let's go," he said.

Chapter 15

The broken statue of Artemis receded into the distance as Bear led the children up the long slope toward the crest, moving through the black ash and raising a cloud that stung their eyes and made them cough.

When they came to the top of the rise, they saw the glimmering water below.

Bear gasped. He knew this place, knew he was almost home. There was the shore, the edge of the cliff, a glimpse of a sandy crescent, jumbled sandstone boulders, and the water sparkling in the morning sun, reflecting the great bulk of Corvus in its place in the sky.

It was like a vision, a dream, come to life.

Except it wasn't the same. Where once the happy neighborhood of spacious wooden homes had stood was more black ash, more little green shoots, more random clumps of wreckage.

Roma was crying, tears streaming down her face.

"Everything is ruined," she said. "Everything burned to pieces."

Bear took her hand and squeezed it, and she didn't pull away as usual, just let him hold it. Bear hoped he was making her feel better. She was only experiencing the same thing he'd felt when his memories had started to come back, and almost every day since, at least for a few minutes at a time.

Shading his eyes with his free hand, he squinted at the distant ridge. There were many uneven piles of wreckage and at least two that seemed a little more regular.

"Look," he said, letting go of Roma's hand and pointing. "Are those a couple of houses?"

The more he stared, the more the two even shapes stood out from the ruins. They looked like rooftops, gabled rooftops and walls, still intact. A pair of houses, he was sure of it. Houses that had survived whatever the Janusians had done here.

All of the children were staring, some also shading their eyes.

"They are," Min, hovering to his right, said. "A few houses weren't destroyed."

"I think you're right," said Roma, sounding a little more hopeful.

"That's where we'll go," Bear said, excited now. "There might be food there."

The town was a wreck, there was no one here, but there was something left, somewhere to go. And they were free.

"Come on, everyone!" he called out. "There's a house over there! A real house. Let's go and see what's in it!"

"Yeah!" Emmot exclaimed. "I bet I can be the first one there!"

He started running, face alight. Bear didn't know if Emmot's enthusiasm was real or a tactic to keep up everyone's spirits, but he suspected it was real, that Emmot was showing his true feelings. Whatever the case, it worked, and he found himself following, going as fast as he could despite not having eaten, trying to outpace his friend. The rest of the kids joined in. A few even laughed.

The house drew closer, and now Bear could make out more details. It hadn't completely escaped damage, and a large patch of black carbon scorching marred one wall, the wooden siding burned away to reveal the geopolymer frame underneath. Otherwise, the structure looked unharmed. Even the massive windows were unbroken.

Emmot won the race, reaching the house first, where he came to a hard stop. Bear caught up to him in half a dozen strides.

"I remember a place like this," Emmot said, voice veiled in wonder. "The door's on the other side."

He ran around to the front. The others followed like a swarm of insects. The house had a roof with three peaks, and beneath the largest was the door, facing the sea. The door hung open.

Bear and Emmot peered inside. A layer of ash extending about two meters in covered the floor, but this looked like it had probably blown in from outside. The rest of the interior seemed fine, untouched by whatever had happened. Bear could just glimpse a great room with a stone fireplace, two low couches, throw rugs, tables, even scattered cushions, printed books and other items, all still there, as if the inhabitants had never left.

"Is there anyone here?" Emmot called.

He and Bear entered the house, making footprints in the ash. For some reason, the other children, including Roma, hovered at the doorway, as if waiting to see what would happen, whether Bear and Emmot would spring a trap or meet some other deadly disaster. Min remained with them.

"Where's the kitchen?" Bear said. "They must have food makers."

He was about to call for Min, but instead let his memories guide him. The house was similar to the one in which he'd lived. There, the kitchen had been behind the great room, and so it proved to be here. And it was intact. The floor was clean, there was a long counter and stools, and a sitting area with little tables for eating. Most important, there in the wall was a large device Bear recognized as a full-capacity molecular assembler.

A food maker.

Emmot ran for the assembler, shouting for joy.

"I remember these! How did I forget about these?"

Bear looked for a chappie maker, but he didn't see one.

"It works," Emmot said. He'd punched several buttons, and the assembler was blinking with little red and green lights. "It has power. Look, there's a menu. Who wants breakfast?"

There were plenty of things on the breakfast menu. Emmot chose pontines—a kind of fish—rice pudding, and sliced char-apples. When he hit the start button, the machine hissed; and a minute later, a plate containing his choices appeared in the assembly area, which was a large drawer underneath the instrument panel.

Bear ran back to the front door.

"There's food," he said.

A few minutes later, the children had gathered in the great room, filling the chairs and couches and the clean patches of floor. Everyone had a breakfast on his or her lap.

Bear sat with Emmot and Roma, next to the fireplace.

"You burn logs in here," said Roma. "Wooden logs. Like in one of Miss Sweet's fairy tales."

"We used to do that all the time," said Emmot. He stopped eating. Large, heavy tears appeared in his eyes and rolled down his cheeks. "I had fathers, two fathers. My dads. Why? Why did I forget them? Why?"

His thick shoulders started to shake. Bear watched in fascination, for he'd never seen Emmot cry or demonstrate anything close to actual sadness. Other kids were crying, too, crying and looking around them in wonder and horror.

It was all coming back.

"It's okay," Roma said to Emmot, petting his arm. "I remember, too. This can be our house now. We can clean it up."

"There's another house just over there," Kalla said, looking out one of the large windows. "We could use that one, too."

Bear tossed aside the strange papery plate the food assembler had given him. For some reason, he felt sick and bitter. They'd found freedom, but he was angry that the Janusians had taken it away in the first place.

⁂

"Maybe we can stay here," he said to Min later, as he sat on the steps leading to the front door, gazing at the ocean. He wanted to go down to the beach, but he was tired. He would have to nap first.

Min bobbed up and down at his side.

"The food assembler is low on raw materials," she said. "It operates on a small fusion reactor, but soon you'll need to fill it."

He hadn't thought of that.

"Can you help us figure out how to use some of the things here?"

"I can, Bear, but don't forget that you still have to rescue me!"

Bear had, in fact, almost forgotten that promise. "I will! But…first you have to figure out where you are."

Min looked relieved. "I almost have it. I'm sure I'll find out soon."

Bear stood on wobbly legs. Never mind the nap.

"I want to go and see the beach. I want to see how close we might be to my old beach. I want to find where my house was."

It didn't matter how tired he was. This was important.

"I'll come with you," Min said.

The ground between the house and the cliff edge was all new grass; and below, Bear saw a stretch of red sand. This was the same beach, he was sure of it, but a little farther up the coast. He just had to find a way down the cliff.

After a quick search, he came upon a straight rail that looked like it had once guided a lift pad to the bottom of the cliff. The pad was missing, but the rail gave him something to climb. Grasping its smooth surface, he searched for gaps in the adjacent rock and was able to pick his way down without any problem. Dropping the last half-meter, he landed in the soft sand.

He was accustomed to not wearing shoes, as all the children were; but the long walk through the forest and grass and ash had taken their toll, and the sand felt good against his feet, like a salve.

Min floated down next to him. He stood still, smelling the salt and gazing along the shore. There was a line of black ash near the base of the cliff, and along the cliff face rested the twisted remains of stairways or lifts;; but otherwise, the beach looked as he remembered it, the same red sand, the same black lines of seaweed.

"Not everything is dead," he said. "There's the seaweed, and all those green plants growing up there. In a while, it'll all come back."

He started walking, and again he had the sensation of having entered a dream. His head was spinning. This was where he'd strolled with Mum and Dad, taken Tayor for romps. Right here. He and his friends had gone swimming and built sand forts. And there had been other kids—cousins... and aunts and uncles. Images of their faces, of their voices, flooded his mind. He'd almost forgotten them. He'd had other family, family who might still be out there.

He started to run.

"Look, Min, look. See those rocks?"

A jumble of sedimentary boulders jutted into the water, and he knew them as he scrambled over their rough surfaces. Beyond was a wider strip of sand, a crescent beneath the cliffs. He stopped and stared. The houses along the cliffs were all gone, but everything else was there.

Jumping down, he walked out onto the edge of the crescent. Min accompanied him.

"This could be a beautiful place," she said. "See?"

A slight breeze freshened, the air off the water cool against Bear's cheek. The waves lapped the edge of the shore, and he closed his eyes to listen. The sounds were right, the smells were right.

He was home.

From far away, it seemed, came the sound of a child's scream, a high-pitched shriek. Bear opened his eyes and looked at Min.

"Did you hear that?" he said.

A loud bang, a distant explosion, made him start. The sound had come from the direction of the house where they'd left the others.

"Did the food assembler blow up?" Bear cried.

Retracing his steps, he scrambled over the boulders and back to the first beach. They could not afford to lose the assembler until they found other ways to feed themselves.

More screams and cries sounded from the house, a chorus of childish voices raised in obvious alarm and terror. Bear's heart froze. They'd encountered something terrifying, something far worse than a broken assembler.

He shaded his eyes against the light, but could see nothing from here, just the three points of the house's roof rising beyond the edge of the cliff.

"Bear, look," Min said. "Someone's there."

A figure had appeared on the beach at the base of the cliff. It was the figure of a tall man in black. The man was bareheaded, and was coming toward them.

"Who is it?" Bear said.

He was unsure whether to stand or run.

The figure drew closer, a young man, thin and handsome, with an olive complexion and short golden hair. Bear had never seen him in this precise guise before, but recognized Mister Verren.

They'd been discovered. They'd been found. He hadn't escaped.

His insides were frozen. He could feel nothing, do nothing.

Verren stopped in front of him and gazed down. His face held no trace of friendship, but was like stone, cold and menacing.

"Bear," he said.

Bear just stared up at the man. This was Verren's proxy. This wasn't the real Verren.

"Did you think you could get away?" Verren said. "Where did you think you would go? As you can see, there's nothing left here. Your old civilization is gone. How many times do we have to explain this to you?"

Bear looked at his feet in shame, shame at failure, at being caught. After all they'd been through. His plan had worked so well, too, but had been for nothing.

He wanted to run, but there was nowhere to go. Besides, flight would do nothing to save his friends.

"We're very disappointed, Bear," Verren continued. "Now this entire operation is a failure, thanks to you. You've betrayed us, you and whoever may be helping you."

There was another scream from the cliff. Bear looked Verren straight in the eye. Now he was angry.

"No one's helping me. Just Roma and Emmot and everyone else."

"Come on, now, Bear. How did you gain access to a private proxy? It's not possible, Bear. Someone had to have reset it, and you don't know how to do that. Please don't lie to me. We saw every movement last night, knew what you were doing from the moment you started. We know things, don't you realize that by now? Now, tell me who helped you."

Bear was only half-listening, because suddenly he felt sick, his stomach full of something heavy, like lead. This wasn't fair. Min was floating there, looking at him, eyes big with shock and surprise. How would he rescue her now?

"Are you going to take us back?" he asked.

Mister Verren put his hands on his hips. "Of course you're going back! What happens afterward depends on how helpful you are."

The waves lapped the shore on Bear's left, the sound of comfort and happiness, the sound of home.

He wasn't going back to the school.

Verran's proxy signal was loud and obvious. Bear found it and followed it in so fast it actually stung, left his real body gasping for breath at the moment he found himself looking through Verren's eyes.

The pain only lasted a second, and then Bear ran Verran's proxy toward the cliff. Verran was gone, and Bear was in full command. Ahead was the elevator rail he'd used to climb down to the beach, and he grabbed it and pulled himself up, climbing all the way back to the top of the cliff. It was easy thanks to the proxy's strength, much easier than it would have been in his little boy body.

Min was with him. She could tell that he'd taken Verran's proxy. "What are you doing, Bear?"

Bear said nothing and looked at the house. Bug machines surrounded it, the black robotic creatures that had kidnapped him in the first place. Now they'd come for them again, and as Bear watched he saw one lift Kalla into the air with its mechanical arms, dropping her toward the compartment in its rear. Kalla was screaming.

"They're proxies," he said in Verren's voice. He could feel their signals, every one of them. They were proxies, and they were machines of war.

He had to get rid of Verren, had to break him so no one could use the proxy again. Without thinking, he turned and leapt over the edge of the cliff.

The rocks and sand at the bottom rushed up to meet him, but he dropped the proxy before the moment of impact. A great deep-throated crunch met his real ears just as he returned to his own body. He saw Verren's proxy twisted on the ground, arms and legs at bizarre angles, sprawled at the bottom of the cliff.

Bear ran for the rail, grabbed it, and started hoisting himself up the cliff.

"Bear, what are you doing?" Min called again, but he didn't look back. He climbed to the top then lay down on the ground, pressing himself into the grass, reaching out for the nearest signal.

He became a bug machine, a battlebot. The house was in front of him, and he saw that one entire wall was now gone, a battlebot having blasted it in. Other battlebots were around him, and some were firing those hot yellow beams into the walls and supports. The house was crumbling, and that was an outrage, the destruction of their new home; but at least he didn't see any of the children inside. They'd all been taken, and several of the battlebots still held squirming little figures in their mechanical hands.

The battlebot was difficult to understand, unlike anything Bear had ever used before. He had four little legs, two arms and several weapons, but the large oval body had no sensors and he couldn't feel it. It took him a moment to figure out how to move, and when he finally got it, the gabled roof of the house had collapsed with a great roar, sending up a massive cloud of ash and smoke, obscuring everything. For a few seconds, Bear was blind.

He charged forward anyway, into the dust, not sure what else to do. It didn't seem possible to rescue all of the children, even if he could see where they'd gone.

Out of the smoke, a dark shape appeared—another bot. It was holding a child, and Bear was shocked to see that it was Roma. She was screaming and trying to pry open the battlebot's metal arms.

131

Bear rammed the other bot, ran into its side and pushed. It almost fell over, but then it righted itself, slamming back down onto all four legs. Roma was tossed back and forth, screaming and crying. The bot skipped to one side, turning to face Bear, showing its two massive round white eyes.

Bear reached out and grabbed the metal arm that held Roma with one of his metal claws, squeezing as hard as he could. The other bot's metal arm snapped off, and Roma fell to the ground with a thud.

The battlebot held up its broken arm as if in shock and surprise. Bear saw Roma get to her feet, which was a relief. She could have been hurt. He hadn't considered her safety in his attack. He had to be more careful.

Locating his weapons—twin plasma cannons—he fired both at once. Searing bolts of yellow struck the other bot square in the middle of its body, and its front seemed to evaporate, white hot flame pouring from the gaping hole the beams had made. The bot tipped backwards.

Bear screamed a war cry of furious triumph, shouting from where he lay on the edge of the cliff. The bot had no voice.

He searched for another target, turning left and right. Some of the battlebots had formed up single file and were marching away. Bear halted and aimed his cannon, but stopped himself before he could fire. The other children were inside those things. They had to be. The bots had filled their compartments and were headed back to the school.

Bear didn't know what to do, how to fight. He hesitated.

Something pinched his belly. It was his real body. Metal hands had taken hold of him, just like before. They'd found him where he'd thought himself hidden in the grass, and a bot had lifted him and was carrying him away. He should have just stayed on the beach.

Something about the feeling of being taken by those horrible steel hands made his mind freeze for a moment, succumbing to terror, and he screamed. He didn't know what to do. He knew there were things he could do, that he could free himself, just take control of the battlebot and let himself go, but he couldn't think straight, couldn't let the thoughts form.

Then he was being dropped into the compartment in the back of the machine. Something touched his side, and he lost consciousness.

Chapter 16

Bear woke in darkness, unable to move. He was back in the dark place, the place of pain.

"No!" he shouted, dragging the word out. At least his mouth wasn't frozen, and he could speak. He remembered the fight on the cliff, the house falling down around him, the smoke and the bugs, Mister Verren. He remembered that he'd failed, his plan completely in ruins.

"Awake, I see," said a voice he didn't recognize, deep and sonorous, yet somehow feminine. "Good. Time for you to answer some questions, my little friend."

He pressed his lips together as tight as he could, determined to say nothing, to give these people no satisfaction. Now that he'd seen what they'd done to his town with his own eyes, it was much easier to hate them. And what sort of people treated kids this way? Used them, kept them prisoner, tortured them when they didn't behave the way they wanted?

"How did you escape?" the voice demanded. "Who helped you?"

That sense of well-being filled him, that contentment, and he knew they were causing it, and that it was false. He resented it even as he enjoyed it, so he just let it wash over him and kept his mouth closed. At least he wasn't afraid or in pain while it lasted.

Then the feeling was gone.

"We can make you feel really good, Bear," the voice said. "We can bring that feeling back, if you tell us how you got away and who helped you."

"Miss Sweet and Mister Verren helped me," he said, intending it half as a joke, and half as the truth. They'd taught him how to use proxies, and that's all he'd needed.

There was a long pause, the darkness growing emptier by the second. Bear actually longed for the voice to return. It was better than this lonely cavernous space.

"How did you escape?" the voice asked again.

"I just opened the doors, and we all went out," Bear said, then clamped his lips together again. It was hard to stay silent for too long. He wanted to boast about what he'd done, tell the voice that he'd stolen Miss Sweet's proxy, that he'd used it to open the doors and lead the other kids to safety. He was proud of his achievement, even though it had ultimately come to nothing.

But another part of him knew the only power he had, that he had ever had, was his secrets.

"I just walked out," he repeated. "I just walked out the door."

"Who opened the door?" the voice demanded.

"Miss Sweet did," Bear said, astonished at his own defiance. But this again was no lie. Miss Sweet *had* opened the doors, by proxy.

More silence. Bear waited for another question, but the minutes went by and none came. Loneliness weighed on him, and the fear returned that maybe they'd leave him here for a long time, trapped here. His invisible bonds made his arms and legs ache, and his stomach was doing its dance. At the same time, he was hungry, so hungry he almost felt sick. He wondered how long it had been since he'd eaten in the house by the cliff.

More time passed, and his stomach grew more and more painful. They were letting him go hungry on purpose. They had him at their mercy, and he was helpless, powerless to do anything.

His thoughts grew darker and darker, turning inward against himself, admonishing himself for his failure, for how stupid he'd been, how he hadn't thought through his actions properly, how he should have anticipated they'd be followed, and how he could have waited, maybe done something different.

And now what would happen? Would Miss Sweet still want to take him to Janus? Why was he here in the dark room? What would they do to him, and to the others?

I could have blasted them all, he said to himself. *I could have taken over every bug machine and wrecked them all, if I'd just found somewhere to hide my body.*

He should have just stayed on the beach, hidden against the cliff.

A sudden flare of light made him squeeze his eyes shut for a few seconds by reflex. There was something odd about the light. It didn't hurt.

It was Min, floating about six meters away. She was surrounded by utter darkness, as if the room had no walls or ceiling. Her hands dangled at her sides, and she looked sad.

"Min!" he cried. He was so relieved he thought he might break into tears, but no tears came.

"This is a strange place they have you in," she said, coming closer. "I'm sorry, Bear, but it took me a while to find it, and to find you. It's not really a place at all."

"I know what to do next time," he said. "If I can get out of here! I know what I did wrong, Min. We can try again, if you help me!"

Min's eyes brightened, and she smiled.

She reached for him with her arms, embracing him, something she'd never done before. What was even stranger was that he felt it, felt her warm arms around him, and his fear and dejection and anger and loneliness disappeared completely, replaced by better emotions—hope and love and gratitude.

She shouldn't have been able to touch him.

"Thanks, Min," he said, almost choking on his words.

"Here I'm almost real," she said, moving away a little, "in this place."

"What do you mean? I thought it was just a closet somewhere."

"No, it's all in your mind, Bear. They're using the thing in your head to create this. The nexus. It doesn't do anything by itself; it's a connection for other devices, something they can plug into; but they have to be very close to you, almost touching. So, they're using this other machine to make you imagine you're in this dark place."

He remembered waking in the corridor after the last time he'd been here. So, the dark room was some kind of dream, a bad dream that they'd created.

"I need to get out of here, Min," he said. "Can you help me get out of here?"

"I'm trying to find out, Bear," she said. "I keep making all kinds of discoveries. And do you know what? I figured out where I am, Bear! I figured it out at last. I've learned. I think that's what I'm supposed to do—keep learning. Now we just have to figure out a way you can still come and rescue me."

Light glared from everywhere at once, real light that made Bear again squeeze his eyes shut. His eyelids glowed red. Voices rose all around him, adult voices, people talking all at once. He slowly opened his eyes and discovered the darkness was truly gone, but this new location wasn't much better than the virtual dark room.

He lay on his back on a hard surface like the table he'd been stuck to before, still immobile, staring at another high-domed ceiling of white panels banded with gold moldings.

Panic seized him. He struggled to breathe.

"Min?" he gasped. "Min, where did you go?"

"He's awake," a familiar voice said. Mister Verren's.

Bear wondered if Verren was mad he had thrown the proxy off a cliff.

"Let me talk to him," said another voice, and it was almost a relief to hear Miss Sweet. "He'll talk to me."

"Well, I don't see why he would. I think he was stringing us along the entire time. Whatever is going on, I think he's always been a part of it."

"What do you mean by that? Who else could possibly had access to these children, and why?"

"Anything is possible. A cognitive transmission of some kind, from a distance."

"Anyone who might have the motivation to do something like that is long dead."

There was silence. Bear struggled to move, but it was no use. He wondered if the table beneath him was like a proxy, a machine with a signal he could control, so he tried to calm himself, to quiet his mind, and listen.

Tones and textures surrounded him, proxies and other devices, but it was hard to tell what was what. The only tones he recognized were those of Miss Sweet and Mister Verren. He could jump into one of them, but there was no point as long as his real body was captive.

"I think we're looking at something we don't understand," said Miss Sweet. "I have no doubt Bear has been keeping secrets, and that these secrets belong to him and him alone. For this reason, I still consider this project viable."

"Come on, Bella," said Verran. "The project is dead. Worse than dead. All of your subjects, with the exception of this one, have been removed. We're only holding on to this one because of the security threat."

"What we are seeing is an extraordinary will," Miss Sweet said after another pause. "We're looking at an exceptional subject. He has no primary controller implanted. What is the basis for his capability?"

"That's my point. It wasn't his will that took over your proxy and mine. That was an unknown technology, one this child can't possibly have developed on his own."

"Which is why we need to study him further!"

Verren sighed. "They won't let you. They're going to shut this down. Your kids are gone, and half this station has already been taken offline. The school has no purpose anymore. They're not going to invest any more time in this."

"They are shortsighted. There is so much to learn!"

"Command sees it differently. If this child is a threat of any kind, he has to go. How he did what he did is secondary."

There was another silence. Bear considered their words. Miss Sweet and Verren didn't believe there was anyone out there capable of helping him, and that meant there were no soldiers, no survivors, no resistance. Bear was alone, and now his captors wanted to get rid of him, just like they'd gotten rid of the others, like Aril and Kanga and Deej and now Roma and Emmot, too. All of them, gone.

He had to get away and get away now. He needed help. He needed Min. Where was she?

"Well, this argument is pointless," Verren said. "We have to go. Bring him."

The distant ceiling started to rotate. Bear was moving, sliding along on the floating table. The dome above moved away, and he was in one of the narrow corridors.

The journey was short. The corridor opened onto another room with a high ceiling, although this one was flat and fashioned from interlocking white tubes—girders or rafters. Bear had never been in this room before.

The table tipped, bringing him upright so his toes just brushed the floor. The table stayed fixed to his back, like a board, so he couldn't move, couldn't run; and although he could blink and move his eyes, he couldn't turn away from what he saw, and that was awful. Awful, and not at all what he had expected.

He was facing a monster.

He had to find the table's signal. Find it now! But what if it was like a door signal? To open a door, you needed to be in a proxy body. So, if he took over a proxy now he could escape.

Escape to where?

"This is our little enigma, then," the monster said in the voice he had heard in the dark room, the strange melodious voice.

The creature was an enormous, horrifying caricature of a man, the skin gray, the face and chin too long, the mouth a grinning cavity filled with yellow fangs, the eyes black pits. It towered over him, hunched and menacing, draped in some kind of brown fur robe, its long arms dangling at its sides. Slender curled horns protruded from its head.

Bear knew the thing was a proxy, that it was really just a big puppet, like the knight and the wolf, like a person in a costume, but he still found it terrifying.

Mister Verren was there, too, behind the creature and to its right. The big room had walls of white and gray rectangular panels and no furniture. Keeping a close eye on Bear were Guardians Two and Four, and Miss Sweet, who today wore her pink face, her hair a turquoise waterfall spilling down her back.

"How did you do it, child?" the creature asked Bear.

Bear's vocal cords seemed frozen. Only his eyes could move, and these he flicked back and forth, to avoid looking at the creature, and to look for Min.

There was no sign of her.

"Of course," the monster continued. "The paralysis remains in effect. Most wise, given his apparent talents. One cannot access a proxy while inside a paralysis field. Or can he? What have you learned? What is the mechanism?"

"Still unknown," Miss Sweet said. "We have only just begun the interrogation."

The creature fixed her with its dark empty eyes.

"This child made a mockery of all of our key systems," it said. "He broke through every security protocol in this station. You are telling me that you have no idea how, and that you did not suspect a thing, and now you're unable to determine the method he used. Can you explain this?"

Miss Sweet gazed back at the creature with a combination of anger and fear, two things Bear had never seen on any of her colourful faces.

"El-Ann, up until now, the child has cooperated fully with my program and has proven to be a superior student."

"Is that so?" said the creature. "I've read and listened to your reports. You admit that his memory suppression failed, and he engaged in acts of defiance."

"Children are mischievous," Miss Sweet said. "His memories appeared to be minimal and did not affect his performance."

The monster barked a single laugh.

"Yes, he performed very well indeed! Better than any of us, and yet we have no idea how."

"If you had not destroyed every scrap of data concerning whatever quant-comm discoveries Sturnus had made," Miss Sweet said, raising her voice, "perhaps we would have an inkling."

The creature turned away for a second, its long hands balling into fists.

"We didn't destroy it all, actually," it said. "Some of it is at Archive."

The hair of Miss Sweet's head suddenly stood out, as if she'd received an electric shock. "Why wasn't I aware of this?"

The monster shrugged and waved a hand. "Just notes and sundries taken from Kamra's office. Artifacts. We don't even know what's there. And it's beside the point. We aren't here to discuss Command policies, but your failure to foresee what this child has done."

Miss Sweet's hands worked at her sides, the fingers fluttering like the wings of a trapped moth. "What this child did is something we considered impossible. It has never been possible, nor is there a known theory to *make* it possible. We do not plan to defend against the impossible."

The creature's toothy grin became a scowl. "Yes. Impossible. This is a problem, isn't it?" It narrowed its strange eyes. "Could we have a traitor? That would certainly make sense. But why? Why would one of our own betray our great project? That, too, to me, seems impossible."

"There is no evidence we have a traitor, El-Ann," Miss Sweet said.

She turned to look at Bear. He saw the motion, and he strained his eyes muscles to meet her gaze. Her mouth was a thin angry line in her strange face, and he could see the hurt in her eyes. For just a moment, he felt sympathy for her, and a little shame that he'd let his teacher down; but the moment passed quickly. He was just an experiment. They'd destroyed everything and used him for their tests. He owed Miss Sweet nothing.

He tried to shout at her, but all he managed was a faint moan.

Miss Sweet flinched, mouth dropping open in shock and surprise. "What did you say? Did you speak?"

Bear noticed that he'd clenched his fists, despite the paralysis field.

The gray creature scowled.

"I see he has a strong will, as you say. I've never seen the like, such ability to resist. Which puts me in two minds. I am not without my sense of curiosity, and I would study him, as you propose, but that is not our aim. My personal curiosity is of no consequence. Thus, we must destroy him."

"We must study him," said Miss Sweet. "We identified strange brain anomalies we have not pursued. Whatever they were doing here on Sturnus, they had developed technologies we don't possess. This child was able to control two proxies, both phase-locked with other people, and did so with no primary controller. I have no doubt this was because of the nature of the quant-comm program here on Sturnus."

The monster's frown deepened. It took two steps toward Miss Sweet, its body hulking over hers.

"You have never understood," it said, "that we don't want their capabilities. We don't want their ways. Our aim was to destroy those very things, expunge them from existence. They are traitors, and their systems are treachery!"

"But what if we could improve—"

"We cannot improve what is perfection! If what you say is true, that there is no outside force at work, no one controlling this child but himself because of some Sturnusian abomination, then we are finished, and our course is clear."

The monster whirled away from Miss Sweet and moved to loom over Bear, peering down at him with those dark eyes. Bear wished he could shrink into the table.

Min appeared at the creature's side. She put a finger to her lips in the gesture for silence.

Bear stared back at the monster, managing to meet its horrible gaze. Min's appearance gave him strength. He reminded himself the thing was just a puppet, just a stupid puppet.

"My one suspicion you are wrong, Sweet," the stupid puppet said, "is that none of the other children have shown the abilities this one has. That suggests an outside influence, working with this one child."

"We don't know that for certain," Miss Sweet said. "Others may have helped in the escape. If Bear was able to hide his abilities, then so could they."

The creature straightened and folded its arms over its fur-clad chest. Behind it, Min's glowing face wore a serene smile. Bear watched her and found he could smile, too, smile at her beauty and light, at the comfort and hope she'd given him since he'd first seen her in the play yard, whoever or whatever she was. He almost believed no evil could truly touch him as long as she was with him. He had nothing to fear from these bad, bad people.

"The fool child smiles," the creature said, with a touch of astonishment and a shake of its misshapen head. "Will he break the paralysis field and attack me in a moment? Maybe he expects to be rescued?

"He knows something we don't. I'm afraid I'm starting to believe he poses an immediate risk, and one I want neutralized at once. We don't have the luxury of further study." The thing held up one massive hand as Miss Sweet started to protest. "I will take your needs into consideration! He can be interred at the Archive, in a severed state. He must not be allowed to ever regain consciousness. Thus, you may examine him and discover the nature of the threat. That is all."

Min had reached Bear's side. "That's where I am, Bear!" she said. "The place she just mentioned. I'm at the Archive! That's where I'm being held prisoner."

"The ship will be standing by," the creature continued, striding toward one of the room's two doorways. "Make sure you are on it with whatever you wish to bring with you. This facility is to be dismantled."

"You can't just abandon this project!" Miss Sweet shouted, crossing the floor to Bear.

"I can, and I just have," the monster said. "This conversation is at an end."

The creature went through the door, and the door closed. Mister Verren watched it and gave Miss Sweet a look of sympathy.

"That's that," he said.

Miss Sweet came to Bear, and he felt her fingers on his shoulder. Their narrow tips dug into his flesh, and he winced.

"I would have given you everything," she said in his ear. "You could have been like my own little boy."

She sounded sad, wounded, but also angry that Bear had betrayed her. And that made Bear angry right back.

"One last thing," Miss Sweet said. "Come outside, into the yard. Verren!"

She started toward the door the monster had gone through, and Verren went with her. Bear's table started to move, remaining upright but following.

"I'm right here," said Min.

Bear's table took him through the doorway, and he emerged into sunlight. He recognized the big field where he had practiced with the wolf proxy only a few days ago. It seemed like more time than that had passed. The large building where the spaceships landed and took off was on his left, the library building far to his right. It was a warm day, the sky blue and covered in a light haze that made Corvus seem dim and distant.

Miss Sweet stopped in the middle of the grass and knelt in front of Bear. Mister Verren took a few more steps and halted, standing a little distant.

"Tell me now what you did," Miss Sweet said to Bear. "I've partially disabled your paralysis field. You won't be able to access a proxy, but you will be able to speak. Tell me now, and we can change what is about to happen."

Bear found he could work his jaw and open his mouth, but he said nothing. Min pressed close to his side.

"They're going to kill you, Bear," she said, sounding worried.

"I know," Bear said. She was right. Whatever Miss Sweet was up to, it would not be to his benefit.

"Then tell me!" Miss Sweet said.

Bear could hear a symphony of proxy signals around him, meaning that whatever the paralysis field was supposed to do, it didn't seem to have done anything to block him, whatever Miss Sweet and the monster may have thought. They'd made another assumption, another mistake, based on Janusian technology.

But Bear was a patient of Doctor Kamra's here on Sturnus; and like his parents, he didn't access proxies the same way the Janusians did. He used a different method, a different route. One that, just maybe, the paralysis field didn't affect.

Bear identified a cluster of signals to his left, in the building that housed the spaceship. They were strange, low-pitched and somewhat unpleasant, and he realized they were coming from the rows of bug machines, the battlebots, that were stored there. He recognized the signals from when he'd encountered them before, on the cliff above the beach.

Could he take one now? What about his body?

This was his chance to strike, but he couldn't fail a second time. He heard the voice of his father—another memory, arising from some deep well in his subconscious—saying *All you can do is try.*

It was something his dad had said all the time.

"You wouldn't believe me if I told you how I did it," he said to Miss Sweet.

"Yes, I would!" she snapped, and then she repeated, in a steadier voice, "Yes, I would, Bear. Yes, I would. I would believe you."

Bear closed his eyes, pictured the battlebots, all just sitting there in a row. Empty. They were no threat to him.

He followed the signal for the first battlebot, and then he was in the room with the other battlebots, looking through those strange eyes, almost like looking through goggles. He felt his four legs, his mechanical arms, and found the plasma cannon. Everything seemed to be working. Just like before.

Now he had to secure his body.

"Bear," Miss Sweet said in her kindest voice. "Please tell me."

He wanted to tell her. He wanted her and Mister Verren to know how good he was, how powerful. He wanted someone to know and tell him they were proud of his achievement, even if it was those two. He wanted to boast, to tell them how much better he was than them.

He turned the battlebot to its left, facing the others in the row. His plasma cannon chirped, spitting out hot yellow beams that stabbed through the inert armour of the helpless mechanical beasts, blasting them apart, one after the other, severed arms and legs flying, pieces of hull casings scattering and bouncing from the walls. One in the middle of the line exploded with a powerful roar and a ball of white-hot flame. Bear felt the heat, felt his own battlebot knocked backwards by the blast, his vision fuzzing, becoming staticky.

Back on the grassy field, Miss Sweet and Mister Verren turned to gape at the spaceship building.

"What was that?" Mister Verren shouted.

Bear's battlebot vision cleared, so he tried his arms and walked a few paces. Everything seemed fine, so he turned around and made for the doors to the outside. They burst open when he struck them with his metal arms, forcing his way through. He saw himself, his real body, standing with Miss Sweet, the foolish white table stuck to his back. He ran toward it, scurrying on the weird spidery legs.

Miss Sweet gasped and leaped back at the sight of the charging battlebot. She grabbed Bear's arm and tried to pull him away, table and all, shouting, "Leave him alone!"

Bear turned his plasma cannon and fired once, striking Mister Verren in the stomach, blasting his proxy into two pieces that dropped to the turf hard and lay there smoking. Miss Sweet let out a scream, and Bear fired again, blowing off both her legs. The legs flew to the sides, the rest of the proxy body dropping and balancing, for a second, on the twin stumps, before falling face-first onto the grass.

Bear reached out with his mechanical arms, grasping the table that was stuck to his body, twisting it with his metal claws, feeling it crunch and disintegrate. His body fell on its side in the grass, and he felt the impact. He could sense the paralysis field was gone, and felt a dull ache from where he'd hit the ground; but he let that fade into the background and used the bot to pick himself up just like that first machine, the one that had kidnapped him.

He placed his body in the compartment in the back of the battlebot. This was a correction to the mistake he'd made before. Now, he was safe.

"What now, Min?" he shouted with his real voice.

The doors to the spaceship building burst open, and two Guardians came out, saw the battlebot, and stopped in their tracks. Bear didn't hesitate, blasting them both, turning them to dust and fragments, the beams also striking the doors and tearing them to shreds.

"The spaceship, Bear," Min said, just her voice in his ears. "It's waiting, and I figured it out. It's just a big robot like these ones, like the proxies. You can fly it! And you can come to the Archive and rescue me!"

"I can't fly a spaceship!" said Bear.

"Yes, you can. I'll help!"

He trusted her, and it was his only option. He charged forward, back through the blasted doors and into the spaceship building.

Surprise was on his side. As he drove the battlebot around the curving corridor toward the open space where the ship was docked, more Guardians came running, so he fired and kept firing, the beams striking wherever he looked, sweeping the Guardians aside, leaving them smashed on the floor, just bits of ceramic, carbon and artificial flesh.

The space dock came into view, and the huge ball that was the ship. On the far side, Bear saw the creature, the monster with the fur coat, standing with two more Guardians and three parked battlebots.

The monster drew a sword—an actual sword—and roared before charging Bear.

For a split second, Bear hesitated, frozen by the sight of this terrible thing running toward him. It must have believed it could beat him. Or was it just bluffing?

Bear fired his twin plasma beams. They struck the creature's arms, blasting them both away, the sword clattering to the floor, but the creature continued to run, so Bear fired again. A yellow beam took off the ugly head, another ripping into the torso, the fur catching fire and flaring for a few seconds. The two Guardians followed, and then Bear destroyed the remaining battlebots in quick succession, leaving them burning and sparking.

He was finished. There was no one else in the space dock.

Reaching into the back compartment with his machine arms, he hoisted himself out, dropping his body on its feet, facing the great ball of a ship.

"Min!" he said, dropping the battlebot signal. "How do I get in?"

Min was next to him. "Just like the school, Bear. Just like the school."

"I need a proxy, then," he said, and took control of the battlebot again, searching for a way to send a door signal. He found rows and rows of the little green boxes, many more than Miss Sweet had carried. He tried one, but nothing happened, so he tried another. After his fifth try, a square door opened in the exact center of the ship, and a ramp descended.

Dropping the proxy, heedless that he might need it or one like it later to exit the ship, Bear ran for the ramp, saying, "Come on."

He'd forgotten Min didn't need to enter the ship in a physical sense. She was with him in his mind, wherever he went.

Chapter 17

B ear walked into the spherical ship. A little stairway led up from the entrance, and at its top was a short passage. The passage had a soft brown floor, its walls beige and decorated with animated pictures of forests, plants, flowers, and animals. As he watched, the pictures changed and moved, one showing a black bird, then a kind of elephant, then some large green dragonflies. The air had a faint hint of grass and earth and something else he couldn't place.

"Where do I go?" he asked Min.

"This way," she said, sliding ahead down the passage to where it crossed another. The second passage was curved, and Bear guessed it was circular, a ring that went all the way around the inside of the ship.

At a point along the first passage was another steep staircase that led up to a short passage. At the end of that passage was another doorway. This doorway was tall, and as Min drifted through it, Bear followed. On the other side was a bright circular room, the wall also a pale earthy colour. A row of dark windows went about three-quarters of the way around it, stopping only for the doorway and an adjacent section to it that was blank.

"I didn't notice any windows on the outside," Bear said.

"They're V-windows," Min said as he gawked. "Video screens that look like windows."

"Is this the control centre?" Bear said, indicating a raised circular platform enclosed within a gleaming gold handrail in the center of the room. In the middle of the platform was a chair and a small white console.

"I can see the schematic," Min said. "The cabin and storage compartments are below. This *is* where the ship is controlled. It's also a viewing deck."

"How do I fly it?" Bear said.

"I think it flies itself. Just tell it where you want to go, like you communicate with the proxies. It works on the same principal. Everything these people make does." She seemed to ponder for a moment. "I think I can fly it. I can talk to it. I can talk to all of its systems. That's good, isn't it?"

Bear took a deep breath. "Okay, so, where are we going?"

"To Archive. That's where I am, remember?"

Bear remembered that Archive was also the place where the monster had wanted to take him, to make him a prisoner as well.

He climbed two golden steps to the raised platform. Now that he had a few moments to think, he searched for proxy signals, finding many, and tried to isolate those that might be associated with the ship. Some of the signals were the type that came from the Guardians, and that must mean several were close by, maybe just outside the ship.

He had to keep them from getting in.

Even as he thought this, footsteps sounded in the passage outside the entrance. Bear swiveled the chair around so he faced the doorway.

"Who's that?"

Miss Sweet halted just inside the room. Bear stared at her with his mouth open. For a second everything—all motion, all thought—ground to a halt. Miss Sweet was in the ship.

It wasn't the same Miss Sweet he'd shot with the battlebot, but one with a pale-blue face and bright-red cheeks. Her flowing dress was like molten gold.

"Bear, stop what you're doing this instant!" she commanded.

"Watch out, Bear!" Min said. "She has something!"

Miss Sweet raised her right hand, and the black cable shot from her wrist. Bear threw himself from the chair, reacting without thinking; and the Snake passed over his head, striking the gold railing with an ear-splitting clang and a flash of light.

Bear grabbed Miss Sweet's proxy signal and jumped in, taking control of her body by sudden and violent force. Pain lanced though his skull, although he couldn't tell if it was in his own head or the proxy's. Clutching his forehead with both right hands, his body lay sprawled on the floor at the base of the railing and gasped for breath. Slowly, the pain subsided.

The proxy was his. He had complete control.

"Where did she come from, Min?" he asked in Miss Sweet's voice.

"Bear!" Min shouted in warning, pointing. "Behind you!"

He whirled his stolen proxy around to see that another Miss Sweet was coming up the stairs. This time, she was turquoise and yellow, her bright face contorted with rage. Bear had never seen her look so frightening; and he jumped to one side, reaching out with his right hand as if by instinct, sending the Snake lashing out like an electric whip. It coiled around the new Miss Sweet's neck, squeezing and snapping, tearing the head free so it fell and bounced down the stairs.

Bear shouted in shock and horror at what he'd done; but of course there was no blood, and Miss Sweet's body hadn't been a living thing. The head rolled to the side wall and stopped as the rest of the body collapsed into the passage.

Bear looked down at the wrist where the Snake had emerged. He'd known how to use it without needing to think about it. Part of the prox-ies' built-in programming, he supposed.

Something struck his left arm, squeezing and pulling. He looked down just as the arm was torn from the shoulder socket by another Snake. He felt no pain, but his shock and fright were bad enough. A third version of Miss Sweet had appeared on the stairs.

This looked like the real Miss Sweet, with the smooth brown skin and long black hair, but it had to be just another proxy. She lashed out again with the Snake, and Bear's proxy's signal winked out; and he was back in himself, watching as the proxy he'd just occupied toppled over, headless like the other one.

The third Miss Sweet was striding up the passage, but Bear grabbed the signal and took control. There was the screaming headache again, but it faded quickly.

He turned just as the fourth Miss Sweet appeared. Now he knew what was happening. Miss Sweet had packed her proxies on the ship, probably while he had been unconscious, or when he'd been a prisoner in the dark room. And if all of Miss Sweet's proxies were here, he would have to de-stroy them all. And there were hundreds.

The fourth put up more of a fight, firing her Snake at the same time Bear fired his. They hissed and clashed in the air, coiling around each other, sparking and flashing. Bear pulled, yanking Miss Sweet off-balance, and she tripped on one of the bodies at her feet, crying out as she fell. Bear struck quickly, first tearing away the right arm that held the Snake, then lashing another head from another pair of shoulders.

More were coming, he was sure of it, so he leapt down the stairs and ran to where the entry passage crossed the curved one, stepping over the parts of the broken proxies. Another Miss Sweet appeared from his left, coming around the curve; Bear struck it down at close range. The next met the same fate.

When a seventh Miss Sweet appeared, it hesitated, pressing against the passageway wall, remaining out of sight.

"Bear, you must stop this," Miss Sweet's voice called. He thought she sounded worried and desperate. "Where do you plan to go? If you go to Janus without me, I won't be able to take care of you. They'll capture you and put you in stasis."

Bear had nothing to say to her. He just had to get rid of her.

Holding on to the proxy, he returned most of his awareness to his own body, got up off the deck, climbed back into the command chair, then swiveled to face the entrance. The curved passage, his proxy attacked, charging around the corner and lashing out with the Snake. Miss Sweet must have expected this, for she struck at the same time, her Snake catching Bear's proxy around the waist just as his Snake caught her around the neck. He felt an impossible pressure, felt something inside his proxy crack, but still managed to pull back on his Snake, snapping Miss Sweet's head clean off once again, just as his own proxy collapsed, torn in two.

As each proxy died, its signal vanished.

Bear waited in the command chair, holding his breath, ready to hijack the next version of Miss Sweet that appeared. A few minutes passed, and none did.

"I'm making a mistake again," he said. If there were more Miss Sweets on board the ship, he could find them, and take them. He could take them all. There was no need to fight. He hadn't been thinking! He could have knocked Miss Sweet out of every proxy, one at a time…except maybe she could have just reoccupied each one as he left it. Maybe it was better to have destroyed them.

He listened, but the strongest signal he could detect was a deep, rumbling series of bass tones. That was the ship itself. There was no sign of Miss Sweet's melodies.

"Min, can you scout for me?" he said. "I need to know what's down around that corner."

"I don't see any more," Min said. "I mean, I don't see any more of Miss Sweet's robots."

"Are you sure? She has a lot more than that!"

Min sank through the deck and disappeared. In a minute, she returned the same way, rising from the soft brown deck covering.

"There's an open doorway down that corridor," she said. "There are boxes and cases in there, several of them open. But no more Miss Sweets."

Bear sat back in the chair. His stomach felt sick, and he started to sweat, his arms and shoulders trembling. He drew in several deep breaths, hoping he wouldn't throw up here in the ship. How would he clean it? Maybe the ship had a way. The Guardians had always cleaned up things like that in the school.

A few minutes later, the awful feeling had passed, but it left his hair soaked with sweat. His clothes had remained dry.

"She didn't pack them all," he said. "She only packed a few of her favourites, I guess."

That meant she was expecting to come back to Sturnus, not leave it for good. Unless she was planning on abandoning most of her proxies. Or maybe she'd never expected her program was about to be shut down, so just hadn't packed them.

"We should go, Bear," Min said. "We should go now, before anyone else comes."

"I don't hear anyone," Bear said.

Nothing on the ship, anyway. There were plenty of signals emanating from nearby, maybe just outside, and the rest in other parts of the city. He had to assume some of them were thinking of a way to take back this ship. Why didn't they just open the door and come in?

He had to lift off at once.

Closing his eyes, he again listened for the ship's deep-toned signal. He could have told Min to make the vessel take off, now that she thought she could do so, but he wanted to do it himself. He wanted to know how, and he wanted to be in control.

The deep bass tone was clear, a pulsing rhythm, almost a percussion. He took hold of it, tried to follow it to its terminus. It just seemed to come to an abrupt end.

He opened his eyes. As far as he could tell, he'd failed to occupy the ship.

"What happened?" he said.

Then he saw that all of the V-windows had come on, showing what looked like the surrounding building, and the edge of the large open area where the ship was berthed. This seemed like the very view real windows would have shown. There was no sign of any more Guardians, nor of anyone at all. Maybe no one knew he was in the ship. No one except Miss Sweet, and all of her proxies were broken.

She had more where she lived. Maybe she was on her way now.

"Destination?" said a voice. Bear couldn't tell whether it was actually spoken or in his head.

"The Archive?" he said, hoping the ship would understand.

"Archive," the ship repeated, its voice strange, seeming to have no quality to it whatsoever, no tone or timbre. Maybe, Bear thought, it was in his head after all.

"There, you did it," said Min. "We're rising, Bear!"

The images on the V-windows changed, gave the image of the ship moving upward, the gray walls of the surrounding structures falling away; and then there was just brilliant blue sky so bright Bear had to squint. Gravitational forces pushed him back into his chair, the weight so great he couldn't move, almost couldn't breathe. It was just as bad as the paralysis field.

All at once, the weight lifted, and he gasped for breath. The V-windows showed nothing but blackness.

Bear stared in wonder. He was in space.

The ship seemed to turn, to roll, the blue ball of Sturnus sliding into view in one of the windows—the whole world, the only world Bear had ever known in a galaxy full of worlds. He was orbiting his planet, his moon, his home, circling, coming up on the dark strip of the night side. The ship glided over a land in total shadow, with no lights to mark the presence of civilization. There was no one left, nothing and no one. No cities, no towns.

If there'd ever been other towns, Janus must have destroyed them all.

The ship completed a single orbit, then threw itself out into space. Sturnus grew smaller and smaller on the screens, and even the mass of Corvus shrank to a bright point, like a star seen at night.

Chapter 18

Bear didn't remember falling asleep, but woke in the command chair, blinking and groggy. He remembered where he was, what he'd done, and a brief sense of pure happiness washed over him. But it was happiness that emanated from the half-remembered impression of a dream he'd been having, a dream that had brought him together with his parents, his friends, his dog, a garden, and a game of rocket ball, whatever "rocket ball" was. Maybe something he had invented in his sleep.

When his eyes at last managed to focus on his surroundings, realization was like an electrical jolt; and he sat upright, grabbing the edge of the console in front of him. The ship. The escape. The awful battle with Miss Sweet. The journey to Archive.

He rubbed his eyes, dizziness and hunger replacing his reverie. He was starving, but also felt sick again. He had to pee.

"Min?" he said, his voice a croak.

"I'm here, Bear," she said, sliding into view just outside the golden railing. "You slept for about two standard hours."

"I need to find a privy," he said. "Is there a privy...a toilet on the ship? And what do I do about breakfast?"

"There is a washroom for the command crew behind you," she said, pointing, "and if you need food, you just have to ask the ship. There are assemblers on board."

The mention of a "washroom" brought an acute pang of discomfort, an odd combination of nerves and physical pain, based entirely on its association with the school, of being herded through the featureless corridors to the Washroom before heading to the dining room. It was a strange reaction. He had never been unhappy there, not even toward the end, when he'd known the truth and wanted to escape. Now, the thought of it filled him with horror. It had been a prison, and he hoped he would never see it again.

He stepped down from the platform to the soft deck. Bits and pieces of Miss Sweet's proxies still lay scattered about, remnants of their battle. Maybe he should clean those up, or ask the ship to do it, if that was possible.

First things first.

"Where's the washroom again?" he asked.

Min drifted to the section of blank curved wall.

"Here."

Bear stared at the wall. He couldn't think of what to do next.

"Can I open the door without a proxy? I don't have a proxy." He jumped up and down. "Can you open it? Oh, I have to pee, Min!"

"Ask the ship!" she said. "Ask the ship for everything!"

He didn't know whether Min meant for him to ask with his real voice, to actually ask, or to make use of the signal, as he'd done before; but he'd become accustomed to the latter, so he reached out with his mind, a curious combination of thinking and feeling, a practice that was starting to become second nature.

After locating the signal, he hit it like he'd done before. When it dropped away, the featureless voice said, "Your command?"

"Can you open the washroom door?" Bear asked.

The wall split along a vertical line. Beyond was a small room with gold-and-white tiled walls, a carpeted floor, a shower and sink, and a moving picture in the wall that showed rivers and waterfalls, the waterfalls roaring and splashing in a pool below. Bear dashed inside, but couldn't find a toilet of any kind, not even a hole in the floor. Unable to reach the sink, and desperate by now, he just peed in the corner. It was all he could think to do. The pee splattered on the carpet and sank into the fabric, disappearing from view.

When he was done, Bear leaned over and stared at what should have been a large wet stain, but there was nothing, not even an odor.

"I'm sorry," he said, speaking to the ship. "I couldn't find the toilet."

He looked around. This was not like the privy and the Washroom in the school. This was more like the bathroom that had been in his house, one that used running water.

Placing his hands under what looked like a faucet, he felt water begin to flow, warm and soothing, splashing over his hands; but when he took his hands away, they weren't wet.

152

His stomach rumbled and pinched. He needed food.

"Hey, ship," he said. "Can I have some chappies? Rustberry chappies with maple syrup? And hydrobacon, if you have it, some cut-up nutmelon and a glass of mango juice?"

These were elements of his old favourite breakfasts.

The ship said nothing, and for a moment Bear thought nothing had happened, that he still hadn't figured out how the ship worked. So, he returned to the command seat, expecting to have to find the ship's signal again.

The requested breakfast was waiting, along with a knife and fork and a set of chopsticks, on the console.

"It worked," he said, slumping into the chair and snatching up the fork. He had no use for the knife or chopsticks.

The food steadied him, took away his lingering sickness, made him feel almost contented. He took his time, eating in silence, watching the sparkling stars in the V-windows, not thinking or feeling much of anything for the first time in a long time. Min hovered nearby, not speaking, seeming to understand that he needed silence.

When he'd finished his breakfast, the contented mood gave way to a sense of melancholy. He was free, but only for the present time. And this freedom didn't mean a return to his happy life with Mum and Dad and Tayor. That life was gone, and so was its replacement—his school life, with his friends.

His friends were all gone as well. Gone and maybe even dead. It was possible he had gotten them killed by making them escape with him.

This idea turned his limbs to ice, made the blood drain from his face. All of his crazy plotting had made a complete mess of things, had made the monster proxy shut down the school early. That was clear. If he'd just gone along with Miss Sweet, gone to Janus and lived there, would the school still be open? His friends still be alive? And what about Aril and the others who had been sent to "another school?" Did such a school exist?

But the more he thought about it, the more unlikely that seemed. Not based on the things he'd heard the Janusians say, from Miss Sweet to Verren to the monster. It had been clear from Verren that a lot of people hadn't liked the school or agreed with its existence, and even Miss Sweet had admitted to only wanting Bear, her star pupil, in the end.

"Well, I tried to save everybody," he said, and that was true, but despair hung over him like a cloud. He thought of Emmot and Roma, gone now, just vanished. His last memory of Emmot was in the house on the cliff, when Emmot had remembered his old life.

Bear was alone. It was a concept just too big to fathom. What would he do now? Would he wander the galaxy, a boy alone in a spaceship with a girl only he could see?

He gazed at the stars in the V-windows.

"Min," he said, after a few minutes, "if we're in space now, how come we don't float? I thought you floated in space. Is this fake gravity?"

"I'm floating," said Min, smiling and drifting by the V-windows.

Bear tried to smile.

"But I'm not," he said. "Why?"

Min paused just under the central screen.

"It's not fake gravity," she said. "It's real gravity, of a sort."

"But this ship isn't that big, and we're inside it. How come it has so much gravity?"

Min seemed to think about this.

"It's gravity caused by the ship's acceleration. As it travels, it accelerates at about half of one standard gravity. Halfway to its destination, its interior rotates within the sphere, which is like a giant shell. After that the ship decelerates at one-half standard gravity. Or variations of this sort of thing.

"The drive is a form of compression drive, which compresses and stretches the fabric of space, shortening the distance between our point of departure and our destination, so we don't travel as far. It's…it's an old design."

Bear only half-understood this. He wished Miss Sweet had taught them more about space travel.

"So, how long will it take to get to Archive?"

"About ten hours at this slow rate of speed," Min said. "Actually, nine-point-four-five hours rounded up, and we've already travelled for about two while you were sleeping, so about eight more hours."

Bear thought that sounded like a long journey. "What do we do for eight hours?"

Min smiled. "We can talk. Listen to music. Have something to eat. Explore the ship."

"Explore the ship first," Bear said, and it felt good to make a firm decision, to have some direction. "That's what we'll do."

"Okay. I can show you around."

But Bear hesitated.

"There's something else I've been thinking about, Min," he said. "How are you being held prisoner at Archive? You said it wasn't a jail or something, or a dungeon, so what is it? Are there guards? Is it like the school?"

He didn't like the thought of having to find a battlebot or something and fight his way in to rescue her. His escape from Sturnus had been exciting, in a way, but also tense and fear-filled, especially in retrospect. He thought he'd done well, had kept his focus and had done what he'd needed to do, unlike on the cliff, when he'd been unable to think.

But despite his success, when he thought about it now, it seemed that he'd also been lucky. The Janusians hadn't understood what he could do and hadn't been prepared. They'd been caught off-guard and had underestimated him because he was just a kid. Next time they'd be ready.

"Should we come up with some kind of a plan?"

"You don't have to do anything, Bear. There aren't any people on Archive right now. No one lives there. It's a place where they store things, things they want to forget about. Sometimes, there are visitors who stay for a few hours or e-days, take things or bring things. Some new things were brought just a short time ago. But now there's no one, just automated systems."

Her description made it sound like a sad place.

"A place where they forget about things? Just leave them there and forget?"

"Yes."

Another reason not to like the Janusians.

"So, you're being kept in a prison cell there, all alone?" he asked.

"Yes, a very small cell. But you can come and take me away, as a visitor, if we can fool the authorizations. I think I can help you do that."

It sounded simple and easy.

"Then what do we do? After I rescue you? Where should we go?"

"Wherever you want to go, Bear."

That wasn't good enough. He only knew of three places where people lived—Janus, Sturnus, and Earth. His hopes were that he could somehow go back to Sturnus, even though there was no longer anyone there he cared about.

"Where do *you* want to go, Min?"

"I think I just have to stay with you. That's my purpose. This ship can take us anywhere."

Bear sighed in frustration. "That means I'm all alone, Min. I mean, I have you for company, and that's nice, but if I need to decide what to do, I need help."

The stars on the V-windows were a billion possibilities, but all of them were empty.

"I want to go back to Sturnus," he admitted, and the longing that welled up inside him made him angry. He didn't want to be sad anymore. "I want to rebuild the houses on the cliff. That's what I really want to do, but I can't do that by myself, and I can't live all alone, and I can't do it if the Janusians are just going to attack again or try to take me prisoner again."

He rested his head in his hands. The loss of his friends, his family, was a cold ache. Min came close to him, smiling, holding out one hand as if to touch him. He imagined he could feel the warmth of her glow, but really he couldn't.

"Are there any other planets out there, Min? With people on them? What about Earth?"

"Earth is a long way away," she said. "A *long* way. This ship could get us there, but it would take longer than you like, I think."

"Then I don't want to go there."

"I've learned plenty of information about other planets," she said, brightening. "I can tell you all about them. I can tell you about Earth if you like."

He shook his head. He didn't really want to hear about any other planets right now. He wanted to know more about his own lost world.

"Tell me about my old moon of Sturnus," he said.

Min's eyes seemed to go blank for a few seconds, and she blinked.

"I need to tell you about Janus first."

Bear sat up in his chair. He didn't want to hear about Janus, either, but thought it made sense that he learn more about it. All he knew was what Miss Sweet had taught them, and he was beginning to think she hadn't really taught them very much that was useful. She may even have lied.

"Okay," he said. "Tell me about Janus."

Janus was an old planet, Min explained. Not as old as Earth, in terms of human habitation, nor of some of the other planets in Earth's solar system, but it was the first planet orbiting another star that humans had chosen to go to, or to "colonize," as they called settling a new world.

Janus was also very large, what was once termed a "super earth" because its gravity was almost twice as great as the mother planet's. The original settlers hadn't considered this a serious issue, since in all other respects the planet had been suitable for terraformation, which was a process by which another planet was made more like Earth.

"Yes, I know what that means," Bear said. "We had to do that to Sturnus, too."

He thought of the statue of Artemis.

Min continued her tale.

Scientists believed that humans could adapt to the heavier gravity of Janus if they had to, because this had been demonstrated in long-term experiments on Earth. At the same time, they were cautious, and only sent robots, machines that could change the planet and start the terraforming process. No one recommended a permanent human colony on the planet, and most of the scientists said it was just a good place to run terraforming experiments.

But there were people who wanted to leave Earth and Earth's solar system, leave and turn their backs and never return. These people were impatient to start all over with something new, and at that time spaceships were better than they'd ever been before, so the time was right. So, off they went, hoping the robots had done a good job, and the planet was ready.

When they got to Janus, they discovered the gravity was a greater problem than anyone had foreseen. The scientists had been right to be cautious. Many of the settlers died, as many as a third, soon after their arrival, most from cerebrovascular accidents, strokes, and cardiac arrest.

"That's when your heart just stops," Min explained.

"That sounds awful," said Bear.

For the others, cardiopulmonary problems also threatened to shorten their lifespans, and many developed vision problems and a vague sense of "not being able to think straight." One group even decided they had to abandon the colony, and so had left for what they thought was a better candidate for terraforming, and that was the largest of the moons of Corvus, a gas giant in the same system. The big moon was a speckled sphere almost the same size as old Earth, but hadn't really been studied until the robots had gotten to Janus.

They named the speckled moon Sturnus, which referred to a kind of bird on Earth. In fact, all the moons of Corvus were named for birds.

"We came from Janus?" Bear said in wonder.

"Yes," said Min. "That's why I had to talk about Janus first."

Within the first decade (that was ten standard years based on the e-year or Earth year, she explained), the number of settlers on Janus was down to a quarter of the original number, fewer than five thousand individuals. That's when things started getting a little strange.

The people who stayed had developed a belief of having been selected to survive, selected in an evolutionary sense, in that the harsh environment of the planet had failed to conquer them. They'd adapted, and thought they could survive anything, and that this made them special, a kind of elite.

From this sense of superiority, a system of government had developed that, while still democratic in form, took on aspects of a theocracy. The driving force behind this neoreligion had been the Hope Mountain Group.

Hope Mountain was a small community that had led the opposition to the abandonment of the colony, and to the settlement of Sturnus. Their philosophy was one of perseverance in the face of all hardship, that the planet was a test, and that only those who could face the test deserved to contribute to the future. This was a code that demanded firm steadfastness in the face of all danger and suffering.

The Hope Mountain Group decided the settlers on Sturnus were traitors to the great project that was Janus, the first extra-solar human colony. They thought the Sturnusians weak, and not worthy of continued existence.

Over successive generations, the people of Janus, guided by this sense of their own immutable destiny, continued to experiment with the human-machine interfaces that had helped them during the long terraforming process. Those interfaces, which became proxy technology, had been instrumental in helping them survive.

Proxy bodies allowed them to overcome the effects of the heavy gravity. While their real bodies hung in sleep bags, fed through tubes and cleaned by the same system used in the Washroom, they could live their lives in comfort and take whatever shape or form they wanted.

Sturnus had developed its own version of this technology based on a different system, one more organic than machine; but to the people of Janus, this was twisted and repulsive. Anything Sturnus did was considered twisted, whatever it was, because they were traitors.

A movement to eradicate Sturnus began. Some opposed it, but eventually their voices became fewer and fewer, and those who were for an invasion became louder and louder.

"And so they attacked your moon and destroyed the colony there," Min said.

"Just because they hated us," Bear said.

Min floated level with his position in the command chair.

"I have other pieces of data—debates and editorial opinions that suggest it isn't that simple. Sturnus was a great success as a colony, and some on Janus saw it as a dangerous rival for resources in the system. They were afraid Sturnus would outpace them and eventually attack and destroy them."

"Why would we do that?" Bear said. "It seems like Janus sounds kind of awful. What's it like there? Cold and rocky?"

Sturnus was warm and green.

"There are three major oceans," Min said. "The majority of the continents are in the southern hemisphere. The planet has two moons, which create tides, and the planet is tilted on its axis, so there are seasons. As a heavy-gravity planet, the surface is relatively flat and smooth. It's hotter than Earth on average.

"There's only one major city on the surface, and that's Hope Mountain. It's built on one of the few actual mountains on the planet. The rest of the habitations are smaller towns, and many are underground, having been built during the robotic terraforming phase."

"You sound like a textbook," Bear said.

"I'm compressing information from many texts," Min said.

Janus sounded like a miserable place.

"I don't think I would have liked it there," he said, "if I'd agreed to Miss Sweet's offer."

"There's one more thing," Min said. "Miss Sweet was a member of the last group to oppose the invasion of Sturnus, a group called No Authority. She has some power in their government, but as a minority. She managed to save forty children for her experiment, to assimilate them into Janusian society.

"The rest of the Janusians didn't like it and just wanted you killed."

"So, Miss Sweet tried to help us after all," Bear murmured.

He'd not been wrong to like her before his memories had come back. He wasn't sure how he felt about her now. She could still be cruel and angry.

"I guess we should explore the ship now," he said. "If that's the end of the story?"

He climbed down from the command chair, left the room, and descended the stairs to the curved passageway. With Min as a guide, he found a dining room, with a white oval table but no chairs, and several bedrooms, although the bedrooms didn't have proper beds. They had hanging sleep bags like those at the school.

Most of the rooms they found (or cabins, he thought he should call them) were storerooms, or cargo cabins. They were all filled with white boxes and crates. Some of the boxes were large enough and the right rectangular shape to contain more proxies, but Bear couldn't sense any more signals, which suggested there was something else inside.

He tried to open a few of them but couldn't figure out how. Min told him she couldn't figure them out, either, which suggested they weren't controlled by a computer but needed a mechanical key to open. Bear couldn't imagine what a key like that would look like, so after a while, he gave up. The boxes probably just held supplies or baggage or maybe just clothes, some of Miss Sweet's glittery dresses. He didn't really care. What mattered was there were no more proxies on board.

When he'd seen all of the ship, Bear tried to clean up the parts of the Miss Sweet proxies that had been destroyed in the fight. The larger pieces proved too heavy, so he just left them where they'd fallen.

A few minutes after he'd returned to the command centre, the ship said, "Warning. Rotation imminent."

"What does that mean?" he said.

"The ship interior is going to rotate in its shell," Min said. "There'll be a loss of gravity for a few minutes as the ship runs under momentum only. Your seat has a strap, and I think you should use it."

The prospect of no gravity was both intriguing and frightening. Bear thought it might be fun to float around the cabin, but Min was probably right that it could be dangerous. Finding the seatbelts, he strapped in.

His timing was just right. His stomach seemed to rise, and his hair stood out. For a second, he thought he would throw up, but then the gravity was back.

"We're decelerating toward our destination now," Min said.

Bear had a snack of biscuits and pink cheese. The cheese looked strange but tasted fine. He watched the V-windows. He was tired, bored and impatient.

After another hour, one of the stars on the central screen grew larger. Bear watched as it continue to grow. It was a pale-blue colour.

"Is that Archive?" Bear said.

"No," said Min. "That's the planet Janus. Archive is its smaller moon."

Bear looked at her.

"What? We're going to be right next to them?"

"No one goes there, Bear. To Archive, I mean. Don't worry."

He did worry. He didn't like the idea of being so close to people he now considered his sworn enemies. And it was strange how Min offered partial pieces of information sometimes, like she couldn't make important connections, or didn't realize those connections were important.

"We're almost there," Min said. "We'll lose gravity again as we prepare to land. I think you should belt in."

The blue dot continued to grow until it was obviously a planet, while next to it another star grew larger and brighter. Soon, that star became a pale-gray object, jagged like a chunk of rock, not the perfect sphere Bear had expected it would be. Archive was more like an asteroid than a proper moon, and he remembered now having seen it before, in the display at the library Mister Verren had showed him.

The chunk of rock grew larger until it filled the central V-window. Bear felt the gravity on the ship grow lighter and lighter, and then he was floating in his belt, his hair again standing out, his stomach rising. He had to keep swallowing.

"Approaching Archive," said the ship. "Authorization required for docking."

"Will they let us land?" Bear said, and then he remembered Min had said there were no people here. This was a place for forgotten and ignored things.

"I can help us land," Min said. "Some of these machines here are old, and I can't talk to them, but the newer ones I can. I can tell them what they want to hear."

The surface of the jagged moon now filled every screen, and Bear saw craters, bumps, and deep gouges or cracks. As the ship drew closer, the gouges turned out to be long windows or openings, like massive rectangular slots. Points of light gleamed from some, and one large one featured what looked like the illuminated outline of a landing pad—a square of blue points.

"I can sense some proxy signals," Bear said, alarmed. "Min, you said there was no one here!"

"There are robots and machines," Min explained. "Don't worry, Bear, I don't see any other ships. The robots are just there for anyone to use if they need to come for some reason. There are currently no people on Archive."

"Except you," he said. "Because you're there as a prisoner."

Min's face went blank. "Yes, I suppose you could consider me a person."

Bear sighed. He wanted to ask what she meant, because he had always considered her a person. He looked forward to seeing for real, for having her as an actual companion.

One of the V-windows had become an ordinary computer screen, and now showed an animation that tracked the ship's progress, showing the approach of the large fissures. A few minutes later they were in among the square of lights, and the V-windows suddenly went blank.

"Docking completed," the ship's voice said. "Access to Archive approved. Atmosphere pressurizing."

Bear was no longer floating, but the gravity seemed lighter than it had been during the journey. Unbuckling his seatbelts, he said, "Well, I guess I should open the door."

Min glided ahead of him as he stepped over the remaining bits of Miss Sweet and made his way down the stairs, then along the straight passage to the first stairs and the door. There he stopped, both nervous and excited about what he might find.

"Ship, can you open the door please?" he said.

"Atmosphere at full capacity," said the ship, and the door opened, the ramp descending to what looked like a polished stone floor inside a cave with walls of rough stone.

Chapter 19

B ear exited the ship by turning around and climbing down the ramp backwards, like a ladder, stepping with care. He felt a little awkward in the
light gravity, and each step threatened to launch him into the air. When
he touched down on the shining floor, he bounced and almost fell over, but
threw his arms out to keep his balance.

"This will take getting used to," he said to Min.

Turning to face the opposite wall of the cave, he saw an open doorway
leading to a wide corridor. Dim but warm lights shone from an unknown
source. The corridor walls were smooth, unlike the rough rock of the cave,
and light brown in colour, the ceiling white and possibly the source of the
light. At the end of the passageway, about fifteen metres away, was another
door, this one closed.

With slow, deliberate steps, trying not to overbalance, Bear walked the
length of the corridor, stopping when he reached a second door. He saw no
obvious handle or latch, and found no proxy to send a signal to open it

Out of pure curiosity, he placed his right hand on the centre of the
door, wondering whether the brown, stone-like surface was warm or cold.
At his touch, the door slid open.

Bear jumped.

"That scared me, Min," he said.

Behind the door was a tiny room, probably an elevator or travel tube,
only large enough for one or two people.

"It only goes to one place," Min said. "The Great Hall."

"Why did it open without a proxy?" Bear said.

"Maybe not everyone who comes here uses one," Min suggested. "There
are temporary living quarters here, for real people."

162

Bear stepped inside the transport, and the door closed behind him. Min hovered at his side. There was no sense of motion, but after a minute the wall to his left opened.

Bear stepped out, gazing around in awe at the size of the room that certainly fit the title of Great Hall. It was a massive cavern, its walls of rough stone, the floor made of something similar to the material used in the yard at the school on Sturnus—a non-glare brown substance that yielded under his feet. The ceiling was so far away it was lost in gloom, the room so large it could have held a football field, maybe two—the real kind, not the small one like they'd had at the school.

In the wall opposite the elevator were several doorways, looking small and far away. To Bear's right, even farther away, was a vast rectangular window, taking up the entire end wall, looking into space. Centred in the window was the gleaming planet Janus.

Bear made his way toward this great window, bouncing along and managing not to fall.

"I think we saw this window from the ship," he said.

When he reached it, he discovered the window had no glass. It was an opening, like a cave mouth, exposed to space. It seemed that, if he wanted, he could have walked right out onto the surface of the moon in his bare feet.

"There's a field here that keeps the air and heat from escaping," Min explained. "Be careful, Bear. You can pass through it from either side if you move a certain way, and then you'd be in vacuum, and you wouldn't like that. If you had an environmental suit, you could do it—walk out and sit on the rocks out there."

Janus hung in the starry sky like a bright jewel, looking much smaller than Corvus, but more inviting with its swirls of white clouds.

"I'll be careful," Bear said. He just kept staring. There was something he liked about this place, some sense of safety. It was even cozy, maybe a good place for a picnic, or to read a book by the light of the planet.

He thought of Artemis, and of his parents. He was not here for a picnic.

"Okay, Min," he said. "Where are you? The real you?"

"The other end of the hall," she said. "Follow me, Bear."

Bear was starting to learn how to walk, and now he was able to take long, drifting strides. It was fun, and he covered the length of the hall, trailing behind Min, faster than he would have thought possible.

Min led him toward a set of double doors in the center of the other end wall, opposite the vast window. As he drew nearer, Bear saw two figures guarding the door—dark humanoid figures, one standing on either side. Neither was moving, but he could sense their signals.

When he reached them, he saw that the one on the left was slender and dressed in plain tight-fitting clothes, a simple tunic and trousers. With its long white hair and pale face, it could have been a man or a woman. The figure on the right was more interesting—a warrior of some kind, in metal armour with steel spikes protruding from its helmet, shoulders, forearms, and the backs of its hands.

Empty proxies, waiting for users.

"You should take one of these," Min said. "But not yet. First we can go into the control room. You can leave your real body there and go into the storerooms with the proxy. It might be of some help."

"I'll take this one," Bear said, nodding at the armoured figure. It was like a knight without a sword.

"You can open the doors," said Min.

Bear touched the doors, and they slid open. On the other side was a suite of rooms divided by transparent walls. To the right was a long space with sleep bags hanging from either wall. The other rooms included what looked like a Washroom, toilets, and a small room with tables and chairs that must have been a dining hall.

"This is in case anyone needs to stay here for a few days," Min explained. "I don't think it's ever been used. I can find no record of it."

Bear was struck by the stark design of the living quarters. It was similar to where he and his friends had lived at the school.

"These people really live like this," he said.

It was a bleak setting compared to his old house on the cliff.

"Here's the main control room," Min said.

The control room was across a narrow corridor from the living quarters. The room was tiny, even cramped, just a square space with white walls and four chairs. In front of each chair sat a console, and hovering in the air above each console was a gray rectangle. The rectangles were V-windows, their screens blank gray slates.

"Sit here, and go back and get the proxy," Min said, an odd tightness in her voice. Bear assumed she was getting anxious to be freed from this strange place.

Taking one of the chairs, Bear closed his eyes, leaned back and relaxed, reaching out to find the signal from the armoured proxy. He found it easily; there was so little noise, just two tones to choose from. The note from the strange thin figure sounded like a reedy flute, while the armoured knight's was deep and metallic.

The knight's body felt large and strong as Bear took control, and he noticed that his fatigue and slight anxiety, factors of his real body, faded into the background. The proxy gave him strength of both body and mind, more so than any proxy he'd controlled so far. Maybe this was why the Janusians did this, rode around in these things. It gave them this feeling of strength, a diminishing of their fear.

"Okay, Min," he said, his proxy voice deep and powerful, the voice of a grown man. "I'm a knight, and you're a princess, and I'm here to rescue you. So, tell me where to find you."

She giggled at that, the first time Bear had ever heard her laugh. It sounded so funny he laughed, too.

"Come on," she said. "There are travel pads."

In the little corridor between the control room and the living quarters, white squares like large tiles were set into the floor. Bear stood on one. Min explained that it would move when he wanted it to move, that it was controlled by tiny motions. He just had to lean.

Bear tried it, leaning a little too far and almost losing his balance as the square started to slide along the floor, but the knight proxy was stable and he easily corrected. After that, it was simple to just let the pad carry him along, down the corridor toward what looked like a blank wall, following Min's glowing form.

The wall opened as they approached, and they passed through.

Beyond was another cavernous room, a space Bear guessed must be even larger than the Great Hall, although it was hard to tell because it was crammed full of things, unlike the Hall, which had been empty. The things were suspended in the air in orderly vertical stacks, as if they occupied invisible shelves. In between these stacks were aisles for the travel pads.

Bear and Min seemed to be travelling straight ahead along what was the central aisle. The light was bright but not glaring, warm and not harsh, and the things in the stacks were easy to make out. They were just…things. Furniture, Bear assumed, maybe taken from Sturnus. There were chairs—rows and rows of chairs made from various materials, chairs of various types, and tables large and small, and stools, and cabinets, all made of wood or bamboo or rattan or something, the sort of real furniture the people of Sturnus had liked.

The travel pad was swift, and soon they came to the end of the cavern, another flat white wall stretching upward toward the almost invisible ceiling. In the wall was an arched doorway. Min passed through this, and Bear let his travel pad carry on after her.

The doorway led to a short, dark tunnel, but the darkness was brief, and soon they'd entered another bright cavern much like the first and just as filled with stacked items. These were paintings and hard-copy pictures, depictions of everything—landscapes and portraits and animals and scenes and just shapes and abstract stuff, and picture frames, and blank frames that must have been electronic or changing pictures. There seemed to be thousands of them.

"Was all of this stuff stolen from Sturnus?" Bear said.

"Everything in this wing," Min said. "There are things from other places here as well, in other storerooms. I haven't looked at everything. I could if you want."

Bear watched one painting as he passed it, a depiction of three dogs sitting together, leaning against each other. The painting didn't seem very well done to him, but it brought another memory—of the paintings Mum would make in her spare time, paintings of small animals, often animals she worked with, and also of flowers. Flowers that were unique to Sturnus. Had any of those been stored here?

Were there things here that rightfully belonged to him? Or had everything been destroyed when his house fell down?

Like the first, the second cavern ended at an arched doorway and a little tunnel. The third cavern was filled with lamps, light fixtures, small sculptures, glasses, mugs, bowls and plates, while the cavern after that contained clothing, an eerie collection of hanging coats and shirts and dresses and pants and tunics and wraps that resembled headless and limbless people.

The next cavern contained objects Bear didn't recognize, boxes of various colours, some with switches and knobs, some without.

"How far does this go, Min?" he said. "How much stuff did they put here? And what for?"

"Wait, I'm just reading it now, Bear," Min said. "I haven't looked at the inventory. There are records, a series of memos. The No Authority faction convinced Command not to destroy everything on Sturnus. This was a compromise, a collection of items for future research."

The fifth cavern was the strangest of all, and was filled with animals. Actual animals. The animals all seemed asleep on their feet, each contained in a rectangular transparent box with blue edges. Bear recognized some as animals his mum would have studied, like yellow wolves, the round-eared bear, certain birds; but others he didn't know, despite the fact they were all mammals and birds.

"Are these alive or dead?" he called out to Min.

Min's face took on the now-familiar blank look for a few seconds. Bear knew this meant she was accessing data.

"They're preserved," she said.

"Are they preserved dead or preserved alive?"

Again, the blank look. "I'm only just reading this information, Bear. They're all alive. I believe they can be revived, based on the metadata. They're in stasis."

They continued toward the end of the cavern. Bear gasped.

"Stop!" he shouted. "Min, stop!"

He leaned back to halt the travel pad, and this time it was thanks to the light gravity that he was able to make an abrupt stop without falling over. Min halted with him.

Bear gazed up at the things that were stored here, behind the stacks of animals in their blue boxes.

It was children. Human children.

Like the animals, they were contained in blue-tinged transparent boxes like blocks of ice, standing in the air, hands at their sides and eyes closed, almost as if they were hanging in their sleep bags. They all wore the plain gray featureless clothing the students at Miss Sweet's school had worn.

For a moment, Bear couldn't speak. The cavern was silent. Min turned back and was staring at him with a look of uncertainty on her face.

"They're alive," she told him. "They're preserved, like the animals."

"Is this where you are?" Bear asked.

He had pictured a jail cell of some kind. She'd said she was in a small cell.

"No. I'm not like these. I'm in a special place. It's not far, Bear. Come on, I think we need to hurry."

"Wait a second!"

Bear recognized the faces of the children closest to the center aisle. These were kids from the school. The ones that had gone missing. The ones who had been sent to a "different school".

Aril had to be here somewhere!

He gave Min a sharp look.

"Min, why didn't you tell me they were all here?"

Min shook her head.

"I'm sorry, Bear, but I'm only just seeing these things. I spent all my time outside, trying to find someone to recognize me, then looking at data else-where. It took me a while to realize where I was. I had to learn."

Bear pivoted on his travel pad, moving it out of the central aisle and along the side aisle that took him past the stacks of silent children. There were three in a stack. He gazed up at the faces, each in repose, eyes closed. When he came to Aril, he stopped.

Aril hung in the air on the top virtual shelf, third from the floor, eyes closed, looking like a lifesized doll. His skin, like all of the kids, was gray.

"They're all here, Min!" Bear shouted. "They aren't dead!"

He started moving up and down the aisle, taking in every one of the preserved children. There was Kanga and Deej, and farther along to the left, where the stacks ended, were Emmot and Roma.

"They didn't kill them, Min!" he said. "Min, we have to save them!"

Min took on her blank look.

"There is a way we can revive them, but that will take some time. You need to find me first. Please!"

Bear hesitated, frozen in indecision. Everything had changed. He wasn't alone after all. He could rescue all his friends, all of the kids from the school, and they could be together as before. They could find somewhere to go together.

"Bear, please," said Min. "I'm afraid something will happen to me. Please rescue me, and we can come back and revive everyone here."

Bear took a deep breath. Both tasks had to be completed. Why not do as Min asked? The kids weren't going anywhere.

"Okay," he said. "Okay."

Min looked at him with sadness.

"I'm sorry, Bear. I'm sorry to be selfish."

Bear smiled at her, and then he laughed.

"Don't be sorry, Min! We can save them all, and save you, too!"

He would rescue Min first, and she could then figure out how to wake everyone. And they'd take the ship, and they'd escape, go far away from Janus and never look back.

"Let's go find where they're keeping you," he said. "Show me!"

Min nodded, turned, and glided back toward the main aisle.

Chapter 20

Bear hated turning his back on his friends, but he followed Min through another little tunnel and into the next cavern. The vast space was identical to the last. How many of these caverns were there? Bear imagined the entire interior of the little moon to be honeycombed by these storerooms and their strange inventory of living things and ordinary objects.

This latest cavern contained toys, stuffed animals, dolls, action figures, blocks and balls, vehicles, and tools—hand tools like hammers and screwdrivers, but also many objects he didn't recognize.

Still another cavern followed, but here Min at last stopped, dropping down almost to the floor of the centre aisle. This cavern contained boxes and containers—boxes made from various materials, some massive crates, others very small, some plain, some ornately decorated. Some were just envelopes or chips.

Min veered down a side aisle and stopped again. Bear followed and came to a halt at her side. She pointed at a small white rectangular box. The box hovered in the air, level with what would have been the second shelf, had there actually been shelves. It looked worn, and had black smudges on its surface.

"This is me," Min said.

Bear stared at the little box. "What?"

Min looked at him, the troubled expression back on her face. "This is me, Bear."

"You're a box? I don't get it, Min. You're a girl."

"Yes. No. Yes." She rose into the air and dropped down again. "I know now. I know now. Accessing data. My name is Min Kamra, Bear. Doctor

Kamra was my father. He was your doctor. Or I *was* her. I was modeled on her. She died many e-years ago. Doctor Kamra built me based on her."

"You're a computer," Bear said, with a sinking feeling.

"It took me a long time to understand," Min continued. "I was designed to learn, to gain understanding, to interact with other computers, other machines, other data sets. Some of Doctor Kamra's notes and data are stored in this room. Yes, I see them.

"The Janusians don't know what's here. They could never access my programming because I can only be accessed through you, and other kids like you, who have the same type of brain systems. The genetic enhancements. So, they just catalogued these items in general terms. They don't care. But I know what all of this is now."

Bear reached for the box, but something stopped his proxy hand in mid-air. Some kind of field, like the paralysis field. A voice came to him, another buried memory, coming back into the light. It was Doctor Kamra, telling him about his Guide.

I named her after my little girl, Doctor Kamra had said. *My little girl who is no longer with us. My little angel. Remember I told you about her?*

Bear looked at Min.

"What I'm seeing, then," he said, "is some kind of interface. Or a computer operating system."

"Yes. I am an artificial intelligence, a quantum computer, modeled on Min Kamra. Hello, my name is Min. I'm here to help you. I know that now."

It seemed to Bear that the stacks and stacks of boxes arrayed on either side of him leaned inward, threatening to crush him. His heart had sunk to his toes.

"How can I see you with my proxy?" he asked. "My brain is back in the control room."

"The proxy is an extension of your brain. It's entangled. So you can see me."

"But...are you alive?"

Min glanced to one side, then looked back to him. "That is difficult to define." She floated closer to him. "It's still me, Bear. I'm...designed to react to my users, like you. To behave in a way that seems comforting."

He didn't know what to think. She'd been his mysterious companion, much more his rescuer than he was hers, and he'd thought she was a person, a living, breathing person, a thinking being who was trapped somewhere. She'd been the only other living person he could trust.

Until his discovery his friends were still alive. That he hadn't gotten them killed.

More memories of Doctor Kamra popped into his head, of the doctor showing him pictures of Min, of the real Min, a smiling girl who didn't glow

170

or hover. Had he ever mentioned her name? Bear didn't remember that. He thought Doctor Kamra must have kept her name to himself.

As you grow older, Doctor Kamra had said, *your Guide will help you learn how to use your abilities. She will have to learn as well, but she will learn alongside you. She will come when you call her and go when you don't want her around.*

Bear remembered holding the printed photograph. He could feel the coated paper between his fingers.

With her to help, Doctor Kamra had said, *you will never be alone.*

As long as this little white box existed.

"All of the children from your school," Min said, "all of the survivors, the orphans, will eventually be able to see me, when their brains reach a certain level of development. So my father intended. Your brain must have developed faster than anyone else's."

Bear couldn't make the knight proxy smile, but his real face smiled in the control room.

"I like how you called him your father," he said.

It didn't matter that she was a computer. She still helped him, still kept him company, and still behaved like a real person. He had no interest in debating with himself whether or not she was real. That seemed pointless. She did what she did.

But the fact she was a machine intelligence explained some of her strange behavior, the way she spoke, the way she missed things, and the way she had learned in chunks.

He should have seen it before.

"I need to get you off this shelf," he said. "We need to keep you safe."

He searched for a signal, some way to remove Min's case from the stasis field, but just like with the paralysis field, he couldn't find anything. The entire cavern was silent.

These machines were different.

"How do I do this, Min?"

"You have to do it from the control room," she said. "If you want to re-trieve something from the Archive, you have to do it from there, with proper authorization."

"I'm already in the control room," he reminded her. "What do I do?"

"I'll join you there."

He left the knight proxy where it stood, returning almost completely to his own body. In the control room, Min appeared in front of him, to the left of the blank V-window.

"Much of the purpose of this room seems to be record keeping and search-ing," she said. "You can light the V-window, Bear. Use your console."

The console featured three squares of some shiny material, and that was all. Bear shook his head, then chose the centre square and touched it.

The V-window lit, turning white. A moment later, three-dimensional letters appeared in the air in front of it, spelling *Janus System Secondary Archive 1.0.0.4.*

"Please state your search requirements," a voice said, a real voice vibrating in the air.

"You want to retrieve an item," said Min.

"I want to retrieve an item," Bear repeated.

"State item catalogue location," said the voice.

"I don't know. Is there a map?"

A map appeared on the V-window. At first, it just looked like a confused jumble of square blocks connected by thin lines until Bear realized the blocks were chambers or caverns, the lines tunnels.

"Indicate level and region," said the voice.

"Which one is it, Min?" Bear said.

Min's face went blank for a second, then she reached out with one glowing hand, pointing at a group of blocks in the top left corner of the V-window. "There. Level One, Section C, Storeroom Number Eight."

"Level One, Section C, Storeroom Number Eight," Bear repeated.

The map zoomed in to show just that section. The image rotated, becoming three-dimensional like the letters had been.

"Select item," the voice said.

Bear reached for the image, found he was able to turn and position it with his hand. Some of the books and other media devices in the school, like his work card, had functioned this way. He could even zoom the image by sliding his fingers.

"Is that it, Min?" he said, pointing at a representation of what looked like her case.

"That's me, Bear."

Bear touched the item.

"Authorization required," said the voice.

Before Bear could scream in frustration and annoyance, Min said, "I've done it."

"Authorization approved," the voice said. "Item ready for retrieval."

"You can use your proxy to pick me up now," Min said. "Or…yes, there are also carts and automated services available for delivery."

"I have you," Bear said.

He'd returned to the knight proxy. Min's little case now glowed a faint pink. Bear reached for it, felt no resistance, and took it in his large spiked hand. It was only about the size of a deck of cards, like the ones he'd used to play with, with Mum and Dad.

Turning on his travel pad, Bear went back to the central aisle and started zipping back through the cavern, through the room with the toys and tools, and into the cavern that held his friends. There he stopped.

"I have you, Min," he said. "Now, how do I wake up my friends?"

He again let his real body dominate. Min was still there with him in the control room.

"The same way," she said.

"I want to retrieve an item," Bear told the console. "A bunch of items!"

"State item catalogue location," said the voice, as it had before.

"Wait, Bear!" Min suddenly said, moving in front of the V-window. Her eyes again had taken on the blank look. "The station has detected incoming ships. Someone's coming to Archive."

Bear almost leapt out of his seat.

"What! You said no one ever comes here!"

Min turned her back, as if she were looking through the rock of the moon and into space beyond. "Four ships, coming from the planet. It's them, Bear. They know we came to Archive. They know we're here."

Bear just stared at her. Every time he thought he'd escaped, they managed to find him. Of course they'd been able to track his ship. He should have realized that. It was really their ship.

The reality that he was just one boy, one boy against an entire planet of adults, struck him with its cruel unfairness. He'd come all this way, had escaped, had rescued Min, discovered that his friends were still alive, and now he was about to be stopped at the last minute, at his moment of success.

He cried out in frustration, a wordless shout, and wanted to smash the console, break it into pieces, tear up the chairs and throw them across the room.

"Bear, you have to think," said Min. "We can stop them."

Bear's hands were balled into fists. Yes, she was right. This wasn't over. The ships weren't here yet. He really had been successful, so there was no reason to assume he wouldn't continue to be, if he refused to give up. He just had to think.

But what could he do? Was there something here at Archive that could help?

"The ships work like our ship," Min said. "They're like proxies."

Bear sat up. Of course.

"I have to see," he said, although that wasn't true. He didn't need to see a proxy to sense its signal. But he wanted to see them.

He left the control room and went back out through the double doors, back into the Great Hall. Bouncing along in the light gravity, he traveled the entire length of the vast room until he reached the opening at the far end.

Janus was brighter than it had been before, more of its daylight side visible. The light drowned out the stars, and Bear had to shield his eyes until they adjusted. He wanted a good view, so he walked out as far as he dared, to the edge of the hall's floor where it became rough rock again.

"The ships will look very small," Min said, again at his side. "You might not be able to see them."

"Are they on this side of the moon?"

"Yes, the Archive station is only accessible from this side."

Bear pointed.

"There they are!"

He could see them. They were small, as Min had said, but almost as bright as the planet, four shining objects just to his right. And they were growing larger, getting closer.

"Can ships land here in the Great Hall?" he asked.

"They have before," Min said, after a slight pause.

"Then they're coming right for us."

He watched them without thinking or feeling anything except curiosity. His ability to feel surprise or alarm seemed to have run out, but that was fine. It was easier to think. Soon, he could make out details, and saw that the ships were similar to the battlebots—landing craft with arms and legs and fat bug bodies.

He found a small rocky outcrop near the edge of the floor.

"Can I sit here?" he said.

"It's safe," said Min.

Bear sat on the rock and rested his chin in his hands.

"All this for me?" he said, watching the ships. A whole planet, mustering so much to capture one boy.

He supposed he should feel important.

"They're afraid of you, Bear," said Min. "They don't understand you, and know that you can undermine the very thing that forms the basis for their entire society."

"They tried to destroy us," he said. "Now they think I might destroy them."

The four ships looked close now, so close he thought he might be able to reach them in a single bound if he were to jump out the window.

He listened.

"I can hear the planet," he said.

Janus emanated music, a single harmonic note, the combination of thousands of signals, maybe millions, softer than white noise, but not by much. It was overpowering, and masked the signals coming from the four ships.

The planet must have been millions of kilometres away. How far away did something have to be before he couldn't hear its signal anymore? Time and space didn't matter, Doctor Kamra had said once. Miss Sweet had said that, too.

It was an interesting question, but not one for this moment. He had to concentrate. No one was coming to help him. He could get up and run away, run into the depths of the storerooms and living spaces and hope no one would find him, but even if he could hide for a while, they would keep looking. He was sure of it.

He had to figure this out now.

The ships were close. He wondered if, when they landed here, they'd have to lower the field that kept the air from rushing out of Archive and into open space, or if they could walk on their bug legs or fly through from their side, just as Min had said he could accidentally walk through from his. Just how strong was that field, anyway? If the ships fired their plasma emitters now, would they get through, or would the field protect him?

He chose what appeared to be the nearest ship, stared at it, and listened. The noise of the planet reached him again, so he tried to isolate some of the tones. An odd, deep group of notes seemed to stand out, so he focused on them, and after a few minutes he determined there were four separate tones, each just a semitone apart. It had to be the ships, but the tones were still hard to grasp.

"I'm hungry," he said, sighing. "And tired, Min. I wish I could go to bed."

A real bed, not one of the awful sleep bags. A real bed like the cushion of undergrowth in the forest, surrounded by his friends.

The ships were closing in. Sleep had to wait. Food had to wait.

He found the tones again. He was sure they came from the ships. Together, they almost formed a dark melody. And then he discovered why it was so difficult to isolate them.

The tones from each ship blended in harmony, like a quartet of musicians playing a single piece. It was as if they were controlled by one source. Could a single person be controlling all four ships? And if so, could Bear do the same thing?

There was one way to find out.

He stood and took a few more paces out across the rough surface, facing his enemy.

"I'm going to take them all, Min," he said. "I'm going to take all four of them."

He followed the melody, and there it was, like a series of twisted lines, braided together. As his mind slid along those lines, he at last found the place where they split, each strand going to one of the ships. He followed one at random, and it led him to the ship on his left, the leading ship in the formation.

He became the ship. It was strange and disorienting, more like a larger version of the bug machines than his spherical ship. From its forward viewing sensors, he could see the moon, see Archive, and he could see the great window where he stood, could mark it by the light that emanated from it.

"Min," he said, transferring some of his awareness to his real body, "there's something strange about this ship. It's filled with proxy tones. That's partly why it was so hard to find, I think."

The ship, he realized, was filled with proxy bodies.

Filled with soldiers.

A communication came in, a voice from one of the other ships.

"Carrier Delta," it said, "we have lost contact."

Bear knew he was Carrier Delta.

"I can take them all," he said again, while standing on Archive.

He reached out for the next proxy signal, the next ship, found it and followed it, maintaining its braided link. It was difficult, and he felt the tension, pressure building in his head, his real head; but now he could see two images via the forward sensors, the cameras that were the ship's eyes, superimposed. It was just like when he'd taken control of two toy proxies in the meadow outside the school.

"It's hard, Min," he said.

It was too much. He could feel sweat on his brow, churning in his stomach, disorientation. He couldn't control more than two.

It didn't matter. He slowed both ships, fired their maneuvering thrusters and turned them. Then he found what he wanted—their weapons, which were quite similar to those of the battlebots. The plasma emitters.

He chose his targets: the last two ships. His first shots missed, the yellow beams lancing out into the void of space, but he saw where they'd gone and adjusted his aim.

His second barrage didn't miss, and the two ships exploded, tiny bits of debris expanding in twin clouds.

Now he had to deal with the ships he controlled. He didn't want to just land them here and leave them. The proxy soldiers inside had controllers somewhere—real people who could only be down on the planet, despite its great distance. They were the real threat.

So, Bear turned the first ship to face the surface of the moon, found a stretch of open rock, and engaged the main thrusters. As that ship struck the surface, he did the same with the second.

"Two new craters on Archive," he said, turning to Min.

He was sweating, and he was weak, but he'd done it. He felt no elation, just a simmering triumph, and pride at what he could do.

"That should give me enough time to get everyone out of here." he said.

Chapter 21

Y ou should rest now, Bear," Min said. "I really think you need to rest."
He knew she was right, that taking control of the ships had sapped his strength. But he couldn't wait. He didn't expect the Janusians to just leave him alone and was sure they'd try again. They'd be even more afraid of him now.

He returned to the control room, again bounding in the weak gravity, going as fast as he could manage.

"Do you think forty kids will fit in our ship?" he said after he'd again taken the chair in front of the command console.

"The ship is designed to carry cargo and a crew of twenty," Min said.

"Then we'll double up," Bear said. "Twenty adults, right? We're small."

His plan was simple and direct—free his friends, board the ship, and leave before the Janusians could send more ships. The only question was where they would all go. That was still the problem he hadn't solved.

He just wanted to go home.

"How do I set them free?" he said, forgetting he'd already started the process.

Min was at his left shoulder, close enough to touch, if that were possible.

"The same way you freed me," she reminded him.

"I want to retrieve some items," Bear repeated, speaking to the console.

"State item catalogue location."

Bear asked for the map, and when it appeared, found the proper location. "Level One, Section C, Storeroom Number Six."

The schematic of the cavern appeared. Min pointed out the proper stacks.

"Highlight them all," she told him.

He did.

꘏

His knight proxy was still in the cavern, waiting, holding the little box that contained Min. Bear took control just as the blue boxes surrounding the children turned red. The children were silent, unmoving, their eyes closed, but the colour shift indicated something had changed.

"Will they wake up when I take them out?" Bear asked, in the knight's ominous voice.

"They will," said Min, now above him.

He positioned himself in front of a girl on the lowest shelf level, a girl whose name he couldn't remember, one of the group that had disappeared first. Her hair, in two pigtails like Roma's, was a dark rich brown. With his massive steel fist, spikes protruding from the knuckles, Bear reached into the red box, took the girl's hand, and gave a gentle pull.

The girl took a step forward and opened her eyes. When she saw Bear's proxy, her eyes widened and her face contorted in fear, her mouth opening as if about to emit a scream.

"Don't be afraid!" Bear said. "I'm not a monster! I'm a friend."

He dropped her hand and moved to the next child in the bottom row. The girl gasped and moaned, her hands held together against her chest.

"You can help me," Bear said. "Take these kids by the hand and pull them out to wake them up. Like this."

The second child he woke was Deej. He let out a yelp when he saw Bear's armoured form looming over him.

"Deej, quiet," Bear said. "It's just a suit, one of the puppets. It's me, Bear, using it. Help me wake everyone in the bottom row."

When the last child in that row was awake, standing with the others and looking around in surprise and confusion, the entire second row dropped, slowly settling to the floor. Bear had wondered how he would retrieve the kids on the upper row if he didn't want to remove everyone from the lower row first. There must have been some other method.

"Where's Miss Sweet?" asked the first girl he'd awakened.

"She's not here," Bear said. "It's okay. Help me wake this next group. You've all been asleep for a long time, and we have to wake you all up so we can go home."

They all seemed to listen, but some gave him skeptical looks, brows knitted. He'd told them who he was, but he wasn't sure they believed him or understood. Maybe they were groggy. They seemed to look on him in the same way they would have looked on the Guardians back in the school.

But they helped, and soon the occupants of the second row of virtual shelves had joined them.

"Don't be scared of me," Bear told the assembled kids. "This is just a proxy, like the toy animals we played with in the meadow. It's a puppet. It's me, Bear. I'm controlling it."

The third row dropped down, and Bear was facing Aril.

"Aril!" he said. "Aril! Wake up!"

Aril stepped out of his box of light and air, frowned at Bear's horrifying appearance, saw the other kids assembled in the aisle, and scratched his head.

"What's going on?" he said.

Bear laughed. Coming from his knight's throat, it sounded menacing, like the laughter of a villain from a story, and Aril flinched away.

Puck was in the next group, along with Kanga, while Emmot and Roma were among the last.

"Emmot! Roma!" Bear said. "It's me, Bear! I'm in this thing. It's a proxy."

Emmot looked angry, glaring around at the cavern, and Roma was rubbing her eyes.

"What happened?" she said. "What happened after the giant bugs attacked us?"

"We all got taken prisoner again," Bear explained. "Now we're escaping again. Follow me."

He walked back toward the centre aisle, not using the travel pads, and the kids followed.

"I hope this works better than your last escape plan," Roma called after him.

He showed them the travel pads. They were accustomed to being ordered about and herded by the Guardians, and they still seemed to react to him in that way, despite his insistence that he was just Bear in a proxy body. They did what he told them to do, and did it without complaint or questions, beyond the repeated "Where's Miss Sweet?"

Soon they were all strung out in a long file, each riding a travel pad, racing back through the astonishing caverns to the control room, where the real Bear waited. Bear saw smiles and heard laughter. They were enjoying the ride.

They walked the last few metres out into the Great Hall. There, Bear dropped the proxy, leaving it in its original place beside the double doors. When the kids saw him, saw that he really was Bear, they shouted his name and slapped him on the arms and back, some even giving him a hug. He felt his face flush, and tears sprang to his eyes, which he wiped away with the back of his hand.

"Okay, everyone," he said. "See, I told you it was me. Can everyone gather in a circle?"

He had removed Min's computer case from the knight's hand and held it in his own, wishing his pajamas had pockets. The children did as he asked, jostling and chattering and laughing, the sound of their voices flat in the enormous chamber.

Bear asked for quiet, and they obeyed him without question or complaint. He told them everything that had happened. He told them what Janus had done, that it had invaded Sturnus and destroyed their homes and taken them prisoner; and that Miss Sweet had wanted to make them part of Janusian society, so she'd tried to teach them how to use their proxies, which was how everyone on Janus lived. Those kids who hadn't been good at it had been sent here to Archive, where they would have stayed on a virtual shelf forever.

He told them he was able to rescue them because he could use any proxy, use more than one at once, and they all had this power, it was just buried inside them; but it would start to come out, just like their memories of home.

Roma was looking at him with fat tears rolling down her cheeks.

"What's wrong, Roma?" he asked.

She gave her face an angry swipe with the back of one hand.

"Nothing. Just as you're talking, I'm remembering things. I remember what happened. I did a little before, but now I remember it all. My family. Where we lived. Everything."

Others were nodding in apparent agreement. Some were also crying. Emmot had one arm around Puck's shoulders, was patting him on the arm.

"Where are my grandparents?" Aril said, sounding outraged. He looked bewildered. "Where did they go?"

"They're all dead," Bear said. There was no use in hiding that fact any longer. "We're the only people left from Sturnus."

⁂

They ate, getting the food assemblers in the living quarters, and used the toilets and the Washroom, and they pulled the sleep bags from the wall and laid them on the floor. No one wanted to hang from the wall anymore. They all remembered their beds, every one of them.

"Is it safe to sleep?" Bear asked Min. He was draped across one of the chairs in the control room, looking out into the corridor where some of the kids were sitting on the floor and chatting, some playing games like they had in the yard of the school. They were falling back on their old habits. He yawned.

"There are many communication signals coming from the planet that refer to you and Sturnus," Min said. "A lot of data exchange. They're arguing about what to do. They call the group that leads them 'Command.' They want to send more ships, but others are worried about the risk. They fear your capabilities."

Min looked blank for a minute.

"Wait. Bear, some of them have suggested shutting down Archive, of killing the power remotely. They can do this, but because it would ruin the station, others have disagreed. They're arguing."

"Then we have to get away soon," said Bear, "in case the bad ones get their way."

He'd wanted to rest, needed it, but once again there was no time.

Roma was coming toward him from the living quarters. She looked unhappy.

"Bear," she said.

Bear knew that tone and sat up straight in his chair.

"What is it?"

"I met Min," she said. "The glowing girl. I met her. She told me you've met her, too. Have you?"

Bear looked at Min beside him in surprise. Min nodded.

"Yes," Min said, "she can see me now, but not this me. She has her own me." She paused. "I can integrate them, if you want."

Bear shook his head. No, his Min was special, just for him. He knew that was ridiculous, that she was a computer, just a box sitting on the console behind him, who'd been designed to help them all. But she'd been his secret for so long he'd begun to think of her as his and his alone.

But wouldn't it be better if she could talk to all of the kids together? Wouldn't that be more useful?

"I think you should integrate," he said. He didn't like it, but it made more sense.

Roma's face brightened, splitting in a wide grin. She looked to Bear's left, to where his version of Min had hovered.

"Hi, Min!" Roma said.

"You'll all be able to see me soon," Min said. "Not just you two. The time has almost arrived."

Bear climbed out of the chair and went into the Great Hall. About half of the children were there. One small group was gathered on the edge of the great window at the far end. A new plan began to form in Bear's mind. If all of the kids were getting their memories back, and they could interact with Min like he could, then they should also be awakening to the same abilities to control multiple proxies.

"Min," he said, looking back over his shoulder to where the glowing girl floated next to Roma. "Can anyone else see you yet?"

"Two others," Min admitted. "Emmot and Kanga."

Bear looked at Roma.

"Can you help me get everyone to gather here, Roma? We need to try something. All of us at the same time."

Roma looked a little annoyed, but she nodded. "Okay. What?"

"I'll show you."

A few minutes later, they were all gathered where Bear had indicated, in a circle again. The group that had been near the window came bounding in, laughing at how high they could jump in the light gravity. When they arrived, Bear motioned for them to be quiet.

"Everybody needs to try something," he said. "Every one of us. See that proxy?"

He pointed at the spiked knight.

"Remember when Miss Sweet made us practice with the toy animals? And we all had to use these little goggle things, the controllers? Well, I don't need those anymore, and none of you should need them anymore, either. So, what everyone needs to do, one at a time, is to look at this knight, and this other thing, and listen for the signal. Find out if you can hear the signal. Everyone line up and take turns!"

They obeyed him, as they'd obeyed him before, but it was also like a game he'd invented. He'd become the new Miss Sweet, although that thought made his stomach flip. He was no Miss Sweet.

"Bear," Aril called from his place in the line. He looked worried. "I was never very good at this."

"It's okay if you can't do it," Bear told him. "You're not going to get in trouble with anyone, right? I just think we need to see who can and who can't. Maybe you all can. Our brains are growing, Aril."

Aril bit his lip. "I'll try."

Roma was first.

"I can hear it," she said, voice hushed.

"Don't tell anyone what it sounds like," Bear warned.

Roma had closed her eyes. In front of her, the spiked knight raised both arms, reached out and touched her hair with gentle fingers.

Roma's eyes opened again, and she turned to Bear with a wide grin.

"I did that!"

"Okay, if you can hear the signal," Bear said, a little irritated that Roma had gone one step further than he'd ordered, but determined to use her actions as a means to maintain control of the situation, "see if you can also move the knight's arms."

Roma danced to the back of the line. The next child also heard the signal, also moved the knight.

One after the other, every single kid discovered they could control the proxy without an external controller. And then it was Aril's turn.

"Just do your best," Bear said.

"You can do it, Aril," Emmot said. "Come on!"

Other voices joined in, offering encouragement, but Bear could see this was just making Aril more nervous.

"I don't hear anything," Aril muttered, just loud enough that only Bear could hear.

"You're not really trying," Bear said. "Try again."

Aril's hair was damp with sweat. He closed his eyes and took a few deep breaths. He was trembling.

His eyes snapped open.

"I can hear it," he whispered. He looked to his left, at the strange proxy with the long white hair. "And I can hear that one, too."

His eyes closed again. The knight raised its arms, then folded them across its chest, then took a step, then another, until it stood in front of the other proxy.

The knight embraced the figure with the long white hair, patting its back. Aril laughed.

"I can do this!"

Bear laughed with him, but he had no time to linger on this one task. Taking two long bounding strides away, he made for the great window, calling on everyone to follow him.

Leaping and sailing through the air, all forty children raced for the window. Bear got there first, holding up his hands and shouting in warning, telling everyone to slow down, that they could jump right out into space if they weren't careful. They all skidded and thumped to a halt.

"What are you doing, Bear?" Min asked, very close in his ear.

"I'm teaching," he said. "I'm training."

He pointed at the blue-and-white jewel of Janus, again half in shadow.

"Everyone look at the planet," he said. "Look at it and listen, see if you can hear it."

Again, they obeyed. They were smiling and happy, as happy as Bear had ever seen them. Happier. They were being given orders; but by one of their own now, not by a Guardian, not by someone trying to control them, but by a peer, and someone trying to help them.

"I hear it," Roma said, and others murmured agreement. "There's music. Weird music. The whole planet."

"It's all the proxies," Bear said. "All their machines, everything they use. It's all the same, it all works the same. And we can use it all."

Now he could sense something else, another shift in their mood. No one spoke, they all just stared at the planet. There was something in their

184

eyes, and Bear thought he knew what it was. It was the realization that they had power, real power, for the first time in their lives.

"Form a circle," he said.

They did.

"We're all that's left of our planet," he told them. "We're all that's left of Sturnus. Those people down there on Janus tried to get rid of us, all except for Miss Sweet. She saved us. That's the truth. But she's also one of them, and was going to let all of you stay here forever and just take me, because I learned how to do all this stuff a little before anyone else."

Now their expressions were grim, but they were listening. He had their attention.

"I was just lucky. I think I was first in the same way that Kanga there is taller than everyone else. I just grew in that way faster. That's all. And for that I was going to be saved. But now we're all together again, and we have a spaceship. I stole it and flew it here, and we're going to have to all get in it and use it again, because those people down there..." He jabbed a finger at the planet again. "...are going to come up here and try to destroy us all over again."

Their anger was building. Not fear, but anger.

"So, I think we need to decide where we go. I have a suggestion. I want to go home. I want to go home to Sturnus, and stay there, and maybe rebuild things. What do you say?"

He was telling the truth. It surprised him to hear the words come out of his mouth, because he was not sure how safe it was to go back, but there was nowhere else. He just wanted to go home.

The kids reacted with an explosion of cheers and cries of assent.

"I want to go home, too!" Emmot shouted.

"Me, too!" said another.

Bear let them cheer, cheer and hug and dance and jump high in the air. He laughed with them, laughed so hard he couldn't speak, and then he noticed a few of them pointing, reaching up and pointing toward the ceiling.

He looked up. Min was there, dropping down slowly, her feet in their little shoes (which must have been copies of the shoes the real Min had worn), dangling just like the first time Bear had seen her. The children watched with wide eyes, some still laughing, but most hushed now, gazing in wonder at this strange apparition.

Min came to a stop just above the gathering. She was glowing brighter than Bear had ever seen her glow before.

Min looked at him. She winked.

"This is Min," Bear announced. "She's here to help us. Doctor Kamra had her made for us."

"I remember Doctor Kamra!" someone said, and there were more noises of agreement.

"She's a computer," Bear said, although he didn't like saying it, felt it was somehow disrespectful; but he knew it was the truth, and he had to say it, and Min didn't mind. "But she's a special computer. She can talk to other machines and computers that are far away, give them instructions and ask them for information. She'll come to you when you call, and help. Right, Min?"

"I will," said Min. "Hi, there. I'm Min Kamra. I've been learning how to do these things ever since I met Bear. And now I'm ready."

She floated among the children, and they reached out to touch her, marveling at how their fingers passed through her luminous form. Bear watched, and any jealousy or possessiveness he may have felt was gone. This was how things should be. It was like his friend was now everyone's friend, and that was good.

He glanced to his left, at the planet. There was one more thing he wanted to do.

"I don't want Janus to bother us anymore," he said. "I want to tell them to leave us alone."

He looked at Min.

"I want to go down there," he told her. "I can hear their proxy signals, even from this far away. I want to go down there and tell them to leave us alone."

Chapter 22

Bear sat in the big window and faced Janus. He listened to the planet, to its distant hum and wail.

"Can I still capture a proxy there?" he asked Min. "It's really far away."

He wasn't sure why this worried him. Maybe because the idea that spatial distance was irrelevant to the ability of two systems to become entangled and phase-locked was just such a strange concept. But he could already hear the signals, so it was only a matter of isolating one and following it to its source.

"What is it that you want to do?" Min said. She sounded skeptical.

"I want to meet these Command people and tell them to go away, to leave us alone, and not to send any more ships after us, because we'll just take them over."

"Do you think they'll listen?"

Bear was a little tired of making plans, but this was no time to rest.

"What if I just pick a signal," he said, "any signal, and then you go with me, and wherever I end up, you go and look to see how far away Hope Mountain is from there, and then I jump into another proxy, and then we keep doing that until we find Command. Can you do that?"

Min nodded. "Yes."

Roma had come to stand at Bear's side.

"Can you all watch out?" Bear asked her. "Watch to make sure they don't send any ships, and if they do, let me know, so I can come back."

"I want to come to," said Roma, but before Bear could object, she added, "but I won't. I get it, Bear. I know you've had more practice than the rest of us. So, sure, I'll keep a lookout."

"I will, too," said Emmot, joining her.

Bear smiled and nodded his thanks.

"Who are the leaders, Min?" he asked. "Do you know?"

"I have that data," she told him. "There are four who sit on the Command Council. The leader is called El-ann, the Chancellor. Verren is another."

"El-ann," Bear said. He knew that name, realized that it was the name of the horrible monster that had wanted to kill him, or abandon him here on Archive forever. "That's the one I really want to talk to."

He listened to the planet, tried to hear a single tone; but it was difficult, and he realized there was a chance he wouldn't be able to do this. If that were the case, they'd just have to leave and hope they weren't followed.

But the longer he concentrated, the stronger the noise of the world below became, and the easier to hear its individual parts. Suddenly, it was easy. It was like the clouds parting to reveal the blue sky. The signals were like coloured hairs, a multitude of curving strands, some thick, some thin, some twisted together. All he had to do was grab one and hold it.

He chose a signal that sounded like a mid-range warbling, and it grew stronger and stronger until it filled his head, filtering out the rest of the sounds. He could see it in his mind—blue and black crescents spinning together—and then he slid all the way down, away from the moon and onto the planet.

He had taken charge of a vehicle or aircraft, flying just below the cloud cover. His vision was vast, greater than two eyes ever could have provided, showing him rugged terrain below, green and gray and brown, hills and lakes and gleaming rivers. Vertigo threatened to overwhelm him; and for a moment he forgot he was in control of the craft's function, and it started to dive.

He tried to pull up, but it was hard, the craft unstable, the air filled with turbulence, so he reached out, listening for another signal; and again there were many, but it seemed not as many obvious ones as before. So, he found another, a fluting melody that repeated, orange and red and gold. He knew when he dropped the aircraft, it would fall and crash, because its original controller had lost access and wouldn't be able to regain it; but there was nothing he could do about that. He just hoped there were no living people on board the vehicle.

He slid along the line of the second signal, rushing in too fast, just managing to slow down at the last instant, avoiding the pain he knew a sudden transfer would cause. The view of the sky and the ground below vanished, and the new view was a street scene. It took him a few seconds to take it in, and he gasped involuntarily, almost stumbling and falling in the new body. This was a humanoid figure, not a vehicle.

Rectangular stones or bricks made up the surface of the street, and the houses on either side were tall and thin and made of mottled plaster, all painted deep yellow, with steep green rooftops. Several people were walking along the street, and they were all short, with green skin, large ears and noses, and unkempt black hair that stuck out like spikes.

Bear looked at his hands and saw that they, too, were green.

Am I a goblin or a troll or something?

He felt like a character from a Janusian story, like one of the many tales Miss Sweet had told.

Min appeared beside him.

"This isn't Hope Mountain," she said. "This isn't even the right continent. You have to go west and a little north. That way."

She pointed.

"Okay," he said, his proxy voice a slithering rasp. "This might be harder than I thought."

There were many proxy signals around him, but all were close, within walking distance. He needed to travel far, but from here in the street he couldn't get a fix on any more-distant signals. He needed height, like a building or a tower or a high hill, a place that would allow him to see far away, and so listen.

He started along the street, looking for stairs or access to a balcony. His legs felt heavy, and he realized the higher gravity was affecting him even through the proxy. A stairway appeared on his left, a way up to one of the rooftops; and he climbed it, taking one step at a time.

At the top, Min waited, pointing again. "That way."

Bear looked, saw a rugged landscape of rocks and prickly trees, like yellowpines but thicker and darker. The forest stretched on to the horizon, but the signals were clear. He chose one at random, one he liked. It sounded like the tinkling of tiny silver bells, and he followed it, felt the goblin drop away from him.

The view changed again.

Looking around, trying to get his bearings, Bear saw that he was in a long narrow room, the light dim. Lined up against both side walls were silent human figures, all standing still. There were figures of all shapes and heights, all human adults and all ordinary-looking, with natural skin tones and hair, their clothing dull colours. Bear realized this was a proxy storage facility, or a closet like Miss Sweet's.

He stepped away from the nook in which his figure had stood, walked the length of the room, and found the door where it should have been, surprised to discover it was an ordinary swinging door with an ordinary mechanical latch, like the door to his old house.

Beyond the door was an outdoor courtyard paved in plain pale concrete. High concrete walls rose all around him, although a ramp on one side seemed to provide a way out. Doors in the walls looked just like the one he had emerged from. The sky was a deep, dark blue, almost purple, and the air smelled of dust.

"Am I closer?" he said, his voice high-pitched and thin. "Min?"

Min was there on his left.

"A little closer," she said. "Still far to go."

Bear started walking toward the ramp. "What's in these buildings? Is it all stored proxies?"

Min rose about two metres, gazing around at the concrete structures. "Wait. I need a machine to talk to, to see. Yes, I have it. There are people here, in other buildings nearby. People resting. Using proxies. They stay in one place. They live there. And yes, this appears to be a storage facility."

"It doesn't look very nice," Bear remarked.

It was just like the school, or the living quarters on Archive.

"They live here," Min said, "but they don't ever leave. They spend all of their time in their proxies."

At the top of the ramp was a concrete platform. Bear saw the other buildings Min had mentioned, their rooftops no higher than the platform. All around lay a landscape of low gray rocks, shrubs, and diminutive trees. A gleaming white rail, the kind used by trains, ran along one side of the platform where he stood. The rail stretched to the horizon, where the silver towers of a city sparkled in the weak sunlight.

"There, Min," he said, pointing. "Is that Hope Mountain?"

Min was a splash of gold amongst all the gray and dull green.

"No, that city is called Last Chance. That's a funny name for a city, isn't it?"

"If I go there, will I be closer?"

"Yes."

Bear listened, stretched out and grabbed a bubbling theme of music, and rode it in, like riding a train.

Cheers, screams of joy and howls of derision filled the air. People around him were standing and clapping or shaking their fists.

"Where am I now, Min?" Bear shouted, heedless of who might hear him, given the people were close—in fact, crammed up against him—and he realized he was sitting in a theatre of some kind, or a stadium, the kind of big open circular place with seats like the classroom at the school, a place where people watched sports. It was open to the sky, the same purplish sky he'd seen at the previous location.

The cheers died, and the people around him took their seats again, but there was still plenty of chatter. Many of the people, or proxies, wore tight-fitting black costumes, the shoulders and arms adorned with streamers and feathers. Bear looked at his arms and saw that he wore something similar—a soft black jacket with green feathers along the seams of the arms.

Below him, the rows of seats sloped down to a large earthen space. In the centre of this space, two enormous human figures, both tall and long-limbed, were fighting with swords. Bear thought the swords must be two metres long. One of the combatants was sky-blue, the other yellow.

In the dust at their feet, two other warriors, one red and one pale-green, lay in pieces.

"They're fighting," Bear said as Min appeared, hovering in the small space between him and the spectator to his left.

Bear knew the warriors, like the people in the audience, were proxies. He could hear their dark, angry melodies even as their swords rang, even as the blue warrior severed the yellow warrior's right arm, and the crowd jumped to its feet again, roaring.

Bear closed his eyes. He didn't like this. It was more the sort of thing Emmot would have enjoyed. He found it too noisy, too mean, and he looked around him to find a new proxy, something up higher in the rows of seats. When he chose one, he made the jump.

The view of the colourful warriors became more distant. Bear looked for an exit, saw doors to his right, listened for a signal behind them, and jumped again.

He jumped three more times before he found a vantage point on the outside of the stadium, where he could look and listen toward the west and a little north.

His fourth jump brought peace, an end to the noise of the crowd. His new body felt small, and he saw that his arms and legs were thin, and that he was wrapped in pale-pink robes. He was sitting on a bench on a grassy hill, and the trees around him made a music of their own as the breeze rattled their leaves. Below the hill was a green lawn, a pond, a little arched bridge, and winding pathways through more green trees. A few other people were there, all proxies strolling the paths, people of all shapes and sizes and colours. One went on all fours and resembled a long-eared cat. Birds twittered and squabbled in the trees above Bear's head. He was surprised to discover, thanks to their obvious fluting tones, that they, too, were proxies.

"You're getting closer, Bear," Min said, descending from the trees. "That last trip was your farthest yet."

Bear liked this garden, and the temptation to sit here for a while was strong, to take a break; but again he reminded himself there wasn't time. The Janusians could decide to shut down Archive at any minute.

He listened and jumped again.

The next location was dark and difficult to make sense of at first. It was a street in a rundown city full of noise and fumes from ground cars that looked like boxes with four spoked wheels. The buildings around him were made of red bricks, held together with cement, and had lots of rectangular windows. People were everywhere, walking, talking, all dressed in peculiar clothes Bear didn't recognize—men in hats with wide brims, women in colourful dresses that showed the bottom part of their legs, and shoes with strange soles that lifted their heels in the back.

"This is like an old place on Earth," Min explained, hovering near three steel buckets with lids. "It's from a story. The people here are pretending to be characters in the story."

"You okay, Jerry?" someone said, and Bear turned to face a man with thinning hair and a gray mustache. He was looking at Bear with concern.

"I'm okay," Bear said, and closed his eyes.

He listened to the cacophony of proxy signals. The signals appeared to be in layers, something he'd noticed before, but now it was more obvious. Each layer seemed to represent distance in space. If he wanted to travel far, he just had to listen through several layers.

He tried it. Eight layers in, he jumped.

He was running, running and panting, his long tongue lolling. He was large and muscled and covered in gray fur, an animal running on all fours. The forest floor was soft needles under his feet, and he emerged into a clearing and came to a halt. A waterfall cascaded from an outcrop on his left, plunging into a river far below.

Bear tried to talk to Min, but all that came from his long snout was a low growl.

Bear thought he was a bear.

"Only a little way now," Min said, rising from below the cliff.

Bear rested his head on his massive paws. Again he listened to the layers, travelling five deep.

Soft music—real music, real vibrations in the air—met his ears. He was in a wide room with a low ceiling, the light dim but warm and golden. He sat in a chair at a round table covered with a white cloth. There were more tables in the room, many of them. It was like the dining hall at the school, only much more comfortable.

Candles burned on the table, and there was a plate of food in front of him, a white plate covered in noodles, and some kind of meat, and green and orange vegetables. Smiling at him through the candlelight were two other people, a man and a woman, both more or less ordinary in appearance, although the woman had tall, pointed ears.

"We're eating," Bear said, looking around for Min. "Why do proxies need to eat? They don't."

All of these people were proxies. He could hear it. The woman across from him gave him a quizzical look.

"Sorry, what was that?" she said.

Min hovered between her and the man.

"Because eating is fun?" Min suggested.

That must have been it.

Bear looked again at the food, but it didn't look like anything he would want, small collections of colourful things he couldn't identify, and covered in sauces; so he looked away and studied the room. Through a wide, low archway, people were dancing, very tall and slender people in an array of colourful and flowing costumes. They held each other, and they danced.

It was like a dream, but the entire strange journey from proxy to proxy had been like a dream, leaping from one unrelated scene to another.

Bear rose from his chair and went to the nearby window. Outside, it was evening, the sky a deeper purple and filling with stars. There was a street, and golden streetlamps, and beyond, a great rise of land, dotted with more lights and topped by the jagged silhouettes of trees.

"This is Hope Mountain, Bear," Min said. "That's the mountain itself. You made it."

"Arvin?" the woman at Bear's table called from behind him.

Bear looked at the dark mountain, and he listened. He jumped.

Now he stood in a dark oval corridor, the walls blue and black and a deep mauve, with strips of gray and silver. Circular holes pierced the walls at intervals. Bear's body felt heavy, but it was strong; and when he examined his arms, he saw they were clad in black, with black gloves on his hands. A mask covered the lower portion of his face and goggles his eyes, and he thought he might be one of the Guardians, or maybe a Janusian soldier.

Min was already with him, glowing at his side.

"This is a strange place, a really strange place, Bear," she said. "There's the city outside, but I can't see any real people in it. There's another city here, underground. Not just under this mountain, but under the whole city and farther away."

"But where's Command?" Bear said.

"Here, under the mountain. You're close…and they're here." She moved around to hover in front of him, her eyes level with his. "They're talking about you, Bear," she said, "and the other children, and Archive."

Bear could go to them right now, locate their proxy signals and jump into one. But he didn't want to do that, because it would mean knocking someone out of their proxy, and he wanted to talk to all of them.

"Can you lead me to them, Min?"

"Yes." She turned to move along the corridor.

Bear pulled back the goggles, hoping there were real eyes behind them. There were, at least real imitation eyes (which he thought was funny), and he blinked in the improved light. What were the goggles for? Maybe protection in a fight.

He trailed after Min. There were many proxy signals around him, but not as many as in the dining hall; and he looked for a cluster of four together, which could be the members of Command.

The oval corridor ended at a conjunction with another oval corridor. Min turned left. Bear followed but paused when he saw a Guardian standing at a door about twenty paces away. The Guardian also wore goggles and didn't seem to react at all to Bear's appearance.

"Come on," Min said.

Min led him toward the door. At last, the Guardian looked at him, and Bear felt an odd tickling behind his ears. The Guardian was speaking to him by means of another type of signal. This was new, and Bear had no idea how to respond.

He attacked, jumping from his Guardian into the second Guardian. The proxy he vacated collapsed to the floor.

"Good job, Bear!" said Min.

Bear found the signal for the door without difficulty, and the door slid open, leading to a long rectangular chamber with a second door at its far end. Along either side of the room were alcoves or bays, and as Bear entered, he saw that each bay contained what looked like a child or infant, suspended upright from a harness, similar to a sleep bag.

"Are these babies?" Bear asked Min, stopping to crouch to get a better look at one. It was the ugliest baby he'd ever seen, with a huge head almost the size of an adult's, a wide mouth, tiny ears, just wisps of hair, and mottled gray skin. It was dressed in a simple white bodysuit that clung to its form.

The baby's eyes opened. Bear jumped back, startled.

"What do you want?" the baby said, its voice gruff.

"They're not babies, Bear," Min said. "They're people, real biological people."

Bear took a few cautious steps toward the second door, a little horrified, and the baby followed him with its eyes.

"Hey," it said, "why are you even in here?"

"Sorry, I made a mistake," Bear said, trying to remain calm.

Opening the second door, he stepped through, but found himself in another chamber full of diminutive people, all hanging from the walls, eyes closed.

"These are people who live and work here under the mountain," Min explained. "Guardians and scientists and all sorts of people. They stay here and live their lives connected to proxies."

"That's what Janusians look like?" Bear whispered, amazed and a little disgusted. He couldn't help it. Maybe he was being mean, because people couldn't help how they looked. But why were they like this?

"Yes," Min said. "The high gravity of the planet has made them smaller over successive generations."

"But I've met real Janusians, and they were tall."

Min looked at him, her expression neutral. "Not all people are the same, I guess you could say."

She led him into another roomful of silent figures, and beyond that was another corridor, running right to left. After that, Bear became disoriented, but it didn't matter as long as he had Min to follow.

They travelled along one passage and then another, up two flights of stairs, one narrow and one wide, until they came to a passage that was wider than the others, its floor a gentle upward slope. The ceiling was also higher, the white walls decorated in geometric panels—squares and triangles. At the far end was a double door made of polished wood, the first wooden door Bear had seen.

A cluster of four proxy signals emanated from behind the door.

"This is the Operations Room," Min said. "Command is in there."

Chapter 23

Bear hesitated. The door signal was there, superimposed over his vision, but he was suddenly nervous. There were no snakes in his proxy stomach, but he could sense them all the way back on Archive.

He had a simple message for these people. He shouldn't be afraid to tell them what he wanted.

He considered knocking but decided against it. Clenching both fists and gritting his robotic teeth, he opened the doors.

The room beyond was large, with a high, arched ceiling, the lighting the same blue and purple as the rest of the underground complex. Along the centre of the room ran a long table, dark brown and gleaming, and at its far end stood four people. There were no chairs in the room.

The four people all turned to look as Bear entered.

Back in his real body on Archive, Bear took a deep breath. With his Guardian proxy, he approached his enemies.

The four members of Command looked annoyed and a little curious. Bear recognized Mister Verran in his black clothing, but he'd never seen the others before. One was a stout woman with short copper hair, her features plain and humourless, and Bear thought she looked like someone who wouldn't tolerate any sort of nonsense or would ever laugh, even at the funniest joke or story she'd ever heard. Next to her was a wide-shouldered man with a long chin. He held his arms folded across his chest and looked the most irritated of the four. With him was a tall and pretty woman with turquoise hair, luminous green eyes, and pointed ears.

"Yes?" said the stout woman.

They thought Bear was just a Guardian with a message or something. Nothing strange or out of the ordinary.

196

He walked the length of the room, Min floating along at his side.

"Hello," he said, stopping in front of Verran, giving him a shy smile, and then facing the woman who had spoken. "I'm Bear. I'm here to talk to you about the kids from Sturnus."

Bear had to admit it was satisfying to see their reactions, and his nervousness quieted a little. Mister Verren looked like he was going to be sick. The stout woman looked affronted, and took a step back, saying, "What?" The large man gaped, arms dropping to dangle like those of an ape, while the pretty woman put both dainty hands to her mouth and gasped.

"Hi, Mister Verren," was all Bear could think to say next. "I'm sorry that I destroyed your last proxy body, but I had to do that. I had to do all those things to get away from you, but now I've come to ask you a question."

The stout woman held up one hand.

"What is this? Who are you?"

"I'm Bear," Bear repeated, raising his voice. "I've taken over this Guardian's proxy, and I've come here to tell you to please leave all of the children on Archive alone."

The members of Command stared. They looked dumbfounded.

"This is impossible," the large man said to his companions, as if Bear wasn't in the room.

The stout woman seemed to collect herself. Facing the large man and gesturing toward Bear with one hand, she said, "This is precisely the threat we have been discussing, here before us. So now he's come to give us a demonstration." She looked at Bear. "Well, boy. I am El-ann, head of this council, and we are not prepared to discuss anything with you."

This was the monster that Bear had vaporized during his escape. Bear preferred her in this body.

"I'd just like to ask you," he repeated, "to leave us alone. We're going home to Sturnus, and we want you to leave us alone. We promise not to do anything to you."

El-ann's face contorted in a scowl almost as ugly as that of her old troll proxy.

"You're just an unruly child," she said, "descended from traitors. We will destroy you and all of your friends. Our fleet is already on its way."

Bear faltered. She was lying. He looked at Min.

"No fleet has left the planet," Min said.

Bear nodded, relieved, and looked back at El-ann.

"You haven't sent a fleet," he said, "and you shouldn't. I can take over any proxy you have, any ship and any body. I can do it. All of us can now. But we won't if you just leave us alone."

El-ann glanced at her companions.

"Kamra's project," said the large man, "had implications we don't understand."

"That is why eliminating its last remnants," El-ann said, "is imperative. Now, get this child out of here!"

"Wait," said Verren, holding up one hand. He smiled at Bear, that old charming smile that had made Bear trust him. "We've studied what you do, Bear, and it's impressive, but we've already figured out ways to defend against it. You can't threaten us."

Bear didn't believe him. They were lying, and not listening, and not being reasonable, and El-ann just wanted to destroy him and his friends.

"You see," Verren continued, "each of us has a core proxy, the body we consider our own. Our main body. Our true selves. It's different from the others, built in a slightly different way. I don't think you'd be able to access those as easily, if at all. And we've decided to build all of our new proxies in the same way."

Still Bear didn't believe him.

"So, are you using your core proxies now?"

Verren shook his head. "No. They're safe somewhere else."

"Where? I can hear every proxy under the mountain, every proxy in the city, every one on the whole planet. Where are your core proxies?"

Verren's smile faltered, just for a second, like a flicker of light and shadow passing across his face. But it was enough to confirm that he was lying. There weren't any core proxies.

"I told you, they're safe," Verren said. "You probably can't hear their signals because they're different. So, we have the means to defend against what you can do. But, Bear…" He held up both hands. "…I don't want us to have to be adversaries. You have a lot of talent. Miss Sweet saw that. You could still join us."

El-ann gave Verren a sharp look, and the large man grunted. The woman with the turquoise hair giggled.

Bear took a step back. This was going nowhere, and was making him angry.

"I don't think you mean it," he said, "and even if you did, I wouldn't join you."

He looked at them, at these four people who had probably stood here, in this same room, months or years ago, and made up their minds to destroy his entire society and kill all of its people.

Why was he even talking to them? He should just take his revenge and destroy them all. It's what they deserved.

He jumped into Mister Verren'a proxy, leaving his vacant Guardian standing motionless, propped against the table. Turning to El-ann in his new body, he said, "Hey."

She looked at him, and he punched her square in the face.

The big man shouted, and the turquoise-haired woman jumped back, hands again to her mouth. El-ann fell backwards and landed on the floor with a shout of outrage and astonishment.

Bear jumped into the pretty woman. The first thing he saw from his new eyes was Verren's empty proxy falling sideways, and then he turned to the large man, grabbing his oblong head with both hands and twisting. The woman's body may have been slight, but proxies were machines, and they were strong. The head popped off with a snap and small shower of sparks.

El-ann had regained her feet. Bear threw the head at her, knocking her down again. Taking two steps to where she lay, he leaned over her and said, "Leave us alone. Leave me and all of my friends alone. We never did anything to you."

El-ann glared back in fury.

"We will destroy you!"

Bear looked at her for a second.

"Try it," he said, and dropped the proxy, leaving the planet, feeling himself snap back across the gulf of space, all the way to where he sat on the floor in the Great Hall on Archive.

The blue planet seemed to hang in front of him, threatening to crush him with its great weight. He didn't think it was beautiful anymore. Now, it was something that meant to do him harm.

Sweat sprouted from the pores on his forehead. His stomach turned over, and he leaned forward, vomiting acid and bile onto the floor. The other kids cried out, some in sympathy, some in disgust, and some in glee.

"Good one, Bear!" Emmot shouted.

Aril was at his side, putting his arm around his shoulders.

"Are you okay?"

Bear's head drooped. The splatter of vomit stank, and although his stomach seemed all right now, exhaustion crushed down on him like the gravity of Janus.

"I think I did too much," he said.

All that jumping from proxy to proxy had seemed so easy, but proxies didn't feel tired, and they didn't feel pain. Your real body carried all that.

"You need to rest, Bear," Min said. "That was awful. Just awful! Those people are horrible."

"Everybody," Bear said, raising one hand like a flag, "I think we need to leave now. We need to get in the ship and go. Right now."

There were murmurs and shouts of agreement from the others. Kids who'd been sitting jumped to their feet.

"I'll help you get everyone going," Roma said. She sounded calm, but he saw the alarm in her wide eyes.

Bear nodded in gratitude.

"Bear, wait," said Min. "Everyone wait."

She floated out through the great window and paused, hovering above the surface of the little moon. All eyes turned to look at her.

"There are more ships coming from the planet. They just launched."

Bear's fatigue seemed to vanish, and he sat up straight. El-ann hadn't been lying?

"How many?" he said.

Min hesitated. "Two hundred."

Bear held his head in both hands. There was no way he could take control of two hundred ships. Right now, he wasn't even sure he could take control of one. Tears pooled in his eyes, and his shoulders convulsed. He didn't want anyone to see him, so he covered his face.

"What's wrong?" said Aril.

"Two hundred ships are coming to kill us," Roma snapped at him.

"That's not what I meant!" Aril snapped back.

Bear steadied himself, took a few shuddering breaths. He looked at the planet. The ships were there, like a cloud of lights, coming toward Archive. He could hear them.

"I'm too tired to take them over," he said.

Roma was rubbing his back. Aril was on his right, looking at the ships. Emmot was on his left.

Emmot shrugged.

"We'll all take them over, then," he said, and he stood, raising both meaty arms. "Hey, everybody! Bear's too tired from all the stuff he's done, so we all have to help. See those ships?" he pointed. "We're going to take them over, and we're going to shoot each other down, and crash the rest into the moon!"

A couple of kids cheered, but others seemed doubtful.

"I don't know how to do that," Deej said.

"Yes, you do!" said Emmot. "It's just like the knight back there. Listen for it, pick one, go in, take it, and turn and start blasting the others."

"There are no soldiers on these ships," Min said. "They're warships."

A dazzling flash appeared amid the cloud of distant ships, and the Great Hall trembled, just a bit, enough to be noticed.

"They're shooting at us," Emmot said.

"I can hear their communications," Min said. "That was a test of the effectiveness of one of their weapons."

"We have to stop them," Bear said, not liking the whine in his voice.

"They're going to destroy the moon," Min added. "They're going to destroy Archive."

"We need to get away from the window," Bear said.

No one listened to him. Emmot stood on his left with Roma. The others had formed a line beside them. Aril was on Bear's right, and Puck and Kanga and Deej, all looking out the great window at the cloud of ships, like a swarm of insects, close enough now that he could make out their details. Large ovoid ships, with two bright blue lights, like eyes, in their bow sections.

Bear saw one of the ships turn, a ship on the fringe of the cloud. It swiveled and moved across the path of the others. A second ship followed it.

Bright yellow beams, like sparks, shot from the two rogue ships, tearing into the swarm, firing on the other ships.

Bear gasped.

"Are you doing this?" he asked.

None of his friends answered. They couldn't speak and probably couldn't hear him. They were concentrating too hard.

More ships joined in the mutiny, curling back toward the swarm. Plasma beams danced and sparkled. It didn't matter if the unaffected ships fired back. What mattered was that the ships were fighting and destroying each other.

Emmot started shouting a wordless war cry.

The swarm of ships became a distant show of fireworks. Ships exploded and tore into dancing motes of light, and then there was nothing but dust.

The fleet was gone.

Emmot raised his fists. "We did it! What a battle!"

He was laughing, and then they all were, laughing and cheering.

"I took over a couple of ships," Aril said. "I didn't get to fire my guns, though, before they were destroyed. I thought it would hurt, but I didn't feel anything."

Bear struggled to his feet. His legs were still wobbly, but the victory had given him strength. He thought of how Verren and El-ann must feel right now, and the thought of their frustration was a comfort.

"I told you to leave us alone," he murmured.

"You know, Bear," said Roma, "we couldn't have done that if they were ordinary ships, and not these proxy things."

"They do everything with proxies," Bear said. "So, we don't need to worry about that."

Roma seemed about to say something else, but a massive shape began to descend from the ceiling above the great window. It was a shutter, a section of wall. It dropped until it reached the floor, closing the window and blocking the view of the planet. The Great Hall shook with the impact.

The children all stared in confusion.

"Why did that happen?" Bear said.

The lights went out, plunging the Great Hall into complete darkness. Several children screamed. The darkness was that of a tomb, broken only by the golden form of Min, although her light wasn't real, nothing but a mental image, and so couldn't illuminate physical objects.

"They're cutting the power," Min said. "The force field that closes the window has a reserve, but when the power goes down, it closes the emergency doors so the air and heat won't escape. Remember I told you they were thinking of doing that? They're shutting down the life support here on Archive."

The lights flickered on again, held steady, then went out again.

"What was that?" said Bear.

"The reserve power is on," said Min, "but it's not enough, so it's diverting to life support and essential systems. It won't last long, and I think they can shut it down, too. This station will be frozen in a few minutes without it. Bear, we have to hurry! Follow me!"

Bear was searching for a proxy signal for the whole station, but none existed.

"Can't we take control of the station and turn the power back on?"

"No, Bear. Remember I told you these were old systems? As old as the first settlement of the planet? Even I can't talk to them. Come on!"

She flew ahead.

"Follow Min!" Bear shouted.

She led them out of the Great Hall, and the children ran after her, some of them crying or whimpering in fear, as if their triumph of a moment ago had never happened. But circumstances had changed. Bear felt his panic rising, an irrational fear gripping him that Min would move too fast, leave him and the others stranded here, trapped underground on a frozen moon.

Min stopped. "Here's the travel tube, but it has a maximum capacity of five people at a time, Bear. With only the reserve power, it won't be able to carry any more than that."

"I'll wait," he said, not liking the words, but thinking this was right. "Get everyone else off first."

"Shut up," said Roma's voice. "Get in the tube, Bear!"

She pushed him and crowded in behind him. He heard the door shut. Min hovered close.

"I'm able to stay with you and with the others in the hall at the same time," she said. "I have them calmed down."

The travel tube door opened, and there was light again, dim emergency lights in the short passage from the transport to the spherical ship. Bear felt another moment of panic, because he had no proxy to open the ship's door, but when he searched for the ship's signal, he found it, loud and obvious.

"Open the door!" he shouted, not knowing if the ship could hear him when he was outside.

"Main hatchway activated," said the voice in his head.

The door appeared in the ship's smooth hull, and the ramp descended. Bear and his friends dashed toward it.

"Get on the ship," Bear said. "I'm going to wait out here!"

He had to see everyone off this moon. Roma gave him a look, and he thought she was going to be stubborn, as usual; but then she nodded and disappeared into the ship.

The next group of five arrived. Bear pointed, saying, "This way," but they were following another version of Min, and seemed to know where to go.

The lights were growing dimmer.

"The power's going," Min said.

"Hurry! Most of my friends are still in the hall!"

The next group of five arrived. That made fifteen. Bear couldn't leave the door to the travel tube. What would happen to him if the power failed? The heat would disappear quickly, diffusing into space, but he thought he would have a few minutes, enough to run to the ship.

Another group of five arrived, and another. The travel tube was swift. Bear's limbs felt numb, and his breath steamed. It was already growing cold. Archive was freezing, but so far his clothes were keeping his temperature steady.

Five more kids came dashing out of the lift. Bear saw Puck and Deej, eyes wide with fear. The door slid shut. Two more trips.

The minutes seemed long. The door opened. Five more kids came out.

The lights in the passage went out. Bear looked back at the ship, which had its own lights. Roma was standing in the hatchway, watching.

"Bear," Min said. "Bear, the reserve power just failed."

He looked at her. There were still five more kids to come.

"Did they get in the travel tube?" he said. "Can you open the door?"

Min looked at him. He didn't like that look.

"I can't. The power's gone, and there's no manual system. The travel tube is stuck halfway here."

Bear felt the cold on his face, his nose. Even his arms were cold. His clothes weren't able to keep up. His toes were ice.

"There's no way to get them out," he said.

It was a statement, not a question.

"I'm sorry, Bear," Min said. "I'll stay with them. I can do that. Until the cold comes, which will be soon. You have to get in the ship now. You don't have a choice."

Bear turned and started toward the ship. Roma was there. She held out her hand.

"Come on," she said.

Bear wouldn't think of the five kids still trapped in the travel tube. He wouldn't think of how they probably felt right now, stranded in the darkness, the cold growing.

They had Min, he told himself. At least they wouldn't be alone.

He climbed the ramp and entered the ship. The door slid shut behind him.

Chapter 24

The control room in the ship was crowded, although not quite as crowded as it would have been if all forty children were there. Bear sat in the command chair, watching the V-windows. The others had accepted him as the "captain" without question.

He wondered if the heaviness he felt right now was the weight of command, a concept he remembered from one of Miss Sweet's lessons. Or just shock, disbelief. They'd lost five kids. Five more children of Sturnus, victims of the Janusians.

Bear vowed those would be the last.

The ship departed Archive, completed a single orbit of the moon and headed for Sturnus. During the long journey, Bear stayed in the command chair while the others explored the ship. When it was time to eat, the children gathered in the control room, sitting on the soft brown floor; and when they slept, some slept in the cabins below. A few even used the sleep bags.

The hours passed.

"When we get home to Sturnus," Bear said, speaking to Emmot, Roma and Aril, his three best friends and now his lieutenants, "we may have to have one more fight, if there's anyone in the city. That's where the ship will land."

"I'm all up for it," Emmot said, but without any joy or relish. Bear knew he was also angry about the loss of the five.

Bear was not up for it. He was tired of fighting, just wanted an end to all of the worries that had plagued him since his memories had first resurfaced. He wanted a rest but knew he wouldn't get it. As long as there was a need to keep Janus from trying to destroy them, he and the others could never let their guard down.

Corvus grew large on the V-windows, and then Sturnus, and then there were clouds and fire outside as the sphere entered the atmosphere. Flames soon gave way to blue sky, and Bear felt an unexpected happiness building in his breast that he hadn't felt in a long time. Home. He was home.

The happiness lasted only a few seconds. The ship landed.

"Alo Base," the ship said. "Landing complete."

Bear had never known the name of the city.

"Well, here goes," he said.

He went down the stairs and into the central passage, but paused before opening the outer hatch. He listened. There were proxy signals, but not many. He could count them. Fourteen.

"There's hardly anyone," he said, surprised.

He asked the ship to open the hatch, and the ramp descended. Bear was ready to do battle.

He found the city abandoned. The Janusians had left and taken many things with them, leaving only a few proxies behind. Guardians, now little more than statues, empty of life. There was no one else.

Bear led the way into the grassy courtyard where Verren had let him practice with the wolf. Min went with them.

"The project was cancelled," Min said. "They have plans to return and dismantle everything, every building."

"They won't," Bear said. "We won't let them. How much is left, Min?"

"The power is still functional, and there is water and food and all essential systems. You can live here for a long time, Bear, if you want."

Yes, they could live here. The city was theirs now. The school was theirs now, too, but they wouldn't go back. This place was good enough, and they could live here until they learned how to rebuild the houses by the cliff, along the sea.

Finding one of the forsaken Guardians near the edge of the field, Bear used it to open the doors to the library. Dropping the proxy, he entered the building. The others followed and gawped at the fantastic room. The books hadn't been removed, and the computers were still there. All the knowledge available to the people of Janus, and now available to the last inhabitants of Sturnus.

"We'll have to change the doors," Bear said. "Just put regular handles on them or something, so we don't have to use proxies to open them."

"Or just leave a proxy outside every door," Aril suggested, with a shrug. "It can be the opener."

"I think I'll live in here," Roma said. "This is the best room I've ever seen."

They explored the city, found many empty living quarters, a few with proxies waiting, silent, on their shelves. Bear found Miss Sweet's quarters, but all of her things were gone.

Although Bear still didn't want to, they went back to the school, and it was intact but silent. He hadn't been unhappy there, but now it seemed like a terrible place. Its walls filled him with a low, seething dread.

"I think we should tear this place down," he said.

Not one child objected.

They went out into the yard. Emmot ran to the play set in the corner, his favourite play set.

"Maybe we can just keep this?" he shouted.

Puck and Aril and Deej all joined him. Bear watched them and managed to laugh, but the sight of them scrambling over the white tangle of pipes made his skin begin to crawl, like insects on his back, as if nothing had changed.

Min was hovering just above the wall, just outside the yard, like she had when Bear had first started seeing her. Corvus was a vast presence behind her.

"Bear," she said, and he heard the note of warning in her voice. "There's a ship coming."

Bear clutched his stomach as a tiny bomb seemed to burst inside him. "A ship? Just one?"

He'd hoped to have more time before the next fight. He was confident Janus couldn't hurt them anymore, not now that every kid had gained their abilities to command any proxy their enemies possessed; but he still thought they should come up with a coordinated defense plan. They hadn't had any time for that, they'd been so intent on exploring the city.

"Yes. Bear. It's Miss Sweet. Miss Sweet is alone in that ship."

Bear hadn't seen Miss Sweet since battling her many proxies when he'd stolen the spherical ship. He listened for her proxy signal, casting his awareness far. He could hear it, behind the ship's signal, several proxies, all with Miss Sweet's signature fluting melody. Four of them.

"Is there more than one person in that ship?" he said.

Min shook her head. "I don't think so. I can only tell by reading the environmental data. It looks like one person."

The doors to the school stood open, including the gates in the wall. Bear walked out into the meadow. He wasn't afraid. He no longer had any reason to fear Miss Sweet, but still didn't want to see her. He never wanted to see anyone from Janus again.

The grass was long, and sprinkled with tiny white flowers. In the near distance, the yellowpines swayed in a freshening breeze. Bear paused a few metres from the yard wall, and the other children abandoned the playset and gathered behind him.

"Min, I think I'll go up there," Bear said. "I can hear the ship. I'll grab one of her proxies and go up there and talk to her, tell her to turn around and go back."

The ship was visible now with the naked eye, a silver ovoid, flashing in the sun. Bear watched it approach. His plan seemed sound, but he just stared at the small craft, his curiosity growing, outweighing all other considerations.

"We need to stop her," Emmot said, suddenly at Bear's side.

Bear shook his head. "Wait. Just wait a minute."

The ship was descending, as if Miss Sweet had seen them. Maybe she had. The gleaming ball dropped toward the meadow, and three articulated legs emerged from its belly.

Slowly, without any noise or wind or fuss, the silver ship landed in the meadow. A minute later, the side opened, a square hatch appeared, and a short flight of steps descended to the grass.

Miss Sweet came out of the ship. Bear heard someone behind him whisper, "Miss Sweet!" The rest of the kids were silent.

Miss Sweet came slowly toward Bear, hands folded in front of her. She was her real self, or the body Bear had believed was her real self, the imperfect one, with the tan skin and the dark hair. She wore a brown sweater and a lighter brown skirt, leather boots on her feet.

Bear thought she looked nice.

Miss Sweet regarded the children, smiling her old smile, although Bear thought she seemed nervous. It was strange to see that sort of thing in an adult he'd once trusted so completely. She was afraid of him, afraid of all of them, and he knew her faults now.

Her attention fell upon Bear.

"Thank you for allowing me to land," she said. "I know you could have stopped me."

Bear felt awkward facing her as an equal, as the representative of his planet. He shrugged.

"Why did you come back here?" he said.

"I want to stay here with you. I want to help you."

Bear glowered at her. After all she and her people had done, she expected them to welcome her back?

"No," he said, shaking his head. "No, this is our planet, and we don't want any more of you people coming here."

She held up both hands.

"Listen to me, Bear. They fear you like nothing else. They hated you before, but now you are an object of terror, which is worse. They no longer want to hear about compromise, and they blame me for allowing you all to live when we invaded Sturnus."

Bear knew she meant Command.

"I was the one who convinced them to let you live in the first place," she continued. "They would have killed you all during the invasion. I tried to do something, anything, to save you. I would have saved more children! I would have saved them all."

Bear wasn't interested in hearing how she'd tried and failed to save more people. This wasn't about her anymore. Min had told him this story, anyway, about No Authority, but it didn't matter. Miss Sweet had been the face of Janus for him for too long.

"I'm sorry, Miss Sweet," he said. "We're not taking orders from Janus anymore. That includes you. We're doing what we want from now on. This is our planet, and no one else's."

Her face fell. For a moment, she said nothing, and Bear shrugged again.

"I loved you, Bear," she said after a while. "I loved all of you."

Bear's hands curled into fists.

"So, now you have to leave us alone!"

The rest of the children had not moved, just stood in a long line behind him. Miss Sweet looked at them.

"You need someone," she said, and he heard a note of pleading in her voice. "You can't survive without an adult to guide you. I can guide you."

"Yes, we can," Bear insisted.

"It's just a fact of your development, Bear! You aren't responsible enough. You have no factories, no way to make clothing, to grow food that isn't manufactured. No understanding of power sources. No way to fix things or build things. New things."

"We have this city you built us."

She shook her head. "It's not a city, it's just a complex of buildings with limited functions."

"We have the library," Bear said. "We'll learn, and when we're older we'll start building new things. And we have Min. She can help us."

Miss Sweet looked confused. "Who is Min?"

Bear wouldn't tell her.

"We don't need you," he just repeated.

He saw her looking at the others, and hoped she wasn't thinking of pleading with them, of trying to turn them against him. He could tell she still had influence, still had power. If she tried to use that power, he would have to do something a little more drastic.

What could he do?

He glanced at her ship, listened for its signal, wondering if there was a way to make her board and just fly away. The signal was obvious, as was that of three proxies inside, maybe bodies she'd brought with her. And there was the fourth proxy signal as well. It was coming from Miss Sweet herself.

"You're a proxy," he said, surprised. "I thought that was what you really looked like."

He saw a flash of a smile, but there was something sad about it.

"Of course not, Bear. I'm still on the ship."

"Is this your core proxy?" he asked.

She frowned. "I've never heard of such a thing. A core proxy. It's one of many. One of my favourites, how I like to see myself."

Realization dawned.

"You've never been to Sturnus," Bear said. "Have you?"

"In order to travel from Janus," Miss Sweet said, "most of the time we came as proxies only. You're right. Our bodies remained on our planet. Space is not a factor for entangled minds, human and machine. However, this time I was forced to come. There's nowhere for me to go on Janus."

She stated this as a fact. Bear bit his lip. He supposed Command hated her, too, now. Maybe they would even kill her. If they were capable of killing all of the people on Sturnus, what was one of their own worth?

His resolve was crumbling, and that made him cross. And yet, he couldn't do anything about it. He was faced with making a hard decision, yet again.

From behind him, he heard muttering and shuffling, restlessness. A few of the children had edged forward. "Miss Sweet," one said. "Miss Sweet."

Miss Sweet smiled at them, but she didn't say anything. Bear looked at their faces, and he saw nothing but eagerness and affection. There was no sign of anger, no sign of hatred.

They still loved Miss Sweet. They still looked to her for approval, and even now they were looking to her for guidance. They'd followed him, would continue to follow him; but Miss Sweet had been like a mother, the only mother they'd been able to remember for a long time.

"Is there anywhere else you could go?" Bear asked.

"There are other human colonies," Miss Sweet said. "Far away. My ship isn't designed for that sort of travel, but I could reach one, in time."

Her voice sounded hollow now, empty. Devoid of hope.

"Maybe you could stay for a while," he said, speaking slowly, his eyes narrowed.

Miss Sweet's proxy started to weep. Bear hadn't thought proxies were capable of that, to produce tears. He supposed they could do whatever their maker wanted them to do.

"On one condition," he added.

She was nodding. "Yes, Bear. What is it?"

"Come out of the ship. Come out of the ship and show us what you really look like."

He was thinking of the ugly, wizened people he'd encountered in the caverns beneath Hope Mountain, and thought she'd be ashamed, that she would object.

But that wasn't how she reacted. She didn't object, didn't say anything, just walked a few steps to one side, turned and stood facing across the front of the assembled children. Her eyes went blank, the life going out of them, and Bear understood she'd left her proxy.

The door to the ship was still open. A new figure emerged, climbing down the steps with slow, almost awkward movements. The children watched in silence.

The real Miss Sweet turned and hobbled toward them. She was small, as small as the others Bear had seen, with a large round head, the hair very fine, silky-white and pulled back and held with a silver clasp. Her face was brown and wrinkled like the bark of an old tree, and her hands resembled tree roots. She must have been very old, much older than she liked to appear.

She was dressed in a robe that hung from her small shoulders, fine cloth in a deep russet, a silver scarf around her neck, and she carried a short staff or cane, also silver. With the aid of this, she approached Bear and halted in front of him.

"It's easier to walk here," she said, her voice a rasp. "I don't use my own legs to walk very often, but the gravity here is kind."

The children gathered around her, more fascinated than repulsed. There was nothing threatening about this ancient and feeble person. A few reached out and touched her robe, touched her shoulders.

Miss Sweet wept, real tears of salt water from organic eyes.

Bear folded his arms. Yes, Miss Sweet could stay here, even live in her old apartment if she wanted. But she would have no say in anything. The children would be in charge of their own lives.

He glanced at Roma, saw that she was smiling, that she was happy.

Maybe this was right.

Bear held out a hand. Miss Sweet took it. Without another word, he led her back toward the gate in the school wall.

About the Author

HAROLD R. THOMPSON is the author of the bestselling "Empire and Honor" series of historical adventure novels, which includes *Dudley's Fusiliers,* *Guns of Sevastopol* and *Sword of the Mogul.* The series details the adventures of a Victorian soldier, William Dudley, during the Crimean War and the Indian Sepoy Mutiny, two of the most significant conflicts to involve the British Empire during the mid-nineteenth century. Although Dudley is a fictional hero, his exploits are largely based on those of actual, although obscure, historical figures, and inspired by the "boy's own adventures" of a bygone age, with contemporary sensibilities and a touch of subversion.

Thompson's stand-alone novel, *The End of the Tether,* is a dramatization of the siege of Yorktown during the American Revolution, and follows a combination of historical personalities, including George Washington, and fictional characters, telling the story of the end of the Revolution from various perspectives.

Thompson's formal education is in psychology and law; however, he studied history as an employee of Parks Canada for over two decades, specializing in British and Canadian military history, and it was during that time he developed the character of William Dudley. At the same time, he retained an interest in science, as well as science fiction, which he considers similar to historical fiction in that both concern times and places different from our own.

He has written nonfiction and short science fiction and fantasy for a variety of print and online magazines. He lives in Nova Scotia and, when not writing or spending time with his family, enjoys hiking and cycling and storytelling in all its various forms.

www.ingramcontent.com/pod-product-compliance
Lightning Source LLC
Chambersburg PA
CBHW020656030726
47498CB00002B/533